The Trees of Calan Gray

THE
TREES OF
CALAN GRAY

by

DANIAL NEIL

OOLICHAN BOOKS
FERNIE, BRITISH COLUMBIA, CANADA
2015

Library and Archives Canada Cataloguing in Publication

Neil, Danial, 1954-, author

The trees of Calan Gray / by Danial Neil.

ISBN 978-0-88982-297-9 (pbk.)

I. Title.

PS8627.E48T74 2014   C813'.6   C2014-900740-X

We gratefully acknowledge the financial support of the Canada Council for the Arts, the British Columbia Arts Council through the BC Ministry of Tourism, Culture, and the Arts, and the Government of Canada through the Canada Book Fund, for our publishing activities.

Published by
Oolichan Books
P.O. Box 2278
Fernie, British Columbia
Canada V0B 1M0

www.oolichan.com

Printed in Canada

for Ruth-Ann

"*Trees are sanctuaries. Whoever knows how to speak to them, whoever knows how to listen to them, can learn the truth. They do not preach learning and precepts, they preach, undeterred by particulars, the ancient law of life.*"

Hermann Hesse

Author's Note:

This book was inspired, in part, by a 2010 CBC interview with Diana Beresford-Kroeger, author of The Global Forest. The book was also written to commemorate the United Nations declaration of 2011 as the International Year of Forests – an open invitation to the world community to come together and work with governments, international organizations and civil society, to ensure that our forests are managed sustainably for current and future generations.

THE LANGUAGE OF TREES

ASPEN

CHAPTER ONE

I always felt the blazing presence of the sky – a summer slap of it against my senses. In that space all was unencumbered, a seamless on and on to the remote and distant. The eye goes there, not by grand imaginings, but to find its place in a world of wheat and toil – the continuous expanse in which things exist and move. House and barn and space played out over and over as if the prairie was all there was in the universe, marooned on a plane between the horizons, alone and adrift under an infinite blue dome, there in the very heart of Saskatchewan in 1964, the godless Gray Farm.

There was not a lick of shade at noon. The sickly lombardy that grew along the driveway cast shadows like fence posts. The barn was full of work and I could be easily found. It was too much for one man and an idle son; not the brood that my father had hoped for. This lack always seemed my fault and not my father's reproductive dysfunction. I was his constant reminder of failure and he never couched his words with me when my mother went to Saskatoon. She went there on her weekly errands and he seemed to save up his grievances. They spit out over the curl of his lips, indictments of how I failed him. "Calan, mark my word, you won't amount to nothin'!"

he would say, as if tempting me to seize the farm life he willed for me, gripping me with his mean eyes that I feared. I could only look down at my clumsy feet at such times and wait for the hard bone of his hand, never against my mouth that would bleed. A welt would rise along the line of my jaw, and it would startle him. I think he always regretted it when he saw what he had done to me. But it was always after. And he would have a story for my mother of how I fell or tripped in the barn, his great laugh spinning away the day. And I the silent accomplice who knew well the sting of reprisal. Something urgent burned in my father. He had a fear of failure, a constant worry of loss and ruination. A farmer desperate to harvest the full measure of the earth, perhaps even to make enough to go south in the winter. But it never happened, just his savage fear of dying without a good year.

I knew that he would find me. I couldn't escape him. He followed the trail I made across the fallow field behind the barn and through the tall grass past the pond to the cool gully on the day when I first felt the language of trees. He was the unwitting spectator to my foolish whisperings under a canopy of mint green leaves. I will never forget his shock, his dismay. I bravely looked up at him that once to see him cry, tears running down the cheeks of a grown man. I did not hate him so much just then for I recognized a deep suffering in him. But still, his tears did not soothe him, did not arouse in him a moment's tenderness.

"What are you doing, boy?" he said, his rough hands reaching down. Hands to pummel me until I pissed my pants.

"Just like to be here," I said with that shrug of mine that never did much good. All insolence and cheek to him.

"Who are you talking to, Calan?" He grabbed my shirt. His twisted face like agony.

"The trees," I said. "No harm in that." There was pleading in my voice now as I strained to get away from him. My shirt ripped but his thick fingers would not be loosed.

"Do you see a goddamn tree worth your laziness? Do you?"

"I didn't do anything wrong, Dad. I only come here to get some shade. That's all."

"I heard you talking to them. It was plain. You come here to talk like an idiot!"

"Just trees, Dad."

"There is no use in it, not a bloody purpose at all. What's wrong with you, Calan? You're ten years old now and you're a weakling child. You can't do a damn thing. You're going to see the doctor. You're acting like you're retarded. I won't have a retard. Do you hear me? Get back to the house!"

He lifted me from the grass and shoved me back on the trail. I ran toward the fields into the glare of his world and looked back over my shoulder. I wanted to be far away from him, Macklin Gray, in that threadbare shirt, his sleeves rolled up above his elbows. His dirty neck. Hanging his head with my shame. But beyond him there was something else in that fleeting moment, that first rush of them to me as if they wanted to come to my aid, a reaching of their own. I could not explain it. A rent in the broad, empty plain, a gouge in the earth, a scrape where moisture gathered every spring. And like some miracle, a grove of trees that shimmered and danced and sang – aspens, thick with chalk white trunks and the sweet breathing of life through the leaves.

Something of chance or destiny drew me to those trees. I couldn't see them from my upstairs bedroom window. I couldn't see them from the barn loft and I couldn't see them from the seat of the tractor when my father thought it time for me to climb up on the big Massey-Ferguson. It pleased him to imagine me driving along the farm track that skirted our fields. He would see me then, I suppose, as a young man working by his side. But I never liked the feel of it, the grind of the engine, the diesel smell and the smell of him – cigarette smoke and sweat lingering. The monotony of planted grids, dust and predictability and the thought of the long days like a slow death.

And then I became aware that I was moving away from him. I was free of him. That green smudge in the distance made me curious and I kept on going, the tractor plodding north, creeping to something so strange, a landscape that seemed out of place – so unlikely. A thick forest sprouting beyond our property. A hidden realm. But I had to go back to him.

So I made the pilgrimage there one day to see what it was – a mystery that seemed to belong to me. Immediately, upon reaching the grove I felt a peace that I did not understand. There was the sense of something old and something unfailing, something stable. I felt safe. I kept going back – in the early spring with catkins like grey woolly worms dangling from the bare limbs and later with the emergence of the freshest green. I would run my hands up the smooth white bark of the trunks, feel the black welds, finger the weeping drills from boring beetles. And the leaves like green hearts would catch a breeze and tremble like tadpoles against my hand. No matter how dry the summer, the grass below was always cool and rank. Tiger lilies rising to the filtered green light made me dizzy and needing to lie down. And the autumn gold that startled me, cheering against a blue sky that I could love again.

In winter I broke through drifts up to my thighs to reach them. They made what was bleak and barren a new world to be explored. The wind blew snow from the prairie – air-born light like emissaries of the sun floating among the trees. There was a hush in the rattling crowns – a wild stillness, a purity of winter that cuts and arrives like dreams and the Snowy Owls resting there. And the trails of fox, their footfall in fine blue wells – a flash of a tail, a wave to me and the outline of wings in the snow where sharp-tailed grouse had been flushed from their sanctuary. There were antelope wary and pawing, sheltered from the wind and cold. They watched me with their vast amber eyes.

Where did they come from – those thousand trees?

Back at the house my father told me to wait in the barn. He had a job for me. My mother had earlier complained about mice in the house and he decided that they must have come from the barn. Spilled grain had caused a population explosion. I could hear their little feet dancing in the dark – searching for food when the house was still. Always a rustle and scratching to ensure their exponential lives. Our obliging neighbour Ole Olsen was more than happy to donate a couple of cats to control them. The expendable ones arrived hungry and without instructions. Soon there were no mice but a dozen cats in the barn, the mice lost in the flattening hierarchy of life.

I stood slackly there as I waited for him, watching the cats loafing on the dusty sills and timbers – black cats, grey cats and orange cats and all the variations. None of them had names. They always seemed so at ease and rested, licking their paws and grooming, stretching, yawning. The younger kittens tussled now and then, tumbling in the sunlit chaff. They were a skinny bunch that never ventured far from the barn.

I noticed their antics as something sublime. I liked the black one with the white feet – paws dipped in paint. The sparrows in the rafters – a kind of one note accompaniment. Those shiplap walls that Grandfather Gray built in 1922, a world to them but apart from a larger world. How satisfied they seemed to live in its containment. Preoccupation with a fly would be an afternoon's work. It was not work but cats living a cat's life. Sleep and play. I often picked one up and pressed it to my ear to hear its calming purr. A little motor idling there. Sometimes the wind would move the barn. Great groans and creaks and the cats would all turn as one, alert, wide staring eyes and ears pricked to account for a shifting world they did not know.

When he walked through the barn door with the .22, I knew what my job was. He approached me with his head down and thrust the rifle into my hands. I prayed for my mother to come home, tried to see the car through the filthy windows. He wouldn't dare be so bold. It was always that heartless part of him when she was away.

"Calan," he said, "you need to put a few of them down. They're starving. We don't want to see them suffer now."

I chanced a look at him. He was playing with a compassion that I rarely saw. I couldn't be sure if he truly cared. "They're no bother, Dad," I said. I always tried to reason with him. The cats watched us negotiating their lives.

"You can keep four of them," he said. "Pick the ones that you want to keep."

How he burdened me with such a horrible task. He didn't need my help. Not a chore to pass on to a boy. It was another attempt to cure me, make me right in his eyes. Killing would do that. Oh, he would slap my back and then go brag to Ole Olsen about what a brave young man I was – pumping himself full of my sick glory.

"Can't we just feed them?" I said. The rifle pointing to the floor. I wanted to let it go, let it fall from my hands.

"Come on now, get on with it," he said, "we can't afford to feed damn barn cats!" His agitation rose in the taut veins of his neck, the blue pulse warned me.

I looked them over. Still they watched us, unaware of their coming murder. I had no favourites now. How could I choose? Such power should never have been granted – the power of life and death in my hands. "I can't," I said shaking my head. I learned not to cry at such times. Tears would anger him more – a sullen detachment was worse. I would withdraw inside myself and offer-up my puny bones.

He looked to the windows – nervous – time was running out. "Come on, kill them Calan!"

"Can't." I hadn't moved at all. His spineless son staring down at the line I drew.

"Damn you!" he shouted. He jerked the .22 from my hands and reached into his shirt pocket and removed a shell. It was a single shot and he pulled back the bolt and thumbed a bullet into the breech and pushed the bolt forward.

He muttered his regrets of my birth and shot the orange one in the head. A sharp bang and it fell over. He ejected the shell and reloaded and shot and reloaded again and again. Bang, bang. They didn't seem to know what was happening to them. All head shots. A grey on a timber shrieked and fell, the thud of its dead weight. He killed the kittens at their play. They died where the sun inched across the floor – blood in tight pools, their little faces squeezing – their eyes pinching painfully as they died. I could see their life leaving their bodies, one by one. The flies found them quickly. He never moved his feet, so deftly he shot.

He left two sitting on the windowsill – all was well in the barn. He knew that I wouldn't do it. He was just confirming what he feared about me. Something was deeply wrong with his misbegotten son.

"Get a sack and bury them, boy," he said.

He never looked back at me. A disgusted man who killed so easily. I often wondered what he was like when he was my age, but he never talked about his childhood. Everything was work to him. Life was all about struggle and suffering, meeting the day with a raised fist. Beating the sun down with a hammer and cursing the moon for its laziness. It seemed that his purpose on earth was to be angry. It would be my mother who would later tell me why.

I carried a shovel and the gunnysack of dead cats to the trees. I had to stop when my arms grew tired. Sometimes I just dragged them along the grass. The sack made a whispering sound over the long blades. I kept thinking about how they died. I would bury them well and found a flat place under the aspens where the grass grew up over my knees. I set the sack and shovel aside and gathered handfuls of grass that grew over the plot that I picked out. Then I took the shovel and cut out a square sod and removed it and dug out enough dirt to keep them. It was hard work and the sweat stung my eyes and ran down my nose and fell into the grave. Part of me – a benediction. Work that was my own, that belonged to me. For them.

I placed a layer of grass on the bottom and then without further ceremony, lifted each cat from the sack and lowered it onto the grass – side by side. The one I liked with the white paws seemed to be sleeping. I just looked at them. No tributes. I covered them with the rest of the grass then placed the sack over them and then the dirt. Finally I fitted the sod into place. I worked until all was returned to the way it had been. Of course, nothing was the same.

The trees, I knew, would keep the cats forever. I heard their praises in the leaves. I felt their blessings in my legs, in my arms, in my belly. I thanked them. And still a cruel world buzzed in my head.

CHAPTER TWO

At supper he was all charm – wanted to hear about her day in Saskatoon.

"Did you get the banking done all right?" he said. "I've never been much good with figures. You know, Calan, your mother's the smart one. She has a mind for it. Isn't that right?" He leaned on his elbows – thick thumbs up on his knife and fork.

"Yes, Mack," she said. She seemed slightly troubled by his good humour. A certain suspicion. She turned to me to see what my face would reveal.

I just stared down into my mashed potatoes until her eyes left me. Then it was his turn. I knew what he was thinking. He was worried that I might burst out with something. Tell her about the cats. Tell her about the ripped shirt and swollen ear that throbbed and burned. But I knew better. I looked up at her and her neat blue dress with flowers and her apron with ruffles stitched to the trim. Her red hair always done up, bobby-pinned away from her kind face. I thought she was the most beautiful woman in the world. She saved the best of her for when we were alone. She could talk to me forever with her Scottish lilt and ways. She never asked me what I did all day, as if *she* knew better.

He went on. "So how did the car run?"

"Oh, it was fine, Mack," she said.

"Handles the dirt roads?"

"Just fine."

"And the blacktop?" Stuffing slabs of roast-beef into his maw as he spoke.

"Smooth," she said.

"I bet Ole Olsen was out in his driveway when you went by. Don't you think so, Calan?"

"I suppose he was," I said. He was testing me. Unspoken conversations there at the table – guarded worlds. A queer game that he always won, turning her away from himself so that he could flush me out like prey.

"The Olsen brothers might be jealous of you now, Calan. A fine car like that."

"I don't care." I shrugged foolishly. His silence lingered like a troubling wind.

"Tell her about the trees," he said coldly now.

"What's this, Calan?" my mother said.

"Nothing," I said. I felt sick to my stomach. The unravelling of what I found.

"It wasn't nothing, was it, Calan?"

How he taunted me. He thought I was such a sickly boy, my mousy hair and cowlick, thin arms and round shoulders inviting, deserving. Would never turn against him.

"What about the trees, Calan?" my mother said. "You can tell me."

"No, I don't want to," I said.

"Tell her, Calan!" He was angry, no posturing now, not a scrap of kindness.

"Calan, tell me about the trees." She took up her napkin and wiped her mouth and then placed it on her lap and sat back.

"You're not going to leave the table until you tell her. Or I'll do it for you!"

I slowly lifted my head. Turned to her. I needed her to help me. But I couldn't say anything. What could a boy tell a mother about something he did not understand himself? What the trees said to me. Not in words. No, it wasn't like that.

"Calan, you can talk," she said. "Just say it." She smiled, an invitation. Her own fears showing now.

"Nothing to tell."

"Calan, tell her!" The slam of his fist on the table. Milk leaping in glasses. The ketchup bottle toppling.

"Mack, you're frightening him." She placed her hand up over her heart.

I knew what was to come. I couldn't stop it. My life was an error to him. He would tell her about their retarded son. But I would not conspire with his claims. I had a beating heart and a tongue to speak. So I told her about the trees. "I buried the cats under the aspens," I said. Some rare mischief in me.

"What cats?" she said.

"Shut up, boy!" His face distorted – sharp-edged, harder still and his eyes that hated me.

"The cats he shot in the head."

"What's this, Mack?"

"He tried to make me shoot them, Mom," I said pleading to her sensitivity. "But I wouldn't. I didn't want to hurt them. They never did anything wrong. Just barn cats."

Then the seething through his teeth and the flash of his hand like a murderous shiv and he took hold of my collar and lifted me from my chair and with his other hand he un-buckled his belt and drew it through the loops in his jeans and dragged me out of the kitchen and up the stairs. My feet scarcely landing on the treads, a punishing strength he had when he lost his mind like that. I was terrified of him – what he became – what he was capable of doing. A raging man could not be stopped until it ran out of him.

"I'll be good, Dad," I pleaded, my hand covering my backside. Whimpering and dragging my feet like brakes. "I'll be good," I cried. "I'll be good."

And there I did betray myself, turned against my innocence, bargaining in order to be spared, to be accepted and to be loved by him – that moment when life is no longer safe, when parents become our worlds and we honour them at all costs. The separation from our soul.

And my mother never said a thing, did nothing to stop him. Never left the kitchen.

In my bedroom he closed the curtains and told me to pull my pants and underwear down and lie on the bed. I cried and sobbed waiting for it. I turned to see it coming. He folded his belt and strapped my bare bum and I cried out for the world to hear. Hot welts across the back of my legs that felt as if my skin had been split open, and blood ran wet between my legs. He strapped me and he grunted like a man at his work, strapped me until he was exhausted, until he hated the brutality in his hands and stopped. He never said a thing as he staggered like a drunk from my room and left me on the bed dying another death.

I cried into my pillow. Another dinner ruined and all I could do was feel bad for what I had done. I had to be better. I had to be a good boy. I turned over on my side and touched the sore spots with my fingers, the raised and painful welts like miserable Braille. There was no blood. I had wet myself and it stung fiercely. Like the salted lacerations of slaves, the mistreated and the impotent. How men could injure. Then something coming. Suddenly I had a sense that I never did anything wrong. I could hear them, a chorus of muted energy. No, please. Go away!

I went to my window, the sun just settling behind the barn. I could feel them, a beneficent presence, waves of soft energy. It was the aspens, not the poor lombardy with their leaves limp and hungry. There was nothing else in the yard.

My mother kept petunias in pots on the porch and a vegetable garden at the side of the house. All else was grass springing from the untrod margins. It was them, over the hills and far away, the aspens and their voices riding the breezes searching for me. But I did not want them now. There would only be his cruel ambition to fix me with his bare hands.

And then I could hear *his* voice below me, through the vent in the floor. I lay down and listened.

"Don't you see?' he said. "Takes after your loony father. He's coming to stay with us, and what is to happen then? Calan has his eyes, green with those bits of amber. Fools eyes. I haven't seen him since Calan was born but I won't forget his queer eyes. Calan has them, I swear. You know he does. You can see it, something wrong with him, something in his head. The collections he has. Labels from cans in a scrapbook. The springs from clothespins – a drawer full. Likely got it from him. You can see it.

"What will we do when your father comes? He will be a ruined boy for sure. Imagine a man who played bagpipes at funerals. He has spent his whole life looking after a stupid tree and painting it over and over and selling the little pictures for a nickel to tourists. What kind of job is that? If Calan has that same trouble then we need to get him straightened out. A doctor to look at him. You know his trouble at school. He can't spell or do his sums. We need to see what's wrong in his brain. Do it, Meg. Take him, damn it, it's his only chance!"

"Mack, Dad was a Forester, you know that," my mother said. "Nothing wrong with him at all and a fine artist, too. Proud to be a piper." She was so impotent against him, his charges. Always her tempering the air, to diffuse the lingering threat of him.

"I'm talking about the boy, Meg. For Christ's sake. Talking to trees. I've seen it. Heard him like he was having a conversation with someone who wasn't there. He'll never set foot there again. I forbid it. It's not right, Meg, I tell you. He won't have a life!"

She must have seen something after all that gave her reason to agree with him – that made her call the doctor. She never stopped him when he hauled me up the stairs and leaned over me with the belt – his spit, a white rime on his grim mouth. She never came to my room to see what he had done. But she called the doctor with some curious affliction that loosened shame in her words. The saddest thing. Retarded by all accounts.

I opened my scrapbook. The flat peaches, pineapple and fruit cocktail. Pears. Soups of every kind – my very own like stamps. And school that confused me.

CHAPTER THREE

I could see the dust in the side mirror and the sleek shape of our new car, a 1964 Ford Country Squire – robin's egg blue with wood-grain and bedecked with chrome. My father kept an old pickup truck for farm work but he had to have a new car every few years. Feast or famine, we would have it, a Ford, but the Country Squire was the nicest, the most luxurious, prestige riding the washboard and potholes toward the Olsen's. It gave me some pleasure I will admit, when my mother slowed to make sure they saw us. Any car coming from the east had to be ours, nothing beyond us but prairie and ponds and a country that I could not comprehend. And the dust was like an announcement, a telegram from my father to Ole Olsen – *by God, I'm better than you!*

I knew this and the thought that I was his emissary on that day troubled me, but still I turned to their house to look for them – Bobby and Ricky Olsen coming up the driveway to see our prosperity, our substance, our standing in the world.

"Oh, look at them, Calan," she said. "Wave. Why don't you wave?"

I only gave them a side look – a bit of a glance and my smug mouth for good measure. How easily it came, that moment to join with him, to herald his inflation, deliver his satisfaction. But with my will I managed a wave to break from his long arms and they just gawked like prairie dogs from their hills, an alert wonder of things unknown to them. They only saw the car gliding by, malcontent about their pinching looks and still my mother waving like one of the Royals.

"Never seen such hard working lads as those two," she said. "Toiling away with their father. Mr. Olsen is mighty proud of them. Fine hockey players, too. Mrs. Olsen told me so. The talk of Clavet. Hard working farm boys. I dare say it'll all be theirs one day."

I looked over to her, that familiar theme of persuasion and manipulation made me shrink. The little deaths of rejection. She was looking into the rear-view mirror. Something on her lip – a bump where her lipstick cracked. She dabbed it with her finger.

"What's that?" I said.

"What?"

"Your lip."

"Oh, that. Bug bite, I'm sure. Nasty little things." She looked at me. "It's nothing," she said. "Never you mind, Calan."

Then she went silent. She turned on the radio. A song that she didn't like, that he liked. Johnny Horton – "Battle of New Orleans." She turned it off. She wanted something else just then, Dean Martin, or Frank Sinatra's "Fly me to the Moon" – somewhere to escape to. I was hoping for the Beatles. He hated them, their recklessness, the outrage of their hair. That winter on the Ed Sullivan Show he leapt from his chair and turned off the television before they could finish "She Loves You".

"Oh," she said, remembering – another diversion, "your grandfather is going to stay with us for a bit. Grandpa Dunny from Scotland. Where I was born, you know. Jules Bear is going to help your father fix up the old chicken coop. Make a nice little house for him."

I wanted to ask her what a *Forester* was, why he disliked him. But she would have known that I heard them, his fears and conclusions. Her indifference. I was just happy that he was coming, happy that I had his eyes. I had only seen a photograph of him, a mane of grey hair and sweeping beard. Fists tucked into vest pockets and a noble rearing back of his head – a black and white impression of a proud man. He sent me a gift once, a rare Christmas present – a book. *Trees of the World.*

"When?" I said.

"It'll be August," she said. "He sold his little farm in Perthshire and bought a 'wee house by the sea' as he called it, on the west coast of British Columbia. It'll be ready for him by Thanksgiving. He's in Victoria now with Auntie Netty. She has a little house downtown, a bungalow really, with all your cousins. But I'm glad that he's there. Since my mother died, your grandmother, he needs the company of family. And Auntie Kate is there, too. No place for him in her apartment. Nurses, you know, coming and going at all hours. So he'll be coming here. We have plenty of room for him."

"Why can't he stay in our house?"

"Oh, it's best," she said, a catch in her voice. "He'll have his own little place."

All that talk about family was confusing, a mystery to me. Where did they come from? Who were they? There was never an explanation, an account. It was if I didn't deserve to know where I had come from. It didn't matter that I was curious. I saw the letters – the postage from Scotland. She never read them to me. She did not acknowledge them, or him. And then I would hear my father. "What did he say?"

And my mother would answer. "You know, weather mostly. Did we plant on time? You know, things like that."

And that would be enough for him, launch him out onto the prairie. "We'll need the rain to let up if there's any chance of that!" He would look out the window as if to confirm his predicament, sneering at the flat earth, never a partnership, a cooperative venture working with the land, but always against it, daring it to spoil another season.

And my mother would turn away with that thin smile of victory, steering a man by what he feared the most. And he would be driven back to the barn to crawl under the big wheels of the tractor with the running gear lying on the straw, bashing his knuckles while I stood there wondering what it was that fired the roaring and cussing, the raw peeling of his hands or my failure to recognize the tools he barked out.

The two worlds of them that never had a place for me – like paddlers in a stream, their oars never drawing together, but each fighting the current that pulled them toward the falls. And I in my flimsy craft tethered to the both of them, going under now and then and thinking any second they would slip a knife through my tenuous cord and be rid of me once and for all.

But now she was talking to me as if I knew the blood and lineage of her family – the McLeods. Not the phantom Grays. Never the past of my father that seemed to dwell in some dark place – an impenetrable vault behind his fierce eyes. It all left me with a profound sense of not belonging to anything, a loose affiliation, a boy staying a while, a contrary boy who arrived unfit for a farm, unfit to kill cats and forbidden to go to *them*. But I had his eyes. I belonged to him at least – Dunmore McLeod.

The prairie rushed to meet us, the brackish ponds pockmarked with the sameness where terns held still in their suspended flight and mallards rested their green heads on their backs as they watched with one eye the broods that followed in strings behind the wary hens. I saw them from my place in my mother's silence – drawing now and then with a pencil and blank notebook. Not creating anything in particular but sketching from some unconscious place where memories and attention gathered a likeness of things, imagined and fleeting. She watched me as we hit the pavement. A sudden floating and shimmering heat wave in the distance, a lake that could never be reached and dauntless prairie dogs dashing madly for the other side of the road.

"What are you drawing?" she said.

I wasn't sure and had to look down at what I had drawn – studied it briefly to understand it. "Just a leaf," I said.

"What kind of leaf?"

I hesitated. "Aspen," I said haltingly. My guilt for uttering the forbidden.

"It's one of them, isn't it, the ones you talk to?"

"Just a leaf," I said.

"Want to tell me, Calan?"

"Tell you what?"

"Tell me about them. Tell me what you say. You'll have to tell the doctor. I won't get mad. I promise. What do you say to them, Calan?"

"Why does he get so mad?"

She opened her purse, removed a pack of Players, and pulled out a cigarette. I pushed in the lighter for her. After a minute it popped and she took the red-hot coil and lit her cigarette. I watched. Her ritual when she was nervous – the cigarette held between her fingers, a smudge of lipstick on the filter and the tapping of the steering wheel. The blue smoke was sucked out her open window.

Clavet appeared. "Let's stop for a pop," she said. "The heat is something else today."

She pulled up in front of the Clavet General Store. Whitewashed stucco and kids' bikes leaning on the outside wall under the Orange Crush sign. Swallows frantic over a mud nest above the door. Peering fuzzy heads. A fat kid with a bolo bat stood next to his bike, a Schwinn, the kind my father bought me. A used bike that I hated the first time I saw it. They were mostly for fat kids, I thought, hard to peddle and unable to keep up to the sleek CCM three-speeds like the Olsen brothers had. The kid could only get about two hits of the ball before it would careen off to the side of the bat. Sweat trickled down his hot cheeks and his shirt sopped under his arms and over the folds of his fat belly. I felt sorry for him, his exasperation, his miserable play. I wanted to go up to him. But I didn't know what I would say. It was just a feeling.

Inside, my mother went to the cooler and pulled a Mountain Dew from the chilled water and wiped it with the towel left for that purpose. She stuck the bottle under the bottle opener and pried off the cap – the metallic clank of it dropping into the tin box. I pawed through the orange popsicles in the freezer until I found a grape. She paid the seventeen cents as she talked to Mrs. Daisy behind the counter. The kids called her Lazy Daisy because she never left her stool behind the counter. She always wore a print dress with daisies. She liked to talk but only to the adults. My mother had a smile the whole time, not like at home. There seemed to be something about being away, a distance from the farm. She became untroubled. A secret life.

When I got outside I cracked my popsicle against the edge of the windowpane splitting it in two pieces. The fat boy was gone but the Schwinn was still there. I slid one half of the popsicle out of the wrapper and gave it a lick. My knuckles got sticky and I licked them too. I noticed a girl looking at me. She was standing by the bikes. She had short dirty blond hair. You could tell that her mother cut it. She was covered in freckles. Scabby knees. I wondered what she was staring at. I must have looked stupid or something. I made one of my squinty faces at her, the kind that my father thought was cheeky. I always told him it was the bright sun. Mostly I wore that look that seemed to cover all looks. I wasn't trying to look that way. I think it was because I was anxious most of the time and that's just how it appeared. She made the same squinty face back at me.

"Do you know her, Calan?" my mother asked noting the exchange between us.

"No," I said. "Never seen her before." She was in my grade four class. Janet Smith. She used to steal lunches from the cloakroom before the morning bell. Thin as a rake in makeshift dresses that her mother modified and passed down to her. Everyone knew. She rummaged like a mouse and the children giggled in their seats. Teased her until a puddle appeared under her desk. She would never leave her seat until all the kids went home. A girl who rarely talked but mostly stared – as if she were studying you – figuring out something. She never bought anything in the store.

I walked over to her and gave her the other half of my popsicle. She snatched at the stick right away. Then she rode off on that Schwinn with a wobbly wheel and looked back at me in the glare of the sun, standing up on the peddles of a bike that was too big for her and stuck out a purple tongue. I couldn't believe it. But I smiled. So rare for me.

"That was nice of you, Calan," my other said, "to offer a strange girl half of your treat like that." She was more puzzled than proud.

"I don't think she has much," I said.

"You know, Calan," my mother said looking out over the prairie, "when my sisters and I came to Saskatchewan every-thing was so new to us. And so much space. But I was the only one who stayed. They were older and perhaps knew better. I don't know." She raised a hand to shield the sun and took a sip from the long green bottle. She looked so young just then, not a care in the world. But as she wiped her mouth with the back of her hand there was something else, a wistful detachment. Did she ever wonder? She stood there leaning on the fender of our car watching cars go by. As if their passing was for her.

Back in the car we passed Janet on her bike just outside of town.

"There's that girl," my mother said. "Must live in that trailer up ahead. There's no other house out here."

I turned and stuck my head out the window as we zoomed by her, her red face and burnt shoulders – peddling all that way. She still had the popsicle stick in her hand. Then she stopped and got off her bike and watched us driving away from her. I could see her through the back window standing there in the sun. It felt like we were leaving her behind somehow, that we forgot to take her with us. Janet disconnected, shrinking until she was no longer there – a shape lost in the pooling heat.

"She stopped," I said.

"I guess she doesn't want you to know where she lives," my mother surmised. "Poor thing."

And the trailer in that isolated space, charred remnants of a hopeful spring. Everything around the trailer was burnt – out to the road – fence posts black and aslant, the scorched frame of a car, incinerated junk in heaps. The only thing untouched was the trailer itself and behind it the familiar beating of trees, there beside a pond – trees, animate and green shaking in the wind and offering a bit of shade in the hot afternoon. I couldn't understand it, the trees protecting the trailer somehow. It was not possible. But I remembered a prayer from when I buried the cats – *protect the weak.* Perhaps it wasn't really a prayer or petition but a thought I had, something that crossed my mind. Like telling a sailor – *may fair winds blow.*

CHAPTER FOUR

In Saskatoon, an oasis sprung from the prairie like a civilized remedy for the isolation of farm life. Bridges over the South Saskatchewan River and great cottonwoods with their feet wet and rooted to the history of rivers stood alongside riparian willows and birches. And downtown maples shaded mothers pushing children in strollers under the curious neon where crowded buildings were stacked with some ambition, some enterprise that was lost to me. And all about a pedestrian play of motion that halted at intersections for cars and trucks jerking in senseless streams bound for unknown places. It was always new to me, a sudden density of life that shocked me, delighted me. Trees that I did not know. I looked for them, down every street, a game I played. Their form in tamed beauty lining the boulevards like bookends, great arching branches touching, holding hands and cradling the miscreant crows. A welcome distraction. And then my mother pointed to a two-story brick building at Queen Street and 5th Avenue.

The doctor was waiting. My mother took me into his office and we sat. The white-smocked Dr. Cooper Douglas smiled and looked down at the chart in his hands – some glimpse into an ailment that had no viral association, no account of broken bones or careless gashes, nothing so simple to set or stitch. I could feel it now, the coming questions – a lens upon my deviations, an exorcism to root out the evil sway of trees. And the doctor who was kind enough when my tonsils damned my throat sat down on a stool beside me and nodded his head thoughtfully.

"So, Calan," he said, "what brings you in today?"

He wanted me to tell him, in my own words, tell him of my secret things, the unanswerable and nameless. And I wondered sitting there with my mother with her arms folded expectantly, waiting for me to answer, why it was me that needed repair and not *him*, and not her with her fat lip? But no, I was the cause and the remedy, the damage to repair. I was a boy without a voice, a reason, nothing rational for him to listen to with his stethoscope. And I sat a long time and didn't answer. Then my mother showed him my drawings and he took them and regarded them casually.

"Are these the trees?" he said. He knew – the infamous.

And I looked at them, hardly turning my head – so afraid to answer, to declare that I had such proclivities, that I admit to some injury inside me and in need of help. So confusing when the natural and benign comes face to face with another world, a world that loathes the mysteries, the unexplainable and the unfathomable. Why did *they* want to make me wrong? Could I trust him?

"Yes," I said finally. There was nowhere to go but with him.

"Interesting," he said, "a view along the stem to the leaves."

"One leaf," I corrected.

"I see many leaves."

"It's only one. I drew how it flutters, wobbles, one leaf in different positions. It's the wind that catches them. And when they all…"

"I see, you ghosted them to show how they move. Actually it is quite extraordinary, Calan. Look at that how they tilt and flatten. It seems that you have quite a gift. So tell me about them." He handed my mother back my sketchbook.

I glanced to her, squinting and twisting my mouth, but I could see that she would not liberate me. She wanted to hear me say it. She wanted to know what it was that drove *him* to fits – from my very lips.

"The trees are by our farm," I said timidly – unwilling but resigned to say it all. "I found them. I had a strange feeling, kind of spooky at first. But it felt…"

"Yes, Calan, go on," the doctor encouraged.

"It felt like something good. There was nothing to be afraid of. I guess it felt like words. But I didn't hear anything other than the wind in the leaves. It just felt like words. So I talked back to them. I spoke out loud. Just like talking to a friend. Nothing wrong with that is there, Dr. Douglas? I talk to them and they talk back to me. I know that I shouldn't. But I think that they want to help me."

"With what?" the doctor asked.

"Help me so I won't get hurt, I guess."

"How are you going to get hurt?"

The rustle of my mother's cotton dress. *No, Calan, No!* I looked down at my hands, the gathering of apprehension, cold and damp. I rubbed them on my jeans. "I think that they saved the girl."

"What girl?"

"You know, Mom," I said turning to her for consolation, "Janet, the girl on the bike. Everything burnt except the trailer and the trees behind it. The trees, I think that they did it."

I wanted so much for her to understand but she wanted no part of it. She seemed weary all at once, sorry to have heard for herself, nothing for her to comfort now. I was in the hands of the good doctor.

"Now, son, you know that trees can't talk," he said. "You must be mistaken. Is that possible, Calan?"

"I never said words."

"But they talk to you?"

"They have their own way of doing it. I don't know how. It's my secret. It doesn't belong to anyone else. I don't want to talk anymore. Can we go, Mom? Can we go?"

The doctor had the look of a man who had just been stumped for the first time in his life. He made a few notes. The grim bow of his mouth. "Calan," he said to me, "can you go out to the waiting room while I speak to your mother?"

"All right," I said.

"She'll just be a minute."

I stopped at the door. I turned and looked right at him. So little sitting there on the stool, never elevating himself above me. "Dr. Douglas, am I retarded?"

"Calan, watch your manners!" my mother scolded.

He had to think about it. "No, son," he said.

I sat in the waiting room. At least I didn't have to bare my sunken chest, my narrow slouching shoulders and feel that fat popsicle stick on my tongue that made me gag. No dropping my underwear so that he could squeeze my balls while I coughed.

When my mother came out she did not seem happy. I was sure the appointment had confirmed my father's suspicions, made me out to be crazy, loony like Grandpa Dunny. I could see her disappointment. I couldn't have told it any other way. But there was something else. She would have to explain it all to him, tell him that he had a son that needed a special doctor, tell him what she couldn't tell me.

And out in the car the fear in her eyes – something terminal, irreversible, that unreachable sense of her. She sat there next to me but her mind travelled to some comforting place – in her past or somewhere imagined in her dreams. I could never tell exactly what it was. She would never just come out and say it. So I speculated with a ten-year-old mind, wondered why she always looked west to the horizon, to the setting sun – to her people. She beheld the distance with such intensity that it seemed to me that she had left the car, journeyed on a prayer or a wish, stole out of her body to see for herself what her longings could bring.

On the University Bridge she slowed to a crawl and pointed to the railing. "That's where they went off," she said.

"Who went off?" I wanted to know.

"Grandpa and Grandma Gray. Some said he just turned the wheel and broke through the railing and plunged into the river. Drowned them both. Heartsickness killed them really. I had to tell you this sooner or later. I think you're old enough now. Your father's brothers, Leonard and George, were killed in the war. Your father was too young to enlist but mostly he was needed on the farm. And then his sister Ida drowned in the pond. She broke through poor ice in the late winter while skating with your father. He couldn't save his little Ida and watched her slip away. He nearly drowned himself trying to pull her out. He ran across the fields to bring home the terrible news, frozen stiff and unable to speak for an hour until he thawed by the stove. Never took off his skates. So Grandpa and Grandma Gray did the only thing left for them. They left the farm and your father and went to join Ida and the boys. There's no sadder story. If there is I've never heard it.

"Your father's not mad, Calan. He has so much suffering in him that it just comes out that way. I don't expect you to like him for what he does. I'd just like you to understand a thing or two. Even that doesn't help sometimes. He never wanted me to tell you. He doesn't like to talk about it. It puts him in a blue mood for weeks. Imagine a sixteen-year-old boy losing his family that way. They even tried to take the farm away from him because of his age. But Jules Bear came to help with all his brothers. They came up from the Reserve. And you know, they made a go of it.

"He wasn't going to lose the farm. That would have killed him too, I'm sure. And I think he farms for them now. Not a day goes by when he's not thinking of them. Jules has been helping out ever since. He won't quit your father. He's paid for his work of course. So perhaps you can see how your father might feel when his only son doesn't take to the farming life. He wants to fix you – like a broken harrow. He can mend anything with his hands. But he can't fix you, Calan. It's not right that you need fixing. I can't tell how much a mother loves her children. But I heard what you said. And you're in need of help that I can't imagine. There're kids that are born crippled. Some die soon after they're born, accidents too, broken necks and backs and not able to walk again. A wasted life. But you're able and your father needs your help. I don't know what else to do. Maybe you'll grow out of it. In a few years be strong as an ox. Throwing bales like Bobby and Ricky Olsen. I'll be praying for that."

Cars started to sound their horns behind us and my mother sped up. All the things that she told me on that day – an accounting of lives, the sorting out of the causes and the effects. She wanted me to know. She let Gray blood flow and I took it in my hands to feel it, the tack of it on my fingertips. Tragic misfortune for me to arrange in some kind of order, some explanation that could make right my world. But it wasn't my world that needed righting. I did not possess the answers to the questions that haunted her so, that look in her eyes, that recognition that hopelessness was the most savage of conditions.

CHAPTER FIVE

The sun broke free of the horizon. It threw lanes of copper out across the wheat. All was ripening well under an August sky that always seemed an ending to me, the completion of things planted and conceived, the culmination of a season's faith that wasn't really faith but an unremitting hope among the farmers on that *flatter than piss on a plate* world.

The windshield of Jules Bear's truck was ablaze when he pulled up to the barn. He got out of his truck and saw me on the porch. A good place to be with bowls of peas and beans waiting for my slow hands to shell and snap. He raised his arm. Swarmed in amber like something painted from a single brush stroke – something from the dirt loosened to walk about in the morning fires, a Dakota man with his pride and denim pants and shirt and a straw cowboy hat and the single braid of his black hair down his back. A bad hip as stiff as a tailgate.

I had been watching my father out in the fields, the posture of him as he fingered the swelling heads of wheat, checking for rust and weevils and hoping like hell that the weather would hold out until harvest. He did that every day, his ritual, willing favour out of the earth, never a petition to God, moving as a mime rehearsed to a role, a rhythm I did not understand though my mother wished for it. But Jules somehow understood him, knew him like the seasons. In a month the combine would be set upon a year's work and they would bring it in together.

Jules walked out to meet my father. When they came together my father threw a hand up on his shoulder. There was much pointing out across the prairie, the way one gives directions to a particular thing. Jules looked out in the direction of his pointing and nodded then swung around as if by some distraction. More pointing. It seemed that they were surrounded by the object of their discussion. In my mind I created a silly conversation fitting for what I could see. *Look, there is that. And over there, something is.*

I watched them walk back down the track toward the house, then momentarily lost in the shade of the lombardy and then re-emerging, larger now, closer to me – close enough to see how my father seemed at ease with Jules – nothing hurried in his movements. A certain unity between them. He stopped and pulled a pack of cigarettes from his shirt pocket. He offered one to Jules. He struck a match and lit them. And they continued, a blue haze marking the passing of moments.

They stopped at the old chicken coop and considered it, the outside, the structure, what they had to work with. They went inside and after a time came out. Jules retrieved a few tools from the back of his truck. My father went into the barn and returned with a handsaw and hammer and a bag of nails. Jules helped him with a stack of shiplap and two by fours. Bats of insulation. Then Jules said something to him and he looked my way, found me wanting on the porch. He stared at me for what seemed a long time as if considering the merits of Jules's suggestion. The mere sight of me was enough to vex him. But he waved me over.

I wanted to be useful, an eagerness to be a part of

something. But it wasn't the work that I was interested in, no skill that I cared to learn. It was Jules Bear. I wanted to know how a man comes to know another man, comes to know his darkness and remains at his side in spite of it. I ran across the yard, my feet unsure and unproven, ran as fast as I ever had, my awkward lumbering that my father turned away from. Spat something foul from his dry mouth.

"Calan," Jules said, "you have grown over the summer." His measured smile, the lines of his burnished skin like knife cuts, set down long and deep. He hung his hat on a nail.

"A little," I said. I felt his kindness that wanted nothing.

Then my father handed me a broom. "Get rid of the chicken shit," he said bluntly.

I suppose he knew that I wouldn't take up a hammer. I stood there on the front stoop and listened to the talk of men and their planning, wary of my father's eye when I took too long to admire Jules Bear. They went inside and closed the door and worked. They spoke as they did so and I moved closer. I wanted to hear the language between them, perhaps the secret of friendship, what sustained them. A crack in the door for my eye.

"He'll be fine in here," my father said. "A simple sort of man. Scotsmen don't need much. He has his funny ways. Meg is making curtains."

"I remember him that summer," Jules said. He packed the insulation and then placed shiplap over the bare studs along the wall. Hammered a few nails. "A man of many stories. He has curious speech. I liked the sound of it."

"Don't you believe them, Jules," my father said, "they're nothing but tall tales. There's a difference. And he speaks a mile a minute. I don't know what the hell he's talking about. And I don't care." He measured more boards for Jules and cut them with the handsaw.

"A man who knows trees. Yes, It will be good to see him

again." Another course of boards nailed – insulated for the colder nights.

My father stopped working and turned to Jules. Threw down the hammer. "Did you just hear what I said? Don't get me started, Jules. I have had it with trees."

"Mack, something on your mind?"

"You don't want to know."

"Then I will just be silent and wait. For you will tell me. You always do."

"Damn you, Jules. You won't believe this, but Calan talks to trees. He claims that they talk back. Don't know what to do. Now that crazy old coot is coming next week. I'm going to have my hands full. He'll be spinning his nonsense. His queer eyes like a senseless dog."

I pressed against the doorframe, my heart thumping the old wood.

"Talks to trees?" Jules never looked up from his work. He took the boards that were cut to length and nailed them. A methodical carpenter present with the wood.

"Talks to them as if they were his friends."

"And they talk back to him?"

"Not words exactly. He says that they talk to him without speaking. He feels them. I'm worried as hell. He's already been to the doctor in Saskatoon. He told him that some trees saved a girl from a fire. Now Meg's taking him to another doctor. He needs to get to the bottom of it."

"Hand me another board," Jules said. "I'm doing all the work and all you're doing is talking." He turned slightly, saw me there.

"They're trees, damn it!"

"What trees?"

"The trees at the end of the top field. Aspens!"

"Aspens. Old trees. The groves are thousands of years old. Old trees."

"So what?" A wall was finished now.

"Perhaps, young Calan has reverence," Jules said. He insulated the opposite wall.

"Reverence. What kind of goddamn word is that? Now you're worrying me, Jules."

"I have prayed, spoken to the four corners of the earth. I have asked the One, *Tunkansila,* to bless my community and all the life that surrounds it. When a boy speaks to a tree or perhaps to Coyote or Bear or Eagle, and if he is reverent, then assistance will come to him in his life. I think Calan has reverence for the land. I don't think that is a bad thing, Mack. Pass me a board."

The door, my accomplice, and the broom a prop in my hands – I wanted to hear it all. A curious word to answer my father's fears, a tone unlike his anger, a word that I did not know. I could sense that Jules understood me just then. And he knew more, but how could I speak to him? I could listen. I could watch him and the flare of my father's eyes. I wondered if Jules could hear the anger in his voice. The danger he was in. But Jules was not afraid – his truth was calm and even. And my father could say nothing more because he could not counter a wisdom he did not understand. He had his sufferings, his ways, the uncompassionate wells that he fell into. The farm was all he had, a farmer all he would ever be.

And on that morning when my mother baked bread while it was still cool and the acres of production swimming gold and boundless, I was the failure that could bring it all down, bring a grand year to its knees when the world found out that Macklin Gray produced a son unfit for a meaningful life. And Ole Olsen would sneer at him with his two mules at his side. Not that I would begrudge Bobby and Ricky their work ethic. It wasn't that at all. I just never had the ability to set out upon a day to make him proud, to emulate him, to be him. He beat that out of me long before I knew the difference between fear and love.

Then my father's voice dropped but I heard it plain

enough. "I hear there might be a special school for boys like him," he said. "He can't do his schoolwork like the other kids."

I fell into the door, my knees sliding. Down.

"Mack," Jules said, a sound like the deflating of will.

But he could never hear Jules Bear beyond the romanticized lore – the fiction of a man who never ran, never quit on him but accepted him all the years. And then all at once Jules came out the door with his hat in his hand, pushed me aside and looked down at me gravely but not menacingly, something that he held in his body, when my father said to him – *boys like him*. And back through the door I could see the shadow of my father leaning against the finished wall with his head down as if shamed – a silence thick with something Jules could not say, things between men when words falter, that deathly stillness that seems to smother the earth. And then I remembered what Bobby Olsen told me – how they came for the Bear kids, snatched them like pups and sent them away to drive the Indian out of them – a factory to turn the little bastards white.

Jules sat in his truck and wouldn't come out. After a time my mother called us in for lunch. She stood on the porch in her apron and watched my father come across the yard with his head down. Walked right by me as if I were nothing at all. A man sinking, wondering what he said to turn his friend away. He rapped on the window.

"Jules, let's get some lunch," he said. "We can finish up the shack later. Come on now. Don't quit on me."

I was there now, invisible on the porch with my mother as Jules finally opened the door and came out of his truck. And that look of hers that did not understand, that did not want to know what it was that my father had done. She turned back to the house and we followed her and took our places at the big table in the dinning-room, the men at one end with slabs of ham and homemade white bread stacked and steaming. A ready jar of mustard.

And I sat beside my mother, some sort of segregation that she conceived that did not stop with me. I would never complain – meat for their hard work. There before me the same bread cut thick and soft and golden crusted. Butter square on a plate and a tin of peanut butter and milk for my thin bones. The warm smell of baking. Those moments seemed to correct a listing world when thoughts fall silent and there is only the satisfaction of food, an unspoken gratitude. In a silence that brought the house to reveal its sounds, great sandwiches were devoured and I might have let out a moan as I stuffed the bread into my mouth, the melting butter and peanut butter slick on my chin.

How the windows lured us away from the troubles that sat down to eat, my mother looking off through the panes to her distance, her escape, and my father to the length of his arm where he heaved his desperation, no farther than the land beneath his feet. I looked to the chicken coop that would keep my grandfather but I did not need a window, a place for wishes or intentions, just out there where my thoughts were drifting like dandelion seeds – a thought to that cool gully and I could feel them. Strange now, a thought and the sudden sense of approaching mystery like flicking a light switch and the disappearing dark. *Boys like them.*

Jules raised his head. His mood was unclear for always his speech was slow and gentle, never faltering from a certain tranquility. But how can one ever know another's inner depths, that place of primordial fear and desperation? I had no sense of Jules's world where words were useless devices to account for an unspeakable hurt. Something in me always wanted to know the truth – wanted me to speak it. At that young age I had come to understand that what someone says and how they really feel, can be very different. Like books that are slammed shut, never to be pried open to reveal their stories. And then *they* were at the door.

"What are their names?" I asked him. A startling question that I heard come out of my mouth. He only hung his head.

"Calan!" my mother scolded, "that was a very bad thing to ask. Watch your place now!"

And my father glared at me – that look meant to show me that he knew what I was up to. He never said a word. He seemed to know that he didn't have anything useful to say. Later I would catch it. But first I had another question.

"What does reverence mean?" I stumbled over the word. I had to know, to see what it would bring, what it would reveal about me. There was something undeniable about Jules. I trusted him.

"Calan," my mother said, "what's got into you?" More bewilderment than anger now.

Still my father watching me stiff with his anger. Jules turned to him and caught his simmering, his agitation and mute hostility. He seemed to measure it against my question, against the morning. Then he slowly turned to me.

"Simon and Gabriel," he said, "they should have come for the summer." Then he folded his hands on the table and studied them. "If we honour something," he went on, "respect it with a deep understanding. That is reverence. To live a life of reverence is a good path to follow. The trees…"

My father interrupted. He had enough. "Calan, go to your room. I will have no more of this foolishness!" He shot out his arm. "Go!"

And from my bedroom window I watched Jules Bear leave and my father standing slackly in the driveway. I hoped that Jules would be back but I feared that I might have driven something between them. How the world seemed so fragile when I walked upon it. And somewhere north where the prairie stalled beyond the great river, I imagined Simon and Gabriel Bear wanting to go home.

MAPLE

CHAPTER SIX

Driving along the blacktop undulations I sat awkwardly in the front seat. There was a fire burning in my legs, scars from his cruel branding. This time he was vicious – I walked him into the uncomfortable truth of Jules Bear, brought it out plain there at the lunch table. With my simple understanding I had asked a question. I knew no other way now. It was the way that Jules lived his life I imagined – quiet, thoughtful, speaking his truth to those who could hear it. And I wondered if *they* had prodded me, somehow made me ask the question.

It was becoming easier to slip into my world of soft grasses and shuddering trees. It would come after a strapping or a harsh word. A severe look from him would do it. In my wondering I thought that perhaps it was a fantasy world created when things can no longer be understood, a way to cope. But the trees did not seem a creation, a projection of a boy's imagined world. They found me, came to me, a message, a soothing wind – helpers, succour for the weak and timid. Why did they come with their mystery?

Jules Bear would know. He knew the ways of the land, the secrets and gifts. I needed to speak to him, to be near him. And yet I feared at times that my father would kill me. I was never strong. He would kill me with his fists, his belt, his anger. I would die and still I would not hate him. My mother had told me his story, the tragic and grim fortune of a boy not quite a man. And I wondered if that was what kept Jules Bear coming back, something that he could see beyond a man's limitations, a shared woundedness. And these things kept me awake in the night. The long worrying dark.

"I need to stop for cigarettes," my mother said.

The only thing she said all the way to Clavet. She played with her hair while she went somewhere that I could not see. Now and then she would turn to me. She had heard the wails and his awful grunts just before the violent slap of leather – an animal engaged in a man's brutality. Soaked the cotton sheets. A battle raged inside her, worked away at her, took her from me. And the radio was silent now. It seemed that even her music could no longer comfort her.

I waited in the car, watched the arc of swallows and their freedom. Back on the road she handed me an Oh Henry chocolate bar and then tapped out a cigarette. She waited for me to push the lighter.

"Mrs. Daisy told me something about the little girl on that bike," she said. Her spirits always lifted after talking to someone outside the farm. "That trailer in the burnt yard. You remember, Calan? Awful. Well, I asked about her."

"Yeah, Janet," I said. A mouthful of peanuts and chocolate.

"She said the little thing is sick all the time. Never has a bath. Socks always a different colour. Shoes with soles flapping like tongues. Seems she looks after her mother. Can you imagine that? Her mother is crippled – braces on both legs. She's house-bound and with a dreadful weight. Mrs. Daisy thinks she has a disease in her brain. Slowly dying is what she said. A bad accident in Prince Albert took the father. Sad state of affairs. That girl shouldn't have to do that. Living like an Indian, I think she put it. And steals from the store. But she can never catch her."

- 52 -

Lazy Daisy. A silent cheer. "She needs help," I said.

"Yes, Calan, she needs help."

"Can we help her?"

"Help her?"

"Yeah – her troubles."

"Well, we have so much of our own, Calan. The farm and all that. It takes everything we have and then some. Oh, I would like to help her. Sure I would. But we just can't be helping everyone."

She had that look, wondering where I would get such a notion – one more thing to add to her worries. And then we passed the trailer and Janet was sitting on the front steps.

"Look at her," my mother said, "that filthy dress covered in soot. A bloody shame. Goodness."

I waved at her when she looked up. I knew that she would. Everyone watched cars go by, always hopeful, as if some miracle had finally arrived. A wish and a dream. Something. Then her little hand came up without lifting her arm.

"Is he going to send me away?" I asked. Just came out. I enjoyed our time alone – the car ride. I could ask my mother things. She might scold me, but the bruise would not last for long. And always I recognized that her answers revealed more about her own fears, things she could not speak about. At such times her sleepy eyes tried so hard to comfort me.

"Why, Calan, of course not," she said. An outrageous question it seemed.

"I heard him say it. There was a special school for boys like me. He said it to Jules Bear. I heard him."

"He was just talking, Calan. Talking with Jules. That's all."

"They took his boys."

"Calan, enough of this. Today we are seeing a special doctor. He'll know what to do. No more talk of this."

"What is a special doctor?"

"A doctor, that's all. A doctor who knows things. That's all."

"He doesn't want me around Grandpa Dunny, I bet."

"Calan, enough!"

We were back in Saskatoon. Thunder above and rain in the streets and umbrellas appearing like pedestrian mushrooms and my mother taking it all in, that feeling she liked, the imagined escaping – one among the many. We found the special doctor at the edge of town, in the basement of some forgotten building, old enough to curl the tarpaper brick siding and not a scrap of green on the property. It was a barren structure, not a crow about the rooftop to praise the bleak and damned. I was damned to be sure as my mother took my hand that one rare time, held it tight down the dark stairwell where the rain overflowed in the eaves and found our gaping necks.

We entered a room like a closet with two chairs. An older woman who seemed without humour sat behind a counter and peered over her glasses that held fast to an impossible nose. I didn't like they way she looked at us as we sat down as if we were vagrants seeking sanctuary from the rain. Something that didn't want us there.

"Dr. Mudd will see you in a few minutes," she said blandly.

My mother forced a smile. A frightful place in the poorly lit bowels of Saskatoon. It didn't feel good. I didn't feel good. The painting on the wall was without taste or consideration, a man screaming – his mouth open like a cavern and behind him a chaos of colour that seemed about to devour him. I looked away.

Old *National Geographic* magazines lay on a table for my mother. She thumbed through them hurriedly. I watched her, saw a naked African woman, with pendulous breasts and a child with a distended belly. A glimpse before she put it down. How did such images end up there. Did the woman know?

The telephone rang. "The doctor will see you now," the woman said.

I followed my mother down a darker-still hallway and

through an open door. A man stood up from behind his desk. He was shorter than most men and what remained of his hair was uncombed – a thatch of prickles. A bow tie listing like a sinking ship. *What now?* his face seemed to say.

"Mrs. Gray, Calan," he said, "sit, sit." He reached out and shook my mother's hand. Then he offered it to me – cold and moist.

We sat opposite him on a brown leather couch. Fat arms. He watched me, sizing me up, wondering. His eyes seemed loosed in his head. I was scared. I feared that I told Dr. Douglas too much. And yet I felt the urge to laugh. I rarely laughed. All this trouble over trees, all this trouble over my reverence. I liked the word – delighted to remember Jules Bear. Nothing to worry about. But if I laughed then he might think me daft – an expression my mother used at times. If I laughed out of turn then surely he would agree with my father and I would be sent away. I would be the perfect boy.

And my mother with her legs crossed and her hands on her lap – composed it would seem, but I could sense her looking up at the high windows, squares of light, to what was beyond – a sparrow beating against the panes.

"Now, Calan," Dr. Mudd said, "I'm going to give you a test today. Not a hard test. It's kind of like looking at sketches. You might like that. I understand that you like to draw."

"Yes. I like to draw. I like to draw…"

He turned to my mother then back to me. "But before we begin," he said, "I would like to ask you about school. You are having difficulty with your spelling and arithmetic. If it is all right with your mother, Calan, I would like you to tell me about that."

"That's fine," my mother said.

All smiles and courtesy. I shrugged. The room was getting smaller. It began to feel like my last chance. I had to show him. "Arithmetic," I said. "**A r**ed **I**ndian **t**hought **h**e **m**ight **e**at **t**obacco **in** **c**hurch."

"Very good, Calan," the doctor said.

"I don't think that Jules Bear eats tobacco," I said.

"It's a tool for teaching children," he said. The slight unhinging of his jaw.

"Roy G Biv," I added proudly. "The colours of the rainbow. **R**ed, **o**range, **y**ellow **g**reen, **b**lue, **i**ndigo and **v**iolet."

"Thank you, Calan. Perhaps your mother can add something. Mrs. Gray?"

"Well, Calan had a difficult year," she said. "His teacher called me in the spring. She was concerned with Calan's progress. He was having trouble with his handwriting. So she had a special blackboard made just for him. You know, to help him."

"Of course," Dr. Mudd said. "Did that help, Calan?"

Dr. Mudd always tilted his head when he asked a question. Just like a crow waiting for the kitchen scraps. I didn't want to tell him about a boy in my class. His name was Phillip and he worked away at a chalkboard at the back of the room. He was unable to keep up with the rest of the kids. Mrs. Percival would come to the back and help him and everyone just turned in their desks and watched. Sometimes Janet would help him form his letters. Poor Philip, his scrawl like lightning bolts across the slate. He never had his own desk, just that board with his name up in the corner. He stood while the others sat. Chalked fingers and dusted corduroys. How he struggled. His reading so painful, his words seem to stick in the quicksand of his tongue.

But in the early fall and late spring out on the soccer field, at recess and at noon, Philip was a marvel, standing on the sidelines while the boys kicked at the ball – his version of Bill Hewitt – giving his rendition of hockey play by play like no other. The boys were transformed, Toronto Maple Leafs all – George Armstrong, Dave Keon, Red Kelly, Frank Mahovlich, Carl Brewer, Alan Stanley and Bobby Baun. But some of the boys had to be Detroit Redwings.

Alex Delvechio and Normie Ulman. I always wanted to be Gordie Howe.

Then one morning another board appeared beside Philip and at the top, for all to see, printed in that perfect teacher's hand was my name – Calan Gray. I just stared at it. Philip was so pleased. I asked him if it bothered him when the kids teased him, called him names and laughed so cruelly. He simply shrugged. "They're not laughing at me, Calan," he said.

"No," I said to Dr. Mudd, "it didn't help." They laughed at me. I didn't understand what Philip said. I cried and Janet stood beside me. They laughed harder still.

"What about friends, Calan?" he asked me. "Do you have many friends?"

"Bobby and Ricky Olsen come over sometimes when they're tired of farm work," I said, "but all they want to do is take their slingshots out on the prairie and kill prairie dogs. Ricky killed one once and propped it up on a stick outside its burrow. I guess it looked like all clear. But it wasn't. They would just leave a pile of them out there. Now I hide when I see them coming."

"Did you kill prairie dogs, Calan?" he wanted to know.

"Why would you ask me that?" I said.

"Some boys like to kill things," he said.

"They're older than me. I suppose older kids might. But they're not really friends. One time Ricky pissed across the Clavet road like a rainbow. He had the wind though."

"I see," he said. He nodded, some revelation in my answers.

And just then the summer seemed to drift toward a future that could not be found, lost to the will of the world. Soon there would be school. But what school? All in the hands of Dr. Mudd and his sketches.

My mother left the room and Dr. Mudd asked me to sit at a table. There were several cards on it. He sat next to me.

"Pick up a card," he said, "and turn it over and tell me what you see. Can you do that, Calan?"

"Yes," I said. His breath like turnips. I felt a tug in my stomach. I didn't know what the test was. I didn't want to get it wrong. If I got the answers wrong then I would be sent away like the Bear kids. I was nervous without my mother. I picked up the first card and turned it over. Black and white.

It wasn't a sketch at all. I could see right away that it was an image with its opposite. I wanted to say snowflake because it reminded me of making snowflakes at school – folding white paper and cutting designs along the edges with scissors. And when you opened the paper you would have the mirror image on each side of the fold. I was thinking too much. And then I saw the cat.

"A cat," I said, "just like the one in the barn." The doctor busy in his notebook.

"Next card, Calan."

Colour now. The one I liked with the white paws. "Blood," I said. I couldn't tell him – shot in the head and blood in its eyes. Why was the doctor doing this? I didn't do anything wrong. I felt anxious. "I buried them beneath the aspens," I told him. "They'd look after them. They told me so."

"Next card."

I could see it looking right at me, that little bull calf at the Clavet Fair. A tiny pen and boys poking at it with a stick and my father laughing. The calf was so helpless. Bawled all day long for a ribbon. "Bull calf," I said.

"Next card, Calan."

I turned it over. It was another animal. There was something fierce there, the way it reared up from the paper. Great stomping feet. And my backside ached sitting on that hard chair. It wasn't an animal. No, it was *him* – the dark shadow of what he turned in to. But I couldn't tell the doctor so. And the word came breathless and crackling. I choked on the lie of it. "Muskrat," I said.

And more cards – shapes, patterns that made no sense, ink blots the doctor called them, but still some element that

I recognized, something that made me fearful. Always my father. I wondered why Dr. Mudd wanted me to see him. It was not a test at all. He wanted to know the mind of a boy who talked to trees. I knew what he was doing. I felt panicky not knowing what my answers would reveal. How unfair it was, a boy impotent before a world of the confused and bewildered. They would decide for me – my wounded father and my mother running away from her unhappy life, and Dr. Mudd imprisoned in that dim place, an archaeologist in the depths of his dig trying to piece together the mind of a boy. He could never leave for the pieces could never really be found. How could one truly know? *Take my hand and I will take you there to listen to the whisperings of trees. Hear the soft purr of kittens rising from the earth. Then tell me that I am broken.*

My mother was silent, not with her distance and longing, but a cheerless and disheartened detachment. Always that meeting after an appointment – mother and doctor. What was said this time? If he said anything at all, she wasn't saying what it was, not even in that vague and deflective way to soothe a frightened child.

We drove through the streets of Saskatoon heading for home. The thunderstorm let up and the sun blinding in the slick streets and the trees row on row dripping little suns. Then up ahead the red flashing light of a police car. My mother slowed – a policeman directing traffic.

"An accident," she said to me.

"What happened?" I asked. I rolled down my window.

"Someone went off the road," she said. "Hope everyone is all right."

Then I saw her, an elderly woman sitting on the curb. She was crying. My mother saw her too and pulled over to the side of the road.

"Oh, she's in bit of a state, Calan," she said. "I have to help her. All alone like that. Stay here now."

I watched her go to the woman, watched her kneel down

and place a hand on her shoulder. She didn't seem hurt, more frightened than anything. Strange, I could feel her distress. And how easily my mother comforted her – a perfect stranger. It was a part of her that I rarely saw, a kindness that was always there, hiding perhaps, waiting to be received. And then the woman pointed to her car up on the sidewalk. Then she pointed to a tree. She had hit the tree it seemed, a great gash in the trunk, the bark peeled away exposing the pale wood. I stared at the open wound, the splinters. And then I could feel it, its own pain that reached out to me. It was not the woman after all; I was certain of it. It seemed so clear just then. It was the tree, a maple tree.

And then all at once leaves began to fall, not one by one, but as if by a sudden shuddering – a release like tears. It was if it came by my looking, by my observation, my awareness of its hurt. I was no longer afraid. There was nothing to fear. It was so simple. I could feel them, as my mother could feel the anguish of the woman, when senses and impressions, for but a moment, are unbound and free. I wanted to know more, what it was that made that possible – something inside me that was growing stronger. It was no longer just aspens, but all trees perhaps.

A tow-truck came and the policeman gave the woman a ride home. In the car my mother assured me that she was not hurt.

"Just shaken," she said. "She got confused by the glare of the sun. Lost control." Then she turned to me. "Why, you're the sensitive one, Calan. She's fine – not hurt at all, though she's a little worried what her husband will say. Wipe your tears now."

I swiped at my cheeks with my sleeve. I felt a vulnerability that I had never felt before, an urgency – a certain desperation to see Jules Bear. And then on my lap, a maple leaf, and the tree shrinking in the side mirror like Janet alone on the road from Clavet.

CHAPTER SEVEN

My mother didn't allow me to go with her to pick up Grandpa Dunny at the CNR station in Saskatoon. I imagined that they had a lot to talk about, grownup talk not meant for a boy's ears. She was nervous when she left – relieved when my father went out to the barn after his lunch, but worried over things, the unknown and unpredictable. She stabbed her cigarette into the ashtray and finished her coffee.

"Stay out of your father's way," she said to me in the kitchen. "I cut a nice piece of rhubarb pie for you. Take it up to your room now, Calan. And you wait there."

I heeded her warning and sat by my bedroom window on that hot August afternoon waiting for the dust to rise up from the road down past the Olsen's farm, eating my mother's rhubarb pie that was so good it made my eyes roll back in my head. A breeze blew through the curtains. I could see him in the distance digging out a culvert that collapsed during the thunderstorm. Now and then he stopped to light a cigarette. He would lean on his shovel for a minute then continue on working with the cigarette in his mouth.

Jules Bear hadn't been back to the farm since that day and I was sorry for it. I wondered if I would ever see him again.

My father had to finish Grandpa Dunny's shack without him and I knew he blamed me. It wasn't the work that upset him. He was a working fool who only sat for his food. It seemed that he lost the only person on Earth that he never swore at or threatened, the only man who he allowed near him. Jules Bear was his only friend.

And now Grandpa Dunny was on his way, my mother's father who wasn't welcome to stay in her own home. It troubled her deeply – out there with her tears, painting the cupboards, made from old wooden boxes, a happy yellow, and hanging the curtains with patterned forget-me-nots. The shack had a pot-bellied stove to warm his old bones when the weather turned cold and a blue enamel coffee pot set upon it, and a kerosene lamp, hot plate and a well-worn braided rug and a painting of a spaniel from the flea market in Clavet. And a red checker tablecloth covered a plywood table, where the salt and pepper shakers and a sugar dispenser posed like a cafe. And cut sweet-peas in a jar, pinks and purples. Two mismatched chairs, an old spring bed, a pale blue second-hand refrigerator that groaned, a discarded sink and old copper piping from a dark corner of the barn completed the scene. Everything had been scrubbed and cleaned. And the bathroom was like a closet. My father dug a trench with a pick and laid the sewer pipe out to the septic field. Bent double for his efforts. And my mother had to help him into the house when the sun quit on him.

I wasn't allowed near the little house. I watched from the garden, pulling carrots for dinner, from the open barn door where cats lolled in the sun, from where I walked up and down the driveway kicking rocks and chasing cabbage whites zigzagging to nowhere in particular, working my way to the tiny window where I cupped my eyes long enough see what she had done. All these things for her father – the loving touches she could do, making something from nothing. And finally the stoop trimmed in forest green – her honouring of him.

The measures he permitted to keep an old man away from him. I wondered why he bothered. He could have just slammed his fist down on the kitchen counter or dining-room table or the arm of a chair, something to take his rages. He could have told my mother plainly that Dunmore McLeod could not set a foot on his farm. For it was his farm and my mother knew that well enough. But he allowed a little house and he allowed it to be a fit home for a while. Some remote and orphaned part of him recognized, perhaps, that Grandpa Dunny was family.

As I watched him bust out the old pipe and drag a length of shiny corrugated steel pipe and work it into place, he stopped and turned to look at that little shack. As if he wondered about his own father, what it would be like if he were still alive. Did he ever dream of a different life? And then he did an odd thing. He sat down right there in the gravel and hung his head down between his knees. And I knew right then that he could not live in a world without my mother. I couldn't watch him like that – my tenderness deceived me, a moment when I might feel sorry for him. And then I would hear it, how he could live in a world without me.

I opened *Trees of the World* as I waited, ran my fingers over the flare of his letters:

For you, Calan
Grandpa Dunny, Christmas 1962

It was written diagonally with quill and ink, a cursive beauty to its form, a style similar to that of my mother. I decided that I would write like that one day. I placed the maple leaf there, saving a memory and a dream. And then I remembered what my father had said about him, words never too far away. *What will we do when your father comes? He will be a ruined boy for sure. Imagine a man who spent his whole life looking after a stupid tree...*

The afternoon wore on. The dust rose out of the west and a Country Squire soon bore out of it, chased it seemed, all the way from Clavet. Then my mother slowed. The dust played out behind her. She turned into our long driveway and my view was lost for a minute. Then the car came up alongside the house. The doors opened and there he was at last, Grandpa Dunny, standing with his cane and a hand on his hip like a fable.

I didn't want to leave the window. I didn't want to take my eyes off him. He stretched his back and looked over to the barn, to the little house and then to my father in the distance. I could see my father standing, facing him, some reluctance that wasn't ready to throw down the shovel. My mother knew the fears that drove him so crazy. She removed Grandpa Dunny's duffle bag from the back of the car, set it on the porch and stood there below me where I couldn't see the hurt and shame in her eyes.

Then she gathered herself, found her courage to pick up his bag and lead him across the yard to his little house. I saw him look toward my father, a fixed sort of contemplation that comes when enemies have nothing but distance between them – waiting for the call to arms. My mother turned to him sharply, saw it too, and stopped him. What she said I don't know, but he bowed his head and nodded. Then he lifted his chin like a king. She opened the door to the little house and Dunmore McLeod entered into the heart of a boy.

At dinner it was odd to know that Grandpa Dunny was so close and yet left alone. The great table had room enough for him. I wanted to see him, listen to him in the worst way. But the welcome would not come easily there, nor the talk, between my mother and father. Nothing could dislodge the feel of it. My father's resentment leaked out of him like a contagion to civility. Then my mother pushed back her chair all at once, not daring to look down the long table.

"I'll make a plate up for him," she said. "He needs to have a proper supper and we have enough."

"He'll have to buy his own groceries," my father said

evenly as he reached for the salt. "I won't be looking after him."

"Potatoes and a slice of beef, Mack, a piece of bread for the gravy." She met him now, the unwavering decision made.

"That's our food, Meg. You can take him into Clavet and he can buy what he wants. A perfect little house. He can cook for himself."

"My God, Mack, why do you hate him so?"

"He's an old fool."

"You haven't even gone to see him. He's right there. My father!"

He looked up from his food. "I won't have you talking to me like that in my own house," he said. Always the escalation. "I won't be scolded. I won't have it!"

"Mack," she said, no longer afraid of him.

He rose roughly from his chair and it fell over behind him. He shouted now. "And he won't be talking to the boy here, not a word!" A thick finger waving at me like a decree, a law never to be broken. The pupils of his eyes were black with his warning.

My mother stood there like I had never seen before. So brave now, defying him like that. Perhaps she did this so that I might witness it. Perhaps Grandpa Dunny had given her strength, courage to speak for herself, something she lost, stolen from her with threats of his violence. But it seemed the more she stood her ground, the harder he pushed back.

I slowly got up from my chair and moved back from the table, wanting to leave, to run away from what I knew was to come. Did he see for the first time that he was losing her? Would he lunge at her and smash that will of hers, strike her down with the back of his hand? But he only sat me down with the jerk of his head when my mother went into the kitchen. She returned with an empty plate and piled on potatoes and roast beef and a slab of bread and butter. There was a silence that stretched between them like a fuse, a moment when life could change so quickly, but a moment freely chosen, a risk that had to be taken. She turned away and left us there and went out the kitchen door.

"Finish your supper," he said to me and sat down.

I looked over to him, a nervous glance. He was sad about the mouth, something beaten about his face. I wondered why my Grandpa would come to a place where he wasn't welcome. There was no room for him in Victoria my mother had said – my aunts and their cramped apartments and houses and his *wee house by the sea* that would be waiting for him. And here he was banished to another little house.

WILLOW

CHAPTER EIGHT

That evening I saw him sitting on the stoop with his pipe. From my bedroom window I watched him dig out the bowl with a wooden match and fill the bowl from a pouch that was tucked into his vest. Then he lit it, took a few great draughts and smoke swirled about his head. He took a long time. He was mindfully formal and careful, as if the pipe were an instrument to foment reflection. Unlike a cigarette that always seemed lit with such haste. It wasn't long before he looked up and saw me. He waved. It was difficult to tell if he smiled for his mouth was hidden beneath the sweep of his grey beard. I began to think how I would see him, how I would talk to him. I would have to know where my father was, the course of his day, what he had planned.

He would rise early when the sun was but an impression of something coming; have his breakfast of bacon and eggs and coffee that my mother made for him. Then he would go to the barn and back the tractor out and leave it idle there as he walked out toward *his* wheat. At the culvert he would light his first cigarette and look down into the ditch for a while. I don't know what it was that drew him to look so long.

Perhaps it was his wilderness, that uncultivated part of him that did not expect anything – a place for frogs and muskrats, something to drain the land when the snow and ice melted in the spring.

Finally he would go there, out along the margins of the golden fields and disappear for a long time. I never knew what he did at those times, but I sensed that it was filled with worry, to be so close to something that could ruin him, to walk beside the full measure of his life and know that it had the power that he had no control over – abundance or devastation like the faces of a tossed coin.

I watched him. I wanted to know where he would be. Something in me could remember and predict, take notice of many things. I gathered information, became a collector of images. I was aware of an order without the constraints of time. I just knew. Perhaps it was a device of survival. He was a prepared man, knew the weather, the seasons, read it all because his very life depended on it. And although I could not read books like the kids in Mrs. Percival's class, I could read with an increasing clarity those prairie transcripts of my father, Macklin Gray.

In the morning my mother came to my room to awaken me. She pinched my toes and whispered.

"Now listen to me, Calan," she said to me as I sat up in my bed, "your Grandpa will be out for a walk soon, past the barn. You know where it is, a trail there by the long grass and willows. You'll be hidden well enough. Grandpa will be waiting for you. He knows, Calan. He knows it all. Go to meet him, every day, have a good talk. You're a good boy – never did anything wrong. But we'll have to know when it's safe."

"I know where he'll be."

"Do you now?" She sat on the edge of my bed.

"He'll go back along the fields," I said, "all the way to the Olsen's farm. The same thing every day."

"Are you certain?"

"He's there now."

"How do you know?"

I couldn't answer her and looked off to the window. "I don't know," I said. "I just do."

She sat a minute, resting with my answer. There was something relieved in her eyes. Then she smiled. "That's a bright boy, Calan," she said. "I'll tell your Grandpa Dunny. Get dressed now and go down for breakfast. There's toast and raspberry jam for you, just the way you like it. Then off you go. It'll be our secret."

"Does Grandpa Dunny have reverence?" I asked her. There was something comforting in that word that belonged to Jules Bear. A word that seemed perfect and pure, unending.

"I believe he does and a proud man of the clan McLeod," she said, "and quite a sight with his tartan draped about him. There's warring in his blood and yes, reverence."

I didn't realize as she was talking to me, sitting there, that she held my face in her hands, cupped my fragility like something cherished and valuable. She never did that, never allowed herself to care that way. In that moment she knew as a mother knows, what I needed. Did Grandpa Dunny bring to her, the remembering of that essential part of her beneath her bruises? But my elation did not come when she left my room. My father was a simple man with a singular purpose, to farm until he bled, until we all bled. And he might have wished me never born and perhaps he would send me away – all these things. But he was not stupid.

I finished my breakfast and ran from the house licking the raspberry jam from the corners of my mouth. I ran past the barn and the idling tractor, past the combine and stiff machinery with their colours long bled out and grass springing up through the frames, and out to the fallow field. The sun was warm on my back and I slowed. I was out of breath. But I ran on, my head down with my urgency. Then I looked up and there he was, standing facing me, a hand in his vest pocket and the other gripping his cane. I stopped. It was easy to think of him – to wonder, to imagine his coming, the little shack to keep him. But to finally be in his presence, to speak with him, just me and my Grandpa Dunny, a man from so far away, from a strange land, a mystery. What would I say? I couldn't move.

"Come," he said, "let me have a look at you."

I stepped forward – looked down at the resting soil.

"Aye, you're a little nervous," he said. "I know how it is. You're a big boy and this is the first time that we have met. And I'm truly sorry for that. But you see, your grandmother was ill for a long time. So here I am and I am pleased to meet you at last, Calan."

His diction was rapid and his speech curious like my mother's but more so. He wasn't as tall as I had imagined, but large around the middle. He leaned back in a manner that seemed to elevate him. And under a chiselled cap his hair was long for a man, to his shoulder. And his beard rested on his great chest. But it was his eyes that I wanted to see. He held out his hand and I took it.

He shook it, not up and down like a water pump but waving side to side like a flag until my arm was like rubber. And he laughed. He seemed to think it great fun.

"Grandpa Dunny shake," he said. "A handshake at a first meeting should be a memorable one. Don't you think so, Calan?"

He laughed and I laughed. I could see his eyes, the bits of colour like my own. I looked long for it was effortless to gaze into a new face when it was full of joy. I could sense a depth in them, an unfettered confidence. I knew that I would never be afraid in his presence.

"I've never shook hands like that before," I said. I remembered Dr. Mudd's formality, his dead fish offering.

"Then you'll always remember."

"Yeah, I'll remember."

"Let's walk a bit then," he said, "under this incurable sky."

We walked along the margins of the field, a screen of willows and grasses taller than our heads. I wondered about his reference to the sky, what it meant. He walked with one hand behind his back, watching carefully all those things left alone. He seemed to be leaving something unsaid, allowing it to come on its own. He looked far off and then down at his feet. His cane uncovering mysteries. A fox leapt in the distance. Then Grandpa stopped and gently thumbed the purple heads of thistle. The rhythm of grass everywhere. He turned to the willows and listened, a rustle there in the breeze. I could hear them whispering like children. He heard them too.

"A man thinks he must carve up the earth," he said resting both his hands on his cane. "It is the wild places where there is life. But a man has to eat, I suppose. Aye, a land without trees. A man needs trees, Calan. We're no different, you know. Not at all. Sprout from a seed. We grow tall, reaching up, up, growing, growing. Soon there is a forest, a family of trees. But if a tree stands alone, if you take the forest away from it, nothing to shelter it from the storms of winter, then limbs will soon break off. Oh, those mighty forces upon it. In time it will rot from the inside. It will die slowly, but it will die.

"A man or a boy needs to start out somewhere, size things up for himself. Why are things the way they are? I suppose we don't think much on the cause of our troubles. We have plenty of time to worry over the effects. Do you understand what I am saying, Calan?"

He spoke of trees. But it was not the aspens or willows that he was talking about. There was something else, a greater thing to know. I recognized it as an important moment in my life. He chose his words for me so that I would understand my place in the world. He was talking about my father. Not to give an excuse for his anger, his cruelty. But it was more of that starting point that he spoke of, an understanding that reached back to the beginning – to that boy who lost his family. And how strange it was, that speech that was so different – a man from the other side of the world, whose words felt much like Jules Bear's.

"I think so," I said.

"You're a smart lad, Calan. I knew it. So it's time to go back. You hurry now. And remember what I told you. There is always something more. We'll talk again. I will tell you of a tree that I know so well, the tree of life eternal. It sends a shiver to tell of it. This cane is made of it. And there are trees that touch the clouds. So off you go now."

I ran with my feet scarcely touching the ground, so lifted was I, as if a gift had been granted me, a piece for the puzzle that was my life – the life that was Gray Farm. I felt grown up, understood now the secrets of life. Confidence soared in my chest. I wanted to shout: *Grandpa Dunny and Jules Bear have reverence!* He heard the willows. He heard their little voices.

But it was all carelessness, as all at once he was standing by the barn, his legs firm and set apart. He was waiting for me. And I fell to the earth. The shock of it, impaled me like an arrow through the belly – his perfect aim.

"Get in the house!" he said.

He sliced me with his eyes as I slinked past him. The back of my neck waited, but the blow never came. As I went into the house I turned bravely and he was there still facing the prairie, waiting it seemed for Grandpa Dunny. I wanted to warn him, call out to him. How swiftly things could foul, always that darkness like an entity that trolled about for moments of good.

My mother was sitting in the dining room crying. I stood there and she looked over to me, her hand over her mouth as if something precious to her had been lost.

"What's wrong?" I asked.

There was an opened letter on the table in front of her and she tried to speak but she choked on her words and could not utter them. I knew that it was there in the letter, something filled with such sorrow. Then she reached out and took my hand and squeezed it tight. The world seemed to be correcting, a hopeful day now all at once undone. And then he came through the kitchen door. His feet were heavy. He came into the dining-room and behind him, Grandpa Dunny. He went to the head of the table, dragging the chair on the floor, making a harsh wail on the hard wood. He sat down. Before him, rising like vile smoke, grew the tension of what he knew. It was about me. Everything at Gray Farm eventually turned to me, found me out. Blamed me. He reached across the table and picked up the letter.

"Sit," he said. An order from his curling lips, some pleasure in that scowl. The swell of veins on his forearm like blue ropes.

We all sat at our places. Grandpa Dunny was at a loss, his sudden ushering into our house, a bewildered man looking to my mother for an answer, my confounded champion faltering before a thing he could not have prepared for, that frightful power gathering in my father's eyes.

"A letter has arrived," he said, "and you all need to know what it says." Then he looked at me and lied. It was so easy for him. "We want the best for you, Calan. Your mother and I, well, we were worried sick. And now we have an answer and you will hear for yourself. You are just a boy and might not understand. But don't you worry. You'll be looked after. The letter is from that special doctor in Saskatoon:

Dear Mr. and Mrs. Gray;

Re: Psychiatric Tests for Calan Gray

Please find the conclusion of my assessment of your ten-year-old son, Calan. I have weighed the evidence with the summary provided by Dr. Cooper Douglas as well as the grade scores and comments from the Principal of Clavet School and, of course, our telephone consultation.

Calan's score for the Rorschach inkblot test was analyzed using psychological interpretation and a complex examination of his perceptions, cognitive mediation and ideation. The goal of the test was to provide personality variables, impulses, motivations and emotional responses and functioning. His answers were unusual and unique, illustrating considerable personality conflicts.

My diagnosis is based on behaviour, noted impairments in social interaction, communication deficits, lack of social or emotional reciprocity and most importantly in this case, the presence of neurological symptoms and disturbances such as the delusional realities that he has displayed.

Calan shows the presence of infantile schizophrenia. Treatment parameters should be established at once and will be provided by the Saskatchewan Psychiatric Hospital in Prince Albert. A referral for admission to the institution is under way. The hospital will contact you directly to ensure the timely arrival of Calan. At that time visiting protocols may be discussed.

I trust this information is satisfactory and addresses your concerns. I must reiterate that it is the well-being of the child that is of the utmost consideration at this time.

Yours very truly,

Dr. Reinhart Mudd, MD

Psychiatrist

"So," he said, folding his hands on the table – his calm seemed to fester and I could not understand any of it, especially when he stumbled over words unknown to him and that phrase *special school for boys like him.*

"It can't be," Grandpa Dunny said. "I know this boy!" He was red about his face and his eyes pushing out of their caves.

"You know nothing, old man!" my father roared leaning over the table. He slammed his fist like a gavel and glared and Grandpa Dunny sat back stunned and unsure what to do.

My mother was defeated, her body slack and trembling and he just sat there, unaffected, unmoved. It was all done for him, finished. How dispassionate he was, his whole demeanour declaring war on us like that, wielding his anger and bitterness in such a way that to fight against it would bring a storm that could never be imagined.

It had been such a fine morning. The parable of the tree standing alone and how it all could be understood, and that fox leaping in the summer grass – I wondered in my sickened bones if it had happened at all.

CHAPTER NINE

A long night of worry, something that couldn't be true. I was just a boy. I thought of Simon and Gabriel Bear. Would I see them? I was so afraid I cried until I fell asleep. I dreamt a nightmare of trees and the wind and my arms like branches and my legs, trunks, and an exaggerated likeness of my father with a great saw cutting them from my body. The wind was laughing and all was cruel, hopeless.

When the sun came up I was glad for it. Then a voice called. I went downstairs. My mother was standing by the kitchen window. She was talking to herself.

"I never called the doctor," she said against the glass.

"What doctor?" I said to her. She turned quickly, startled to see me there.

"Oh, Calan, nothing… but it's not nothing. No. The letter, don't you see, he read it, and he didn't understand the word. I never had a *consultation* with the doctor on the telephone. I didn't talk to him about you. He called the doctor himself. It was him." She looked down at the floor, stared blankly. "What did he do?"

Then she turned away from me and went out the kitchen door. She walked slowly over to the garden and moved among the carrots and peas, down the rows of radishes and beets, a piece of the earth that belonged to her. I watched from the window, her apron over her summer dress, the breezes playing with her hair and her listless hands. She had given up it seemed. She turned inward where even the joys of her garden could not enter.

There was a knock at the door. I opened it and Ricky Olsen was standing on the porch. His mother had sent him over for a cup of sugar.

"That grubby Janet wrote your name on the side of the Clavet General Store," he said bluntly. "It made me want to puke." He couldn't wait to tell me that. He kept looking over his shoulder at Grandpa's little house.

"So." I shrugged.

"Don't you care?"

"No."

"You're so weird, Calan. You must have felt her up or something. My mom says that you have a gnome living with you. Is he in there?"

"What's a gnome?" I asked, still wondering what *felt her up* meant.

"Jeez, Gray, don't you know anything? A gnome is like an elf or something. My mom says that they're full of mischief."

"My Grandpa Dunny lives in there. And he's not an elf."

"Are you sure? Ask him to come out."

"I'm not allowed."

"There's nobody in there. You're so stupid, Gray." He stepped off the porch for a better look.

"He's in there."

"Well, go get him then."

I didn't know that Grandpa was standing by his door, in the shadows. He was listening.

"I said that I'm not allowed."

"Not allowed to see your own grandfather?"

"It's not like that."

"Like what?" He turned back to me with his challenge.

The sun was at Ricky's back now and I could see Grandpa Dunny coming off the stoop. He was twirling his cane and his eyes were smiling.

"Do you really want to see him, Ricky?" I asked. I had a feeling that he wouldn't forget my grandpa.

"Yeah."

"Well, he might be an elf. I've never seen one. And he might be full of mischief."

"What a retard, Gray."

Grandpa came up behind him and touched his shoulder then stepped around him unseen as Ricky spun on his heels, this way and that.

"And what do we have here?" Grandpa said circling him. "I'm put in mind of a poem by Robbie Burns. You may not know of him but I'll give you a bit of it:

To a Louse

Ha! Whaur ye gaun, ye crowlin' ferlie?
Your impudence protects you sairly:
I canna say but ye strunt rarely,
Owre gauze and lace;
Tho' faith! I fear ye dine but sparely
On sic a place

Ye ugly, creepin', blastit wonner
Detested, shunn'd by saunt and sinner!

"And on it goes. Look at you, Ricky, with hair like snow and eyes like the sea. Oh, my, my, you're in grave danger. You see where I come from in the Isle of Apples, the fairy folk, the immortals in their barrows and cairns, their green little world, are spirits of the dead and changelings, too. I've been there myself. They steal children and replace them with fairy children. So you watch when you're about, be careful of things you might see underfoot or any queer light that might attract you. If you're lucky they will just have a prank for you."

Grandpa spoke quickly, his words like riddles rising from a gurgling stream. I felt dizzy by the movement of him, the fantastic imagery. My mouth fell agape. Ricky stood like a boy who had just freed a genie that he could not put back in its bottle. Then Grandpa, still walking in his circles, snatched the slingshot from Ricky's back pocket.

"And what use has this?" he said.

Ricky swallowed. The gnome was not done. "It's my slingshot," he said.

"And what do you do with it?"

"It's for aiming at stuff," Ricky answered looking out of one eye. "Birds and prairie dogs."

"And from what wood is it made?"

"Just willow that grows along the ditches."

"Ah, willow, you say, a tree rich in the lore from the old world, a sacred tree of the ancients. The wind through the willows inspires poets and the bark reduces fevers and sweaty feet. But some say when the dew settles in the early hours like honey, that the Celts would plant willows above their departed ones, the dead, so that their spirits would rise up in the saplings and be with them forever. And I wonder who is locked in this willow sling?"

Ricky peeled off on his bike. He left without his sling-shot, left without the cup of sugar. My mother came from her garden and took Grandpa's hand. She had tears still wet on her cheeks, not from her sadness, but from his whimsy to help a boy think upon his manners and another to smile. There at Gray Farm where joy had no memory and happiness was a futile longing.

"I dare say that Mrs. Olsen will have a time of it now," my

mother said light-heartedly, "spreading the gossip the way she and Mrs. Daisy…." Her voice trailed off all at once.

All gaiety died in her eyes as she met him down by the culvert, my father sitting up on his tractor. It wasn't moving. He was looking our way. Even over that distance you could feel his displeasure, his intimidation as if space collapsed and he was seething there among us.

"A few days and he'll be away," she said evenly. "Overnight in Regina, a meeting with the Wheat Board. Once a year he goes."

"Aye, then it's time," Grandpa Dunny said. He put his arm around me and gathered me against his bulk.

"But I fear what he might do," my mother said.

"There can be no doubt now, daughter," Grandpa said. "My grandson will not be sent off."

"There's an army rifle that he keeps behind our bedroom door. He's taken it."

"Then we must heed him and give him no reason to wonder."

"Calan, you must do whatever we say," my mother said, "even if you're afraid. Can you do that?"

"Yeah," I said.

"Let it be done," Grandpa said with the grand lifting of his head.

"We're going to need help," she said. "I've been thinking long on this, all the minutes of my days. I will call Jules Bear and pray to God."

It seemed that she was looking down the barrel of that rifle as she stood there wondering if he would knock her down. It was plain now that Grandpa Dunny had not come to visit that incurable sky or to walk along the ditches and admire the willows and thistles. He was not a man to swallow another man's bile.

My father watched us like death. I waited for the explosion. It could come easily, like killing cats. Then my mother pulled me away.

CHAPTER TEN

On the morning my father was to leave on his trip to Regina we surrendered our lives to the prairie breezes. I knew that there would be no turning back, no undoing what my mother and Grandpa Dunny planned in their moments together – a plate of supper, words exchanged on his stoop. A look. Pointing to the stacking clouds with their black underbellies and more words that had nothing to do with crop damage or the clothes on the line that would never be drawn in.

There was too much to think about. I needed a distraction and played with the cats in the barn. I stroked their backs and scratched their fine chins. I gave them names and forgot them right away. But the cats heard as I spoke the names aloud, each cat seeming to know they mattered to a boy who would not hurt them. Sparrows watched with eyes that seemed too small to see much but they always knew at once when grain was spilled.

I stood there in my father's barn where the light was always so muted, the dark so undeniable. It seemed so temporary; a strong wind might bring it all down. But it was home to a thousand crawling things. If it weren't for the blood on the floor and the sharp clap of the .22 distilled in that space and his loathing railing endlessly in the rafters, I might have found the barn an enchanting place to be. A solitude to enjoy, but his presence was always there ruining it all.

I walked about the yard, the garden, out near the Clavet road. I looked back to the house. I wanted to remember how it looked against the reaching plain, the white shiplap siding, where our lawns came right up to the foundation. And the roof of green shingles, a pitch steep against the winter drifts. The front door was never used, only the back door where the porch served in so many ways: a place for muddy boots; a place for my mother to sit in a wicker chair with a bowl of peas on her lap; a place where the clothesline ran out to a pole, a place where tree swallows returned in April to reclaim the birdhouse crowning the top of it.

Back along the driveway the lombardy withered. I wondered what bothered them so. Their great columns had known a certain vigour as they grew up with the farm. I recalled the day in Saskatoon when the woman drove into the maple tree and its injury somehow touching a quality I had. I asked them what it was that made them sick. And then almost at once there it was, a gentle nudge, a push then a language in my head that I could understand. A translation. They spoke in waves, no words, but waves of energy. Their mystery came slowly to me, chose me. The trees spoke as one.

I turned and there by the ditch where the grass had soured were the remnants of winter salt used for the driveway. The salt was too close to the trees. The brine parched their roots. I went to the barn and got the wheelbarrow and shovel. I pushed it past Grandpa Dunny on his stoop with his pipe. I did not look at him, nor did I glance toward the kitchen where my mother always stood. I moved the salt away from the trees and scraped the soil until it could breathe. Then I heard the sound of the tractor and felt my father watching me. He didn't seem to mind what I was doing for I had never worked so hard. I was flushed. Sweat ran from my temples, blisters lifted raw from my soft fingers.

My father parked the tractor in the barn and walked by me like a stranger as I put the tools away. I stayed by the dusty barn window and watched him go into the house. He came out a short time later with my mother. He was carrying an overnight bag. He was about to leave it seemed. Grandpa Dunny was in his house. My mother stood alone with my father. I could see her pale skin, the hollowness in her cheeks. I could feel my own churning stomach. How could she manage, standing there, waiting and fearing?

Then he looked around with the wariness of a wild thing. His eyes retreated into his head, a darkness gathered in the wells. We were hidden from his sight. Nothing to provoke him but our absence. He turned back to my mother, set his bag down, took hold of her bare arms and tried to kiss her. She turned her head slightly and offered her cheek, not her lips. He said something to her as he held her. She tried hard to smile, to put on a dutiful mask for him. He seemed reluctant to leave her while he stood so close to her smiling like that. So how many times had she misled him and how many times had she paid the price when she didn't?

He let her go.

When he turned the Country Squire around in the yard and headed down the driveway, she didn't move. She crossed her arms and held her bruises. I could see the shaking in her shoulders like the quiver of wings. Slowly she crept to the corner of the house and watched for dust rising in the distance. Then she walked briskly down the driveway out to the Clavet road. She had to be certain he was gone. I left the barn and stood by the house. She looked so small against the prairie, insubstantial, a feather against the wind. She could float away and disappear so easily.

She turned back and began to run in that awkward way that we shared. She called out to me in full flight, frantic, her dress sucked against her thin body.

"Calan," she said, "up to your room. There's a suitcase in

your closet. It's all packed. Get it and wait on the porch. You must take us to your trees. Jules Bear is waiting!"

How delighted I was to hear his name. He was waiting for us. But Jules Bear was my father's good friend. I was confused. Leaving was furious and urgent. I had not imagined what it would be like. I had never dared to dream about another life the way my mother did.

Then my mother ran over to Grandpa Dunny's little house and banged on the door. "Dad," she cried out to him, "come now!"

Grandpa Dunny stuck his head out the door then quickly disappeared. Something seemed comical in it all, like a cartoon, a surreal morning at Gray Farm. But there was nothing to laugh at as my mother nearly kicked the kitchen door down. She never altered her stride, her purpose. "Hurry now, Calan," she said running to her bedroom. "I fear he'll come back and catch us like thieves in our own house!"

I found my suitcase, opened a drawer and removed my sketchbook and *Trees of the World*. I put them in the suitcase and made for the door. Then I turned to look at it, that room where I had lived my whole life. There was a Roughrider pennant on the wall and a picture of Gordie Howe from the *Star Weekly*. Nothing else, only the bed where he hurt me with his belt, his bare hands. The sight of it gave me an empty feeling, a feeling of something wasted. I left it all.

My mother came down with her suitcase. Grandpa Dunny was waiting on his stoop with his bag. They looked at each other across the yard, reaffirming what they were about to do. Grandpa walked out and we turned north toward the fallow field. Our walking was more like running. It was all I could do to keep up with them, Grandpa with his spirited strides, pushing with his cane – his resolve like a legend and my mother with bruises mauled on her arms, not so determined now but stricken with what she was doing and knowing that we could no longer stay.

We followed the trail along the willows through the tall

grass, refugees escaping tyranny, past the green-headed mallards exploding from the pond.

On we went, birds all about us, inverted chickadees and drilling sapsuckers in the willows, sleek waxwings gorging on saskatoon berries and the alarm of a killdeer from somewhere on the trail ahead of us. Butterflies and all manner of bugs in the backlit sun and a hawk turning against a pearl sky. How strange a feeling this sense of adventure.

"Where's Jules Bear taking us?" I said hurrying to keep up.

"I only pray that he will," my mother said.

"Where?" I insisted.

"Mind your mother now, Calan," Grandpa Dunny said.

"I couldn't tell him, don't you see?"

"He doesn't know we're running away?"

"I couldn't risk it."

"What if he's not there?"

"Then we're in a fine predicament."

"Calan," Grandpa said and stopped and turned to me, his lively eyes now inflexible. "It'll all be fine. You must trust your mother. Do you understand? There's no going back."

I nodded and my mother fell silent walking on with her greatest fear, that it would not be Jules Bear who would be waiting for us.

It was warm at noon along the trail. We walked single file now. I was busy with the worries of a boy, my adventure swept away out over the prairie like dust. I was left with the images of that dream when he cut away my limbs, my treeness severed from me like a surgeon amputating disease. I was so fearful I could not hear *them*.

"Calan," he said turning back to me, "how far now?"

I moved up ahead and stretched as tall as I could. The grass had grown over the summer. "There," I said as if I were sighting land from a grass sea. I glimpsed the movement of the aspens, saw the easy sway of branches and white trunks. The birds fell silent. My mother and Grandpa Dunny stepped up alongside me. There was only listening now.

CHAPTER ELEVEN

Someone was down in the trees. There seemed to be many voices, a chorus of sadness and a song above the voices filtering through the limbs. I could not hear the trees. There was only the song and a sense of weeping green blood. It was the song of a man grieving, a primal chant for the dead and forgotten. The trees were his comfort but I did not hear this from them. There was a world behind the world and it was this world that spoke to me. The trees understood this. I could not hear them for they were the song singing for the dead.

"What is it?" Grandpa Dunny said.

"I don't know," I said, "I think it's Jules Bear."

"Are you sure, Calan?" my mother asked.

"*He's* not there."

"How do you know?"

"The trees would tell me."

"There's a suffering wind about the trees," Grandpa Dunny said. He thumped his cane. "But I dare say it is not *him*."

"All right then, Calan," my mother said, "take us now." She took my hand the way she did that day in Saskatoon when the rain poured down our necks.

I led them down the trail to the green light, the landscape

gently falling away from the prairie and my mother cautious as a deer in an uncertain wood, her liquid eyes and ragged breath wanting to pull her back but on she went. It seemed as if I had never been there before. What had changed? Then Grandpa Dunny with his keen eye and his cane out in front of him like a sword stopped me short.

"There he is," he whispered, "a man there among the trees."

"Who is it?" my mother said.

"I can't be sure. He's standing in the shadows."

"What should we do?"

"Be still."

The struggling wind and dead branches rubbed like a hinge above us. The drum of a flicker some distance away and the disappearing sun in opaque streams falling over our shoulders. Then I felt their sweet arms around me, holding us all. The shadow moved and Jules Bear stepped out into a column of light.

In that prairie hollow there was still a quiet resistance in my mother. What would she say to him? But Grandpa Dunny seemed to know what a man stood for, what purpose drives him. He stepped out ahead of us and set his bag down on the grass and met Jules Bear like an old friend.

"Aye, Jules," he said, "so good to see you again." He held out his hand and Jules Bear took it.

"Yes, it has been a long time, Dunmore," Jules said.

I could see wet creases on Jules's charred face and the dark stains of tears on his shirt. I knew that he was the singer and I knew that he was the sadness.

"I wasn't sure if you would come," my mother said nervously. Her hand came up and touched the veins in her neck as she examined the dense grove and the shadows where the grass writhed in the gusts and then up the slopes to the light peeling along the prairie rim.

"Mrs. Gray," Jules said, "I know why you called me. I could hear the question you couldn't ask. And I am here with my answer."

"Thank you," my mother said. She thoughtfully touched his arm.

"Where do you wish to go?" Jules asked.

"To the train," Grandpa Dunny said. Nothing more.

The sunlight ceased all at once and rain began to fall, dripping down from the high leaves and rumbling now overhead and a compressed smell electric. It felt as if dusk were coming.

"We will wait until it passes," Jules said.

We stood in a circle around a thick aspen with our suitcases and bags in our hands. The prairie storm would rise and pass in a minute. Soon the sun would reassert itself, so we waited, slumped like sheltered horses. Grandpa Dunny lit his pipe and the sweet smoke warmed us.

"There was singing," I said to Jules. "A sad song."

"Yes," Jules said after a moment, that hesitation typical of him – thought before speech. "Your trees, Calan, have the spirit of the Creator. My own Grandfather spoke of such things. What you hear and what you feel is Spirit. It is the voice of *Wakantanka*. There are few now who hear this."

"Aye," Grandpa Dunny said, "it is the truth. I have touched the mystery. There is no loneliness in trees."

Jules Bear nodded. He seemed fond of Grandpa Dunny. But his dark eyes swam with his sorrow and he could not speak to it. His words had made plain what was known to him and what the people of the plains understood and believed to be true. I felt the rush of relief, to hear of something so perfect and beautiful and to know that it always had been. Yet I wondered about what he did not say, that lament loosened from his throat and lost in the trembling crowns.

Then something rose against the morbid sky like a spectre. I rubbed my eyes because I wouldn't believe them. But still it loomed there. Then it gave a savage bawl with arms stiff and legs like piles pounded into the earth, a nightmare soaked to the skin like something drowned but not quite dead and its eyes boring holes into our heads. My mother's legs gave out and Grandpa Dunny held her. He seethed and spat and I could see that he wanted at *him*, wanted to claw up the slope with his sword and cleave him once and for all as if he had his tartan slung over his shoulder, the triumphant cry of clan McLeod.

"You can't leave me!" he shouted down at us.

"Let us pass, Mack," Jules called back to him.

"Jules, what are you doing?"

"The only thing I can do," Jules said.

"You bastard!"

"Mack."

"Do you all think I'm stupid?" my father went on, a wild rant. "I stopped for cigarettes and Daisy said that Mrs. Olsen called her, all worried that I had forget something. She had seen Mrs. Gray follow me out to the Clavet road. Damn you, Meg. I went back and you were gone. Even that old fool!"

"Stop this and let us by," Grandpa Dunny said.

"Shut up, old man!"

"Please, Mack," my mother pleaded.

"Get in the car!" He shot out his arm.

My mother sobbed and my legs melted like candles. We crowded behind Jules Bear and then Grandpa Dunny lunged forward but my mother caught his arm. "No, Dad," she said to him.

"Come," Jules Bear said to us, "stay behind me." He took my mother's hand and we all followed him in a chain up the grass slope.

I wondered where in the tall grass he hid the rifle. I knew what he was capable of. Our path passed below him. He stood taut, ruthless and coiled. The sun broke through the drift of clouds and steam rose up his back and shot out the top of his head. He stood for a moment smoking and backlit, and then all at once he sprang. He scrambled down the slope and stood before Jules Bear and blocked his passage, his brutish chin thrust out. All seemed lost.

"I'm taking them home, Jules," he said, the whites of his eyes flashing.

Jules did not move, did not falter. We waited below him strewn like the tail of a kite, hanging on with our fingers, impotent, waiting for Jules to lead us on before we were delivered forever to the grave of cats. My mother looked pale, bloodless, her mouth like cracked porcelain. The threat was so real the heat from it burned in my chest. But Jules Bear knew him, knew the cold will of fear and the futility of rage.

"Let us go, Mack," he said.

"You can't quit on me now. All I've done for you!"

"Let us go."

"Why are you doing this to me?"

"I have no cause but my own sanity."

"You make no sense, Jules."

"There is no sense in this world."

"Step aside!"

"My sons did not come home for the summer."

"What are you saying?"

"I have lost everything. And you don't know."

"Step aside, I'm not going to ask you again!"

"I have nothing now," Jules said. His chin buckled and he could not stop the tears that were close to his lips.

"Look at you, you're crying," my father mocked.

"I am not afraid to die."

"What is wrong with you?"

Jules looked away revealing the vulnerability that was his strength. He was not afraid. "I cry because you do not know me," he said. "I cry because my sons ran away from the residential school. They ran to the river. They wanted to come home. But there was no way to do this. The men in robes watched them. They watched Simon take Gabriel's hand, his little brother, and walk him out into the river. They watched this. They watched Simon walk Gabriel out into the deep water. They watched the water slowly swallow them. Simon and Gabriel did not try to swim. Now they are gone. They were just boys. They saw them as Indians who had little value. Now I have no sons to hear my story. I have no sons to listen to what is true about them. I cry because your heart has turned to stone. You will not send your son away to drown in the river. You will no longer hurt your family with your past."

Jules Bear stepped around my father. My father did not try to stop us. We did not turn back to look at his madness as he railed at us, his words like dust against the wind, his condemnation dying in our ears.

"Jules, we have a field to bring in," he called out to our backs. "You can't quit on me. Damn you. Damn you. Damn you to hell!"

We stumbled along through the grass. When we reached Jules Bear's truck we loaded our bags and suitcases in the back. I sat on Grandpa Dunny's knee in the cab by the window. We were all damp and trembling. Jules Bear turned the truck around in the tall grass beaten down by the rain. I looked down as we passed the Country Squire, that fine car that I would never see again and saw the Lee-Enfield across the back seat and the glint of the barrel.

We bumped down the old farm road to Elstow, each of us silent, alone with our thoughts. Wheat ran seamless away from us although I could see blemishes of knocked-down grain from the storm. Now and then I looked at the side-mirror expecting to see him charging up behind us. But something told me that the trees were holding him in the aspen grove. Perhaps it was Jules Bear who harnessed the wind and their Spirit was present in him as he set us free.

Jules began to tell a story, a memory of my father. I didn't want to listen. I wanted to plug my ears. But there was always a purpose when Jules Bear spoke.

"When I was a boy there was a fire on the Reserve," Jules began. "Our house burnt down to the foundation. My family escaped but two of my cousins were killed. There was nothing to fight the fire. We had no home. We stayed with relatives. This was very hard on my family. Then a strange thing happened. James Gray was a farmer who had three sons. They lived near Clavet. One day a truck pulled up in front of our burnt house. It was loaded with wood and supplies. And James Gray and his sons began to rebuild our house.

"I do not know where he got the money but every week they would come and saw and hammer and up went the house. James Gray built us a house in the spring of 1940. A few years later many tragedies struck the Gray family. Soon only a son, Macklin, was left."

"He never told me that," my mother said.

Jules Bear gripped the steering wheel with both his hands. "Sometimes a man with all his good powers," he said, "will choose destruction rather than resurrection."

"Aye," Grandpa Dunny said.

"What will he do?" I wanted to know.

"I do not know," Jules Bear said.

We drove through Clavet and passed the general store and there it was crudely painted on the white-washed stucco wall.

JANET LOVES CALAN GRAY

"Who's Janet?" Grandpa Dunny said.

"Just a girl," my mother said.

I looked for Janet sitting on her front step but she wasn't there. My mother could have pointed to the burned yard and the sad trailer where Janet looked after he mother. But she merely turned to me with a drowsy smile. I mattered to someone and it felt good. And I wondered what would happen to Janet and if I would ever see her again. It seemed the most important thing in the world to me just then.

YEW

CHAPTER TWELVE

He stood on the CNR platform in Saskatoon holding the pipe Grandpa Dunny gave him. He was admiring it. Then he stuffed tobacco into the bowl. He never looked up as the train pulled away. I suppose it was the way of Jules Bear. Perhaps in that way we were never really leaving. But I could feel the end of something as I sat there with my face pushed against the glass, watching him fade from my sight, at first recognizable and then a form that could have been anyone. I looked away because Jules wasn't just anyone. He was a man who could not be easily forgotten, with his soft words that seemed to make all things right, if only for a moment.

The maples along the streets that followed the railway had begun to turn to crimson, the cottonwoods by the river yellowing. Saskatoon began to fade, receding into my memory as the *Super Continental* picked up speed. We passed the rural patchwork in the late afternoon where combines were working the coppering grids like impossible insects and my world was expanding like a ripple, rushing to the west coast. Grandpa Dunny was reading the Saskatoon *Star-Phoenix* newspaper. How easily he settled in. He didn't seem to be bothered by his undertaking, the rescue of his daughter and grandson. Now we were on our way to his *wee house by the sea*.

"Look at that," he said, "a new flag for Canada."

My mother sat across from us. How sleepy she looked. She smiled and cast her eyes down, massaging her finger where her wedding ring had been before she put it away into her change purse. She looked up now and then to gaze out the window at the changing landscape. I noticed that it was not the prairie she looked at. She was staring at her own reflection in the glass, as if she wondered who it was that was sitting there. She never spoke of her feelings for my father. She never came out and said she hated him. I only knew she was afraid of him – a life of fear. His rough love battered her. Was he always like that? I watched her. Her future was my future. I didn't want to see her so sad.

"I've seen the flag," I told her.

"Have you now?" she said. She seemed to like my assertion.

"It's a maple leaf."

"Now that's fitting," she said.

"I've seen maple trees in Saskatoon."

"You know, Calan, it's back east where the maples are. A real show they say in autumn."

Grandpa Dunny closed his newspaper. "Not everyone is happy with a new flag it seems. I'll wager that those with their allegiance to the Brits won't be satisfied with a homemade flag. John Diefenbaker, a Conservative, from this very province is not happy at all."

"I don't pay much attention to politics, Dad," my mother said, "but we love our John."

"I don't know what the fuss is about," Grandpa Dunny said. "I think Canada should have its own flag. A proper flag for this country."

"I like the maple leaf," I said. "Are you a Canadian, Grandpa Dunny?"

"Well, I soon will be," he said. "As I see it, in Canada,

most people are from someplace else. I think that's what brings them. A man has never seen such space." He returned to his newspaper.

My mother was asleep now. Her arms were crossed at her wrists. Her head was tilted to one side, her vulnerability exposed to me. She was losing weight. Her arms were nearly bone and her shoulders no longer filled her dress. A brittleness consumed her and I feared that she could crumble at any moment, leaving an empty pool of cotton.

Then I felt it, a presence that was new to me, a disruption from inside her. It seemed to broadcast a message to me. Immediately I felt tired. The presence drained me, and then it was gone. Perhaps it was just my worrying. I wondered if Grandpa Dunny noticed her fragility, but he seemed only interested in his newspaper, learning to be a Canadian. I missed Jules Bear. He would know what was wrong. I closed my eyes and felt the subtle shifting of the train. The muted clack of wheels seemed like a speeding clock of iron taking us to some other time.

I don't remember going to the sleeping car. It all seemed so dreamy, the sensation of motion, a constant going west while I sat or slept. I soon forgot where I was in the world. In my dreams there was an unmistakable sense of being carried away, of flying over unfamiliar places.

I awoke feeling the same current of steel under my feet. I dressed. Grandpa Dunny was waiting for me and led me to the dining car, steadying himself with his cane and the *Star-Phoenix* tucked under his arm. The people in the car seemed pleased to be there. Their voices murmured pleasure all around us as I slid into the booth beside my mother.

She sat with a cup of coffee. She faced the window with her elbow resting on the table. Her arm angled slightly away and she held a cigarette in her fingers. The spiralling strings of smoke rose in a drift of blue haze along the ceiling. She often sat like that back on the farm when she had a moment to herself. She always seemed reflective, perhaps distant, but she was always calm when she smoked a cigarette. However, it was only the appearance of ease, a moment when her world seemed a tolerable affair. She smoked often. Sometimes she smoked without using a match, lighting one cigarette from the butt of another.

A steward brought porridge and orange juice to our table, breakfast for Grandpa Dunny and myself. There was nothing for my mother.

"What are you having, Mom?" I said. I was worried more than ever now.

"Just coffee, Calan," she said sweetly. She played with her hair, childlike.

Grandpa Dunny sat across from me. He watched my mother. I wanted him to say something, tell her that she had to eat. He said nothing and started on his porridge. I couldn't understand his inattention after what we had been through. She needed help. We had just left our home, walked away from the only lives that we knew. There was no talk of tomorrow, what we were going to do. It all seemed reckless somehow. I wanted him to tell me it would be all right, that everything was going to be fine, that my mother would get well, that there was a better life waiting for her, for us.

"Sometimes, Calan," he said putting down his spoon and leaning over the table, "when a man is fixed upon a task, his mind and body pressed to do a certain thing, there can be no thought of what comes next and no regrets of what has been. There's only the one thing he can do. And then, after that great thing has been done, there will come a time for the man to be alone with his thoughts. In those still moments his reckoning of the world can return to him. Man or woman, it makes little difference. Now is such a time. Your mother has been through a great ordeal. Both of you have. You have suffered. You are old enough to hear this, Calan. Don't be afraid. Everything we'll need will be waiting for us. We may not know how things will be, but we can trust we'll have the courage to face whatever it is. Now we are here. It's time to be patient with ourselves. I will look after your mother, Calan. She is my youngest daughter. We'll get to the bottom of it, whatever the ailment, but there is nothing to do until we get to Victoria. I quit my tobacco and it's all good health now. All right then, finish your porridge like a good Scotsman."

He reached across the table and placed his hand over my mother's cigarettes and pulled them away from her. That action seemed to bring her back.

"Have you seen what's out the window, Calan?" she asked me. "Something you've never seen. Come close and see for yourself."

There was a dark smudge beyond where my mother sat. Outside the dining car window a bank of trees flashed by. The world looked uprooted, pitched to the sky. The earth was reaching up to a walled in wilderness and a line of fresh snow a thousand feet above us. The train moved down a serpentine valley along milky creeks and rivers and across bridges and spans. The Earth was not flat at all. It was green, green, green, thick and strange. The trees were perfect in their symmetry. What were they? Their form and layers as they ascended the steep slopes seemed like a well-laid plan, something never ending. There were millions upon millions of trees, I was sure. Above the snowline the trees vanished, gave way to the ragged crowns of the Rocky Mountains white with new snow against September's polished brilliance.

"After your porridge, Calan," Grandpa Dunny said, "there's the domed cars for sights such as these. *Sceneromics* they call them, a great window to view the mountains and the valleys. With any luck you'll see a goat or a moose. Perhaps a bear. Fantastic animals I can tell you. We're in British Columbia now. And Calan, you'll hear them, the trees, lad, the score of God's own choir."

I just looked at him. The enthusiasm in his eyes seemed

too much at times. He was not a simple man. He always had a laugh and a riddle. Yet he was a measured man when he needed to be. There was something else in his eyes that wasn't just mischief, there was an uncommon strength when he smiled. And only a fool wouldn't see that firm hand on the hilt of his sword.

Grandpa Dunny was right about the domed cars. I stayed there all day, not leaving my seat for lunch or supper. The ever-changing wilderness of trees, trees, trees was a sanctuary for my senses. Their song in my head was an affirmation, a declaration of their place in the world. I had to leave the car when the stars shone out of the blue-black sky. Grandpa Dunny came for me. He fed me a sandwich from the dining-car galley then helped me into bed. My mother was already sleeping.

"Why do I hear them?" I asked. He stood in the aisle. All was cramped and dim, and full of the voices of strangers. He leaned into my berth..

"Well," he whispered, "I suppose it's time for you to know. I was waiting for just the right moment. I can see that it is here. There is a tree, Calan, I know so well. You will remember I said so that morning by the willows. I was the custodian of the Fortingall Yew, a sacred tree, an ancient tree located at the very centre of Scotland. The Monarch of Antiquity they call it. It is 5000 years old, the oldest tree in the world some say and I believe it. It is the immortal tree of life. A tree so thick, fifty-six and a half feet around, that ten men can join their outstretched arms around its girth. A tree so old has its legends and lore. It is said that Pontius Pilate, the son of a Roman Legionary some 2000 years ago and the man who would grow up to crucify Jesus Christ, played under it as a child. But I know something more about it that you will understand. In all my days and years in its service, I could feel its intelligence. I could feel its language just as you; Jules Bear and his people know of such things as well. You heard him speak, Calan. It is true.

"A lifetime is but a blink of an eye in its presence. Yet I spoke to it and I listened and I often wondered why others couldn't hear the voice of that elder yew. Your mother was not alone. As a young girl she thought me a grand storyteller. Perhaps I was just that. But its message is true, the earth is a living thing. All things have life, from stones to feathers and fins to heather. All are sacred and divine creations. You have the gift. You can feel the energy of life, in all its forms. However, the gift can be a curse as well. So you must heed what I tell you. You will be overwhelmed with your senses and at such times you must tell me what you feel. For now then, don't think on it and be off to sleep."

He kissed my forehead and left me, but the more I tried not to think, the more my mind went to work imagining the sacred yew. Thousands of years old and still in its place, witness to an unending stream of happenings, the rise and fall of civilizations, death and rebirth, the joys and sorrows of existence woven about its flanks, the Fortingall Yew, the Monarch of Antiquity. Then I saw the image of a tree standing alone against a battering wind, a parable of a man's destruction. I saw my father slack and ruined. I had not left him. He was near. He lived inside me.

CHAPTER THIRTEEN

The landscape we passed through seemed curious to me – all shades and textures. Dense forests on the humped shoulders of mountains made a verdant hide which changed to sparse wan hills. Slow green rivers merged at a city. The train stopped for passengers coming and going. Then we continued down, skirting cliffs burned with russets and ochre, down where the sun was but a shy impression and the shadows kept the frost all day long, down where rivers joined once again and roiled madly in through narrow gates and then spilled muddy out into a broad valley that seemed to never end.

The mountains were oddly blue, a smoky distance and we followed the now leisurely river through farms and towns, across trestles and new waters. I watched tugboats, rafts of logs and mills gushing cinders from inverted cones. I saw fishermen on gravel bars heaving their lines, shoulder to shoulder like queer wading birds. Somewhere Vancouver was ahead of us, the end of the line, the city by the sea. Then the towns merged, the endless houses crowded the treeless slopes above the river. I would always remember the drizzle and raindrops against the viewing panes inching like translucent worms. I would remember the trees and the smoking woods. I would remember Grandpa Dunny pointing to the bulky eagles with their great white heads, unmoving in the high limbs of massive cottonwoods that grew along the clay banks. I would remember the gulls and crows squabbling over spent salmon in the isolated pools along the bars. I knew that I would draw those scenes one day, that I would remember that dripping gallery of impressions.

When we stepped off the train in Vancouver, the salt of the ocean stung my nostrils and tasted briny on my tongue. The air thick with these flavours. As in Saskatoon, the buildings rose in stacks five high, shutting out the sky. The people in the streets rushed about under black umbrellas and the traffic lights bled red and green on the pavement.

Grandpa Dunny held a newspaper over my mother's head as we hurried from the train station to the bus that would take us to Victoria. My mother was still in her summer dress with a sweater wrapped around her shoulders. She dragged her luggage through puddles while rain slapped her pale legs.

"Hurry, Calan," she said, partially turning to me in the driving rain. "Hurry now."

The bus by the curb on Station Street was taking on passengers. Someone was standing near the bus leaning against a streetlight pole with his shoulders gathered and his head stooped the way that people stand in rain. The sight of him stopped me cold. He was smoking a cigarette. He was soaking wet and had one hand in his pocket. He looked right at me. I knew the shape of him, how he looked when he was angry or sullen or seething. I knew how he smoked, the deep sucking of his cheeks, the pulling of the cigarette from his lips. His head, his face angular, hard and cold, his hair kept short and proper. But his eyes were the most telling feature of all. They demanded something, things I could never realize because fear always immobilized me. I stood unable to move, the rain running raw down my neck.

In the open door of the bus my mother turned back to

me, impatient now. Grandpa Dunny held her arm. "Calan, get on the bus!" she shouted angrily.

I stood still, staring at him, waiting for him. He couldn't possibly be there. I thought I had outraced him, expelled him from my thoughts, filled myself with a miraculous new world. Then my mother saw what stuck me fast. She dropped her suitcase and left Grandpa Dunny at the bus. She ran to me and took my hand. She trained her eyes on him, a mother ready to give up her life for her child. He flicked his cigarette and began to walk toward us. My mother crouched, sheltered me while we waited for what was surely to come. But he didn't stop. He walked right on by as if he never saw us shivering with our cold blood. We watched him. Such likeness in his features but it was not him, just a man walking toward a woman just off the train. They embraced. We were stunned by the story that we carried with us, our fears casting a shadow of him, projecting a dream we could not awaken from.

Grandpa Dunny was waiting for us at the bus. He hadn't moved. He saw it all, our mistake, allowed it to unfold without interference. But my mother gave him a look for his indifference and he caught her meaning sure enough. He smiled to assuage her then he knelt down to me. He took hold of my shoulders in that way of his when there was something to be said. Everything had purpose and meaning to him. There was not a word or gesture that did not matter. All things were part of a grand design. He never said it was God's divine hand. He never repeated a pious quotation, or a piece of scripture. His speech came naturally as a breeze stirring leaves. His wisdom radiated from his eyes and in his touch.

"Calan, lad," he said, the wet strands of his hair curling on his cheek, "you know, I've seen my dear Margaret three times today."

The Pacific Coach Line's driver stowed our luggage and we settled into our seats. Soon we left the city, crossing viaducts and bridges over that slow river. We passed gushing stacks of industry, went through a tunnel and out onto farm-land stretching out to the ocean. Crops were still in the fields. "Spuds," Grandpa Dunny said from behind his *Vancouver Sun* newspaper, his curious eyes studying his new country like a mindful student. "They say that W.A.C. Bennett was a tough negotiator during the Columbia River Treaty," he muttered.

His words found a way inside me, bound for some good that he wished to cultivate. I was clay in his hands in com-pensation for the guidance that I never had. I was too young to understand every lesson, every story but he seemed to trust that his words would settle into their proper place, simmer-ing in my idle mind, still sorting out the past and the future. I looked and listened because I could do those things and not be made wrong for it. He was a patient man. My mother with her dreamy smile deferred to him now, allowed her own father to be a father to me.

We neared the ocean. Outside the window the sun broke through a grey wall of weather. Shards bore out of it, in rays across the neat fields and all was golden the way the sun can transform the light of the late afternoon. A ship waited in its berth. The *Queen of Saanich* held her great mouth agape for buses and cars as willing motorists and drivers fed its empty gullet. Once aboard we left the bus. My mother found a seat and rested there looking out at the saffron sun falling into the ocean while Grandpa Dunny had a mind for some indoctri-nation. He led me outside. There was something frighten-ing on the upper deck of the ferry with Grandpa Dunny, the wind in his hair and beard and a fervour about him driven by the sight of the sea.

"The ancient McLeods had lands in the Isle of Skye in the west," he said. "They were seafarers. But our family is from Aberdeen – cousins and uncles crazy for the ships and ports, my brother Daniel himself piloting the *Queen Mary*. My fa-ther had a team of Clydesdales and delivered barrels of beer to the inns and pubs. I was the one who wandered inland. I don't regret it though, but I must say that it feels like home to be here on the steamer-track among the combers and gulls.

"You will have family like you've never seen, Calan. It's a fine thing to be surrounded by your loving people. I'm not saying that families are without their squabbles. No, not at all. And your cousins might take a while to get to know you. You must give it time. There's good and bad to most things in life. The answer to that is to put your attention on the good. A tall order it is, Calan. But a worthwhile endeavour nevertheless. The high road, I like to call it.

"Now, lad, lift your chin and put your face into the stiff breezes. They'll draw your tears but feel them full. Tell me if they don't stir your McLeod blood. A glorious wind over the sea can set a man straight and give him his bearings. It can cleanse you through and through, give you a good clearing of the head. Now hold onto the rail, close your eyes and let the sea welcome you home."

I was holding on for dear life, my knuckles white against the guard rail as I braced against Grandpa Dunny's *stiff breezes*. They seemed like a hurricane to me. They pried at my fingers trying to pitch me into the froth and foam topping the bottle-green swells far below me. *Home*, he said, a word now without meaning for me. It seemed that I had been away forever, away from the prairie that was a fixed place, unmoving. A secure and familiar monotony. Oh, to stand still for a minute to let that sky impress me with its eternity. An oppressive quality, I had thought. But the diversity of landscapes of British Columbia with its fluid transitions carried me farther still. There on that ferry, I wondered if I could do it, if I could make a new beginning. Or should I could release my grip on the railing and slip away? Slip away. A prairie boy after all.

It seemed to me we crossed a vast ocean. The *Queen of Saanich* slipped by islands and bays, past fat sea lions lounging on a lighthouse rock. The western horizon was smeared with ribbons of the setting sun that bled orange and reflective between the treed islands. Finally the ferry landed at our new home, Vancouver Island. Eagles watched in the decaying light from their fine perches over the blackened rubble of the broken shoreline while dark shapes of slouching birds waded in the shallow pools. Herons, Grandpa Dunny called them.

In the dark the bus took us farther still until the urban lights of Victoria revealed a world against the black-knit void, unknown streets in an unknown city. Somewhere we had a family. I had no sense of place anymore, no sky leaning over me, no rivers to follow, no waters to keep me, and no comfort in the shadows of trees lining the wet streets. I was lost on the west coast.

I held my mother's hand as we left the bus and walked up Hillside Avenue toward Cedar Hill Road. That's where my auntie Netty lived. A family, our *loving people* waited for us. I was nervous. Grandpa Dunny was chatty and my mother's mood improved while I felt sick with my worry. Soon Grandpa Dunny pointed to a house with stairs and a broad porch, a veranda as he called it. I wished I were someplace else. I didn't want the attention I feared was waiting for me.

We climbed the stairs and stood under the porch light. Grandpa Dunny rapped on the front door with his cane and bellowed out our arrival. There was a great disturbance inside me as people rushed at the door. Something pushed me back down the stairs. I closed my eyes, reached for its enduring presence, and held my bony arms fast against the Fortingall Yew.

ARBUTUS

CHAPTER FOURTEEN

It was a frantic place to be, a living room filled with grownups hugging and crying. I stood by the door with our luggage. My cousins had their slick hair parted and combed. They wore plaid shirts buttoned to the neck like good boys. Four of them sat on the chesterfield in the rising order of their height like stairs, their welcome rehearsed. They stared at me as if I were an alien who had just dropped by from another planet and not another province – *Greetings from Saskatchewan.* The way they squinted their eyes and wrinkled their noses, rankled. I felt they hated me.

The mob of aunts and uncles turned to me and gushed their praises of how I'd grown. But how could they know? It seemed to me that I was the smallest in the room except for the poor orange cat that was trapped against the living room window. One cousin on the end seemed like a shrimp. Still they pulled at my cheeks and patted my spinning head in a way that seemed to delight the cousins.

"You remember your auntie Netty and Uncle Reggie, Calan?" my mother said to me. "And Auntie Kate and Uncle Al."

I nodded but I felt I had never seen them before in my life. I could have walked into any house on that street. *Who are these people?* I wondered until I did remember, vaguely, a wedding photograph that I found in a drawer on the farm. Yet there never seemed to be a moment when she could talk freely about her family. I learned not to ask. And the photograph couldn't convey Uncle Reggie's blustering laugh that shook the windows and the paintings on the wall and made my brain rattle inside my head. He was a Victoria policeman. A Jell-O shiver in his belly. My uncle Al, his arms folded, smoking his pipe, had a thoughtful look in his eyes. He seemed amused by it all. I liked him right away.

I remained by the door. I couldn't see a way inside the room. I had no will to be *surrounded by my loving people.* It all seemed too much to me. I couldn't reach my mother with her sisters doting on her, searching out the illness in her pallid skin and child-bones, lingering with their looks where flesh had once been and then looking to the other in the secret code of sisters. How they touched her, held her, my mother melting into their arms, their cherished little sister.

Auntie Kate seemed tired, overwhelmed perhaps from the long hours of work in the hospital. Auntie Netty, a stern version of my mother, suddenly fired off a missile of threats to the boys punching each other on the chesterfield. She was a yeller and singled them out by name. I could see the youngest one, Kenny, was nearly in tears. She never lost sight of them – they were like a grass fire that might get out of hand. They worried me, those Bratt boys.

Then Grandpa Dunny stood before the cousins shaking each of their hands. The slack-armed side-to-side *Grandpa Dunny shake* that belonged to me. I felt betrayed. How could he? I was the only one.

"Now, boys," he said, "take Calan downstairs. Help him with his suitcase."

The dreaded moment had arrived. "No, I'll take it," I said. I wasn't going to let them touch my things.

"Get settled then, Calan," Auntie Netty said. "There's a

supper of ham and scalloped potatoes waiting in the kitchen. Boys, be on your best behaviour now. We have special guests."

I could see what the brothers thought of me as they all scrambled down stairs and disappeared in a wake of mocking laughter. The aunts and uncles left for the kitchen while Grandpa Dunny helped my mother. Then he turned to me and saw my hurt, my trepidation.

"They're good boys, Calan," he said. "Go now and get to know your cousins."

I remained by the door of the now empty room. They had all left me like the discarded shoes. Leaving home and setting out for the *wee house by the sea* had seemed a simple plan on the face of it, but I could sense complexities arising from it that could never be known – a world of moments that could not have been foretold.

So I rested there in the space of that living room on Cedar Hill Road. It was if I needed the stillness and my own thoughts to interpret what had happened only moments before, what was said, what secrets crept among the *loving people*. The room was filled with paintings and photographs and fine figurines, a tapestry of collected things in a cluttered beauty. There was a floral couch and chair, tables with warm-lit lamps and a television set in a polished wooden cabinet. A painting on the wall above the fireplace nearly filled that space. It portrayed a swan attacking a fallen ballerina or perhaps it was the swan that was dying. It was a painting of feathered form and shadow that I didn't understand. The death seemed lovely.

Back on the farm our living room was desolate, unused, bare without a soul. But now all about me there seemed to be a richness that wasn't present before. My sensitivity couldn't recognize such qualities with all the competing energies. Standing alone was a marvellous thing for me. My mind stopped racing to understand, to sort out. My fear fell away. The orange cat brushed by me. Warm and wonderful smells came from the kitchen. Life pushed me on, down the stairs to the cousins waiting to devour me.

At the top of the stairs with my suitcase in hand I looked toward the kitchen. The grownups all seemed to be in a good mood now. From my distance I admired their smiling faces, the blend of new voices, the sound of pouring drinks, the progression around a table of food. And always there was Uncle Reggie's laughter. I paused, not knowing why. I suppose I was captivated by what a family could be, by their curious joy. A family lived there. They had lives. I thought of how I moped about the farm without anyone except my mother. As if that were all there was in the world.

Suddenly my mother was lying on the floor. How strange, I thought – the sound of her hitting the floor seemed to come after. There was a delay between the image and the sound. Like the roll of thunder that follows a lightning flash. There were bodies standing over her. Auntie Kate knelt on the floor beside her, taking her hand, lifting her head. I heard loud visceral gasps of fear. I stood there processing things. My mother was not well. What was wrong? She had finally arrived where she wished to be. She had made it. Yet she lay on the cold linoleum with loving hands desperately trying to coax life back into her ruined lungs.

Uncle Al walked toward me, his head down as he approached. I could hear Uncle Reggie on the telephone – his urgent diction. The sisters stood over the youngest, talking to her, "Come back, Megan," Auntie Netty called through her tears, "Come back." Auntie Kate pushed on my mother's chest but the damage was done.

I felt Uncle Al's hand on my shoulder. He ducked down to steal my eyes away from the kitchen.

"Calan," he said, "go downstairs. Be with the boys. An ambulance is on its way. They will look after your mother. There's nothing you can do now."

I looked past him. I could see her hand, limp, resting on the floor. The frantic sisters and Grandpa Dunny watching it all as helpless as he'd ever been. But she wasn't there. I had a sense that she was gone and that the ambulance was coming for her body, not for her. But she was not dead. Then I heard Uncle Reggie's big voice and Uncle Al stepped aside.

"Downstairs!" he said. He stood before me like a wall. No laughing now. A fierce, twisted compassion.

"She's not there," I said to him.

He had that stunned-owl look that comes from something unexpected, when words do not match understanding. Uncle Al bowed his head.

A part of me wished to die, there with the cousins in the basement staring at me. A low timber ceiling and a bare light bulb. Comic books and clothes were scattered on the concrete floor. Buddy and Jimmy, the middle cousins, stood like prize-fighters with boxing gloves like swollen red stains over their raised fists. I didn't want to get to know them.

"You can have Kenny's bed," Jimmy Bratt said. "It might smell like piss, though."

"Shut up, Jimmy!" Kenny said.

"Watch it you twerp or Buddy will use you for a punching bag."

"That Butchie is in for it," Kenny said to distract Jimmy. "Tell him Buddy, tell Calan what you're going to do."

"Don't you ever shut up, twerp?" Jimmy said.

"Do you want to know?" Buddy said to me. His eyes flared.

An ambulance wailed in the distance, growing stronger. I couldn't think. I wanted to crawl away. Sit in the dark. So I shrugged, the only language I knew just then.

"Butchie Burnum wants to fight me," Buddy said. "He gave Jimmy a good lickin'."

"Did not!" Jimmy protested.

"Sure did," Kenny said.

"Both of you shut up!" Buddy said. "Dad bought us these gloves so we can stand up for ourselves. That Butchie wants me next. He's going to be sorry that he messed with me."

"Grandpa Dunny has a Volkswagen Bug," Kenny said. "It's parked in the lane. Buddy can start it."

"You're going to get it now, you little twerp," Jimmy said.

"Larry smokes," Kenny said.

"Shut your traps!" Larry the oldest said. "Dad's coming."

Uncle Reggie came down the stairs like gloom. "Stay down here for a minute," he said.

He found me in the dull light standing by Kenny's bed. He didn't know what to say with all his sons watching him.

"I'm hungry," Kenny complained.

"You'll have to wait," Uncle Reggie said.

"I'm starving."

"Shut up, Kenny," Jimmy said.

"Boys, Auntie Megan is sick," Uncle Reggie finally said. "The ambulance has come for her."

"What's wrong with her?" Larry asked.

They were all sitting on their beds looking at me. They were a subdued bunch now.

"Calan, do you want to see her?" Uncle Reggie asked. His big voice wavered.

It was a hard question for him. There were no rules about such things. "Yeah," I said to him.

"Up you go, then. I'll put a cot for you beside Kenny's bed."

At the top of the stairs I saw her. She was on a stretcher covered with a white sheet. I saw the outline of limbs, a shrouded face. The attendants secured straps. They didn't speak. The aunts sat on the chesterfield with Grandpa Dunny between them holding their hands. Uncle Al stood by the fireplace with his pipe. I felt the painting of the swan and the ballerina creeping up my back. Then everyone saw me standing there. That Jimmy Dean song, *Little Boy Lost*, began to play in my head. *Where's my daddy, where's my daddy…?* That sad refrain. But he was nowhere. He wasn't anything at all. How I hated his intrusion just then.

CHAPTER FIFTEEN

I awoke to a square of light on the floor. At first, I didn't know where I was. After a moment of confusion the awareness of what had happened slowly seeped into me. Gone was the possibility that it all had been a bad dream. The sun did come up. The floor above me creaked like a pinching saw, footsteps moving away. Soon the cousins would be up. I could hear them stir. I didn't want to be run over by the rousing bedlam of the Bratt brothers and hurriedly dressed. As I did so I could feel a presence outside. Quietly, I went out the basement door.

It was cold and I shivered. A curious chill found its way under my clothes and at once the sea was in my nose, tingling. I saw a red Volkswagen Beetle parked beside a garage. Bikes were stacked together. In the corner of the backyard there was a tree that seemed to be on fire. I rubbed my eyes as I walked toward it. Raucous crows dispersed like blown shingles. I felt uneasy, fitful. The sky was grey. Clouds, like pads of steel wool, hung low and thick and moved rapidly across the sky. Somehow the sun found a way through and bathed the tree and its glossy, green leaves in the queerest light. The tree leaned. Its great twisted branches spread like flaming, stiff hair, and its roots fastened to an outcropping of rock. The trunk captured all of the sun. It was smooth, a glorious, bloody orange and in places scales peeled away exposing a raw inner wood. As I stood there before it, beneath it, I was no longer afraid.

The light fell in ripples down the trunk, crimson waves pulsing, alive. Then the light shifted from one part of the tree to another, flashing, like the blinking lights on a Christmas tree. I was warm now. I felt a bright heat on my face. I sensed the tree's energy and something else. I knew it was kind. There was no mistake. I knew it as one knows a sparkle comes from the sun.

There was a rattling in the tree branches, a beating of its leaves. An energy seemed to rise taking the light with it, rising up through the limbs to the very top, upward still until the sun itself was lost behind the clouds and all was flat and still. And then loneliness, so sudden and sharp fell upon me, a sunless world devoid of life and purpose. I no longer had an identity. I was no one. I could only feel a stitch in my belly – shards of emptiness. And I cried as I stood there with my slumping shoulders before that tree, blubbering that I should have been the one to die, worthless little boy, motherless child. Then someone came. I turned. It was Larry. I quickly wiped my eyes with a knuckle.

"Did you see it?" I asked him nervously. I had to search for an explanation.

"What?"

"The light in the tree."

"Ah, that's just the way it looks," Larry said.

"What's it called?"

"An arbutus."

He looked away. I wondered if he was waiting for my tears to dry. It seemed that I didn't need to explain anything to Larry.

"Geez," he said, "that's awful what happened to your mom. On your first day here and all. That must feel like crap."

"Yeah." I couldn't lift my head to look at Larry. Words

were inadequate to speak to the hopelessness that I felt, deeper than anything on the farm. Then there was always my mother. Even as she struggled, she was the living bedrock of my life. And when conditions were about to extinguish her once and for all she scooped me up, and with Grandpa Dunny set out to make our lives right again.

"My brothers are goofs," Larry said all at once. "They don't know anything. Kenny's just a squirt. He picks his nose and eats it. Disgusting. He's a little ratfink. He thinks it makes him seem older. And he's got a big head like a pumpkin that makes him fall over sometimes. And Jimmy, he's so skinny that if he stands sideways you can walk right by him without seeing him. Buddy's athletic, good at sports. He's always showing off his muscles. I won't arm-wrestle him. Everyone wants Buddy on their team. He's a good fighter, too. It's hilarious. Buddy beats up Jimmy and Jimmy beats up Kenny and Kenny cries to Mom and then I catch it. She'll yell, 'Larry, what's going on down there?' Then I have to keep them in line, with a pinched tit or a gonchee-pull. I'm not tough. I'm big. Dad calls me husky. I hate that. I talk my way out of fights if I have to, or I stare a kid down. But I'm not tough. All together I guess we're tough. I hear them say, 'look out, here come the Bratts.' Just look mean and most kids will leave you alone. Think you can do that, Calan?"

I knew that Larry was sizing me up. He could see that I didn't have much muscle on my bones. I wasn't much of a threat. He was worried about that fact, his cousin from the prairies unprepared to walk among the budding pugilists of Victoria.

"Yeah, I have a look," I said, thinking of my sullen mouth that vexed my father. There was nothing tough about it. It was simply fear disguised as something more. I thought animals might have that ability. I supposed that's what Larry was getting at.

"Show me," he said.

Larry Bratt was a boy who knew and accepted his place in the world. He watched over a brood of cowlicked and freckled brothers struggling to find their own place. I was beginning to understand that it was not Auntie Netty or Uncle Reggie who were raising those boys. It was Larry. He was leading the way, shielding his brothers, taking the teenage slings and arrows to spare them. And he was leading me away, for just a while, from my broken heart.

I gave him a look to satisfy his counsel. In his eyes there was curiosity, and then in his mouth, dismay. Larry wasn't convinced.

"Look," he said, "I guess you have to go to school. Not today. Maybe not tomorrow, but one day. And I won't be there. I'm in grade nine. I go to Victoria High. The other clowns go to Oaklands Elementary. You have to hang around Buddy. That's it. That Butchie Burnum will get you. I'm not kidding. I don't want to scare you, Calan, but he's a real dink."

"What's wrong with him?"

"Butchie – he's just mad. He flunked last year. Now he's stuck in grade seven."

"I'm in grade five."

"That don't mean nothing to Butchie. Any day now, Buddy's meeting Butchie after school at the paper shack. Everyone's talking about it. If Buddy whips him, then maybe Butchie will back off. But if Buddy loses, then that Butchie will be picking on everyone. Girls too."

"Why don't you fight Butchie?" I was worried that Buddy might lose.

"Can't, he's younger than me," Larry said. " I could take him if I had to. But I'm in high school. It's just not done. It's up to Buddy."

In what new world had I arrived, with characters plucked right out of a dream, a comic book storyline? Butchie Burnum seemed like a monster, something fanged, lurking.

"I've got to get ready for school," Larry said. "Remember, stay close to Buddy."

I watched Larry go back into the house. Then I turned back to the tree, that magical tree. I could feel its life like a blessing now. What had happened was not so clear – the sun finding its way through the clouds perhaps in the way it always did. There was nothing miraculous about that. Yet somehow the tree made me think of her. It had lifted me. I had felt safe and then it was gone. I wanted to wait there all day until the sun appeared once again, for me. But I had to go, too. They would be waiting for me, to reassure me. *Everything will be all right*, they would say. But how could they ever know?

In the kitchen the cousins were bent over their bowls of porridge. Auntie Netty stood at the counter over an assembly line of school lunches: four stacks of bologna and mustard sandwiches, four pairs of jumbo raisin cookies, four apples and four brown bags with the cousin's names marked in pencil, except for Larry. Something about high school, I imagined. I watched her. She wore an apron like my mother. They were so much alike. I couldn't stop looking at her. Then she saw me standing there.

"Well, good morning, Calan," she said. It crushed her to look at me. "The boys will be off to school as usual. No sense having them underfoot. And you can do what you please. We'll have to decide when you'll go to school. I'll have to see that you get registered. So we'll need to talk, not right now, but in a while. Uncle Reggie is at work and your Grandpa Dunny is out doing errands. He'll be back shortly. Now you sit down and have your porridge." She was trying so hard.

There was a chair for me at the table, at the end beside Kenny, my place in the Bratt pecking order. The cousins blew and slurped, heaps of porridge stuffed in their maws leaving no room for words, but their eyes danced all over me, their thoughts wondering, I supposed, about my circumstance. They might have been thinking about their own mother, perhaps with a renewed gratitude for the things she did for them. How quiet it was now. A radio played, but still there was a silence, a withdrawal from the ordinary. Order had been disrupted. It seemed that normal life in the house had left with my mother.

Mourning had a weight to it. It stopped the tongue, rationed words. Yet Larry seemed unaffected when he laid it all out for me under the arbutus. Now there seemed to be an honouring, respect from sons to their mother, an understanding. How she suffered over their lunches as they plunged their spoons. A rough bunch, I thought, but they had manners. And they knew when to *shut their traps,* as Larry would say.

I couldn't eat. I stared into the bowl at the melting brown sugar and the mountain of oatmeal rising above a sea of milk. Life went on, but part of me was unwilling to go on without her. Nothing came to counter my resignation, no reassurance from Auntie Netty that *everything will be all right.*

CHAPTER SIXTEEN

Auntie Netty said that I could do what I pleased on those mornings when the cousins were at school. So I went to the backyard and stood under the arbutus. In rain and sun the leaves were wet and bright as faces. I touched the tree's garish bark. I wanted to hear its language. I listened but the only thing I could hear was my own worrying. I had always worried, something I learned on the farm, waiting for my father to come in from the barn. I didn't worry about him, never about him, only about what he would do. More than that, I worried about my mother, what the day would bring her. Why couldn't it have been happiness? That's all she ever wanted. I worried when she baked, when flour spilled and dusted her cheeks. I worried when she turned to the window, afraid she would leave me when she could no longer resist what called to her.

I worried about the barn cats long dead and the ones left behind. I worried about Janet and her stitched and pinned rags, looking after her ill mother, scavenging in the cloakroom like a hungry mouse, ignoring the looks from the other children, some little pride burning unshakable inside her. I worried about Phillip and his blackboard. Would he ever be able to write in a scribbler? I didn't worry about Bobby and Ricky Olsen, those hard working brothers, hockey players, model sons. Instead, I worried about the prairie dog that Ricky shot with his slingshot and propped up on a stick. I feared for the furry colony that watched with their prairie dog empathy.

I worried about Simon and Gabriel Bear who were already dead. The image of the brothers walking into the river and no one moving to save them haunted me. I worried about Jules Bear and his sadness. I was afraid of what my father might do with his Lee-Enfield, blue and deadly in the backseat of the Country Squire. Why was it there? Why hadn't he shot us dead and buried us all beside the cats beneath the aspens?

I worried about the swan attacking the ballerina, about the size of Kenny's head, about the bruises on Jimmy's willow arms and about Buddy trying to start Grandpa Dunny's car. I worried that Larry was trying to be brave, that he smoked and that he would die one day. I even worried about Butchie Burnum. How could I worry over a bully, a bully who picked on kids, wished to beat them up for no good reason?

I couldn't stop. There was always more. The orange cat tossed out of the house, the sparrow stuffed in its mouth and the wobble of its limp head. I worried about Auntie Netty bustling in the kitchen, fretting like my mother. With her pale, Scot's skin I feared she could drop dead just like that and the cousins wouldn't be able to go on without her, and Uncle Reggie would sleep all day with the curtains drawn. Auntie Kate worried enough on her own and I imagined that Uncle Al soothed her with his sympathetic looks while he stood calm and composed with his pipe. I worried over so many things, a stream of things that could happen, that had happened, things that couldn't be stopped. I worried because I had seen the worst of it. I knew that bad things happen even if you pray, even if you're good.

I worried about Grandpa Dunny. It seemed that he had

forgotten me. When our eyes met in the kitchen, he would turn away. He couldn't look at me. Perhaps the shock was too much for him, but I needed his kind words, something to carry me, something more than Larry's practical tutelage, those day-to-day things to keep a boy out of trouble. I needed a broader view, a glimpse of greater meaning. I needed a tangible affirmation of life before I curled up under the arbutus, to become a root or stone, stripped down to nothing, to become nothing, to die with my worries because what I worried about most of all was my frightening thoughts. I wished *him* dead, my father, smashed to a bloody pulp.

Standing under the arbutus, I heard a car start in the lane. It was Grandpa Dunny's Volkswagen. He got out, stood beside it and looked at me across the yard. White bats of exhaust gathered, thinned and vanished. He called out to me.

"Calan, can you come with me? There's a place that I want to show you. I think it'll be good for the both of us."

Then Auntie Netty came out with a jacket. "It's too small for Kenny now," she said, "but it's still a good coat. All the boys wore it. You'll need it up there. There's always a wind."

Too small for Kenny. I wondered if it would ever be too small for me. I waited for her to come across the yard. She helped me put it on and zipped it up to my neck. It was made of knitted grey wool with brown eagles on the front with stitched white heads. I liked the feel of it. It was warm.

"We call them Indian sweaters," she said. "Go now with your grandpa."

I thanked her. She rested her hand on my shoulder and smiled. I could feel her wanting to wrap me up in her arms but she turned and went back into the house. Everything she did reminded me of my mother, the way that she spoke, how she moved and the same upright strength and words that were her own.

The Volkswagen jerked onto Hillside Avenue. Grandpa Dunny swiped at the windshield with his handkerchief.

"Foggin' up," he said. "Funny bit of a car, don't you think, Calan? Wee motor at the back."

He fiddled with the radio dialling up a sequence of stuttered songs. There was nothing to his liking and he turned it off. *Blaupunkt* it said.

"Where are we going?" I was curious to know.

"Find our bearings," he said. "You'll understand in a few minutes."

The Volkswagen plodded along like a bug, its namesake, upwards through neighbourhoods of fine houses cut into stone slabs with garden thickets, showy arbutus and larger evergreen trees. Then we were at the top of a hill in *Mount Tolmie Park* a sign read. Grandpa Dunny parked the car and removed his cap. He got out and I followed.

We stepped over the curb and stood near the edge of a mountainside of bare rock. I saw a fearlessness about him now. The wind rushed at us and took his beard and shook it. His mane of hair was blown back like beaten grass. His eyes teared and his tears ran down his cheeks. He reared back with the force of the wind and placed his arm across my shoulders. The wind tugged and pulled at me and he kept me from taking flight. Suddenly I could see an expanse in all directions – mountains, forested hills, the sea, and the city below. Victoria with its tall buildings crowded a harbour and the sky about us like the far-seeing prairie. Thin clouds hurried by and the sun shone on the water, luminous and shattered.

"Now look around you, Calan," Grandpa Dunny said with a great sweep of his hand. "This is the west coast. This is where we are, surrounded by the sea. And there, Vancouver, beyond the islands, and those mountains across the waters of Juan de Fuca Strait, the United States of America. And farther still, the Pacific Ocean, thousands of miles across it to China. Here the sea is always near. This is the place to start a new life. There are forests like no other place on Earth. Get a feel for it. This is the place to come when you're feeling down, when you're looking for home. It is a grounding thing to gaze upon the forests and waters like this. Our eyes always want them. Something inside us recognizes that our spirits are part of the trees and the oceans. We need them for the health of our souls.

"Look beyond the city, there across the harbour, Parry Bay. That's where we'll live. My house is waiting for us. Any day now, it'll be ready with its new roof of shingles split from blocks of cedar. It'll be a good place for you, Calan. Auntie Netty has her hands full with the boys. I'll drive you to school. You'll see them everyday. No worries. Just imagine now, lad, a rocky beach and salty pools brimming with astonishing creatures the likes of which you've never seen.

"So, don't you worry now, lad. I know you're going through the hardest thing, to lose a mother like that – and my daughter. A man or a boy can never be prepared for such a shock. We're never ready for a loved one to die. It'll take time…"

His hand came up into his mouth and he bit on his knuckle. He struggled there to guide me, to reassure me when words could do nothing of the sort. But his words persisted. They had hope in them, wisdom and lore.

"Grandpa, there is a tree in Auntie Netty's backyard," I said looking up at him. "Larry told me it's an arbutus. Like those ones." I pointed down the hill, to a gloss in the leaves.

"A marvellous tree, Calan," he said solemnly. Then his face brightened. "A tree that holds fast to rocks. Legend has it that the people here took hold of it during the great flooding of the world. That tree never gave up its grip, fastened it was, and it saved the people."

"After my mom died I went to it," I told him. "I felt it. And it lit up all red and shimmering. I think that she was there. She did that for me somehow. Do you think that it could have been her, Grandpa?"

"Aye, there is nothing strange about such things," he said, "but we cannot say for certain that our deceased loved ones are present among us. Still, I will tell you that it is so. Don't just believe such a thing, Calan, but know that it is true. Your mother came to comfort you in the way she chose for you. Oh, it is most fitting of her, your mother, to come to you in the spirit of that tree."

"How do you know?"

"Well, I'll tell you this, when your grandmother passed on it was a sad time indeed. But I had to carry on with my duties. I tended to the Fortingall Yew, talked to the tourists all day long about this and that. One day I had time for myself and I decided to take a hike. I went up into the hills. There along the trail to Schiehallion, the fairy hill of the Caledonians, was a bird that seemed to be always near me as I walked. Several times its wings brushed my cheek. The bird stayed near me. When I stopped for a bite of lunch, it stopped too and I fed it sunflower seeds from my hand. That bird kept me company. It made me feel not so alone. How strange it was, I began to think. And then I realized that it was a bullfinch, Margaret's favourite bird. She often said so. We kept a little feeder for the birds and bullfinches brought her great joy. Yes, I thought, it is Margaret coming to tell me that she is all right and not to worry. And why not? Some will say that you're daft for such notions. But I say that it is a perfect thing, a most loving gift and a moment to cherish. So, yes, Calan, I am certain that your mother visited you."

"How do you know so many things?"

"Whatever I see in front of me I must know it," Grandpa Dunny said. "I read and read until I know its secret. I believe that life is always trying to teach us. It makes little difference if it takes the form of a rock, a tree, a bird or a creature of the sea. I look and I wonder. I sketch and paint what I see, what I feel, because there is nothing but seeing and feeling to a man in this world. And there are times when seeing is not only with the eyes. It is in nature where I draw my strength. It is not religion that I speak, but of life itself."

He looked down at me, ruffled my windblown hair and could see that I was trying to understand what he said, what life was teaching and where it was taking me. It was more than I could comprehend, that wonderful oration on the hill. And I could tell by the light in his eyes, the bits of colour, eyes like my own, that he wasn't quite finished.

"So there's things to be done," he said. "Your aunts and uncles are preparing for the funeral, in just a few days, on Monday morning. Now we had to notify your father and Mr. and Mrs. Olsen and Mrs. Daisy at the general store. It is the proper thing. We could have said nothing at all, just got on with it, a private service for the family. We had a dreadful time of it, Calan. We sat up late into the night. We said that your father doesn't deserve to know, that he has no rights in the matter. But your Auntie Netty is strong-minded, loved your mother dearly. She wouldn't have it. In the end we decided that we wouldn't call him directly. Instead, we placed an obituary in the *Clavet Weekly*. That would be it. It would bring it all to a close, nothing left undone. No danger in that."

No danger in that. Why hadn't they asked me what I felt, what mattered to me? "Grandpa," I cried, "when we left him in the trees there was a rifle in the back seat of his car!"

CHAPTER SEVENTEEN

It was my first time in a funeral home. I sat in the front row on a hard pew beside Grandpa Dunny in his kilt that exposed his hairy knees. Auntie Netty and Auntie Kate sat beside him holding hands, their veiled heads bowed. Behind us sat my uncles and cousins. Others sat across the aisle and I wondered who they were. Everyone was stiff and formal. I wore a dark grey suit and tie that Auntie Netty bought for me. No hand-me-downs would do here. The cousins were smart in their suits and shiny Brylcreemed hair. An organ played a mournful melody, which made me feel old and slouched. I wanted to leave but there was something necessary here that I had to understand – my family joining together in crushing sadness. So I straightened my back and looked up to the high ceiling and coloured glass. In the chapel, sound was amplified – the organ, the random coughs, the murmurs. There was a statue of Jesus on a cross. His face was twisted in a grimace. He had gashes in his ribs and wore a crown of thorns and painted blood. It all made a dismal scene around my mother's body. A reverend, solemn in his gown stood to one side, patiently waiting to begin the service.

I stared at the burnished wood of the coffin. I imagined her lying there with everyone watching. She wouldn't have liked that. The coffin was open with sprays of flowers, tiger lilies, and tall white candles lit and aglow. If my mother were really there with us she would be pleased with the tiger lilies. They were one thing from Saskatchewan that never hurt her. The singular orange beauty and innocence of that flower symbolized all that was good about my mother.

The reverend stepped up to his pulpit and spoke of God's mercy and the sacrifice of Jesus Christ. He looked down at us in the front row, set us apart from the world, slack and stricken with our grief, and said with such conviction and gall that my mother was in a better place. How was that possible? She had just arrived to be with her *loving family*, with a chance to live the life that she deserved. I was angry. I glared at him, hoping that I might stop him from saying anything more about her. He didn't know her. He began a prayer. We bowed our heads but I watched him with one fuming eye. Finally he was done. He clasped his hands before him, stood aside and the organ started up again with a jarring groan. I hated it. I felt it was trying to crush me, filling that place with morbid sounds. And then an attendant with a sympathetic look approached us and motioned us to our feet.

I followed Grandpa Dunny out into the aisle. He turned toward the coffin and I understood we were going to view my mother and say goodbye . I felt Auntie Netty's hand on my shoulder and Auntie Kate's on the other, shepherding me from behind. I sensed their kindness and the burden of their loss, their little sister dropped like something treasured down a deep well, never to be retrieved. As we passed the coffin, I experienced only the fullness of the moment, its unmistakable silence. Grandpa Dunny paused. I heard him gasp against the stillness. There was to be no lingering with her. And I didn't want to look. I didn't want her old suit of bones to be my last image of her. I believed she was in the trees as real as a loving thought.

I looked because I could not help it. I could not fight against the faint possibility that she was waiting for me. She was in a white cotton dress, a necklace and matching earrings. Her hands folded over her breasts. Her hair was neatly brushed and a tiger lily rested in her made-up grasp where grains of pollen spilled, a russet stain on her dress. She did not look as one would imagine, asleep in a satin bed. No, her life was gone. It had vacated the painted pallor of her cheeks and lips. Only the likeness of someone beautiful remained – mother, sister, daughter. Auntie Netty and Auntie Kate leaned to kiss her cheek. Then we stood apart as the rest of the mourners, the uncles and cousins, moved up the aisle to pay their respects. Those brave cousins, aghast and fascinated, with their dutiful hands at their sides.

Grandpa Dunny left me there with the aunts. I knew where he was going. He had told me that morning he would pipe us out at the end of the service. He warned me that the sound of it could undo the most gallant of men and not to worry what came out of it. What could he mean? I had heard a bagpipe once in Clavet at some celebration. It made a queer caterwauling sound in the distance. My mother had stopped to listen. "Your grandfather is a piper," she had said. "He said that the sound of a bagpipe can raise the dead."

I wondered what was to come. Grandpa Dunny slipped behind a curtain and began priming the bag, urging the thing to life, as if that were what he wished to do, rouse my mother from her sleep.

The attendant pulled back the curtain and Grandpa stood like a glorious vision of a man with his pipes against the pulse of the drones. He stepped toward us as the first notes of *Amazing Grace* lifted up into space, Grandpa Dunny in his Balmoral cap, Argyll jacket, horse-hair sporran, his McLeod kilt and hose and the polish of his Ghillie brogues. He seemed a God, the otherworldly sound reaching higher, filling the chapel with the drones and the skirl of the pipes. He came up to the head of the coffin and stopped and paid his tribute to his youngest daughter. The sound was relentless, an oddly soothing howl and lament that outdid all sounds. It struck my heart like a dagger, creating a mood of its own. So deep and swift it was, that no measure of thought or speculation could supplant it. The piper and his pipes seemed to be one inseparable thing, the emotive gatherer of grief, a piper's dream to set us free from the temporal world.

Grandpa Dunny stepped toward the aisle slowly and deliberately, leading us with visions of resurrection and glory. Our tears gushed as his piping lifted the pain of our family, flung it against the wood and panes and across the borders of time, until the very air suffered, until we all stood around him in the reception room, wilted and spent. He piped until the last notes fell like stones and the drones faded like a final outbreath. He was awash with perspiration. The high colour in his cheeks drained and pooled about his neck. He was unsteady on his feet. Every scrap of McLeod that he could muster, from the ancients to the modern liberties of Scotland, he delivered there like a sacred offering in the service of my mother.

At the reception strangers came to take crustless bread and fancy cakes with their tea, drawn perhaps by the piper's call. How could they all have known my mother, I wondered? They had come I began to understand, for Auntie Netty and Auntie Kate. They were neighbours, coworkers, and acquaintances, all with gracious attention and thoughtful words. The reverend stood shaking hands. My cousins were tentative with the pastries, their restraint initially worthy of admiration, until at last it was too much for them and their greedy hands darted to the trays like thieves. They had lost their manners, but tried to conceal their sticky, giggling mouths. I wondered at the fluid security that allowed the Bratt boys to move from one moment to the next.

I felt weak. I trembled and stood by Grandpa Dunny,

unwilling to move, to engage the others, to be among the cousins with their smirks. I could not forget the emotion and sensation, the image and sound of the piper, my grandfather after all. I heard it still, the blaring pipes in my ears, in my head, burning in my heart – the sight of him, the sight of her. People began to drift away. The room emptied and Auntie Netty herded the cousins out of the funeral home. Uncle Reggie was waiting with their car at the curb and they piled in.

I walked with Grandpa Dunny to his little Beetle. He placed his bagpipes in the back seat. We didn't talk. He started the engine. We sat there as cars left one by one. The cousins gawked at us from the back seat of their car. Grandpa Dunny was a joke to them. The black hearse was parked at the rear doors of the chapel. We were alone. Something that had seemed as if it would last forever was over. The two of us sat in that queer red pod of a car like seeds.

A fine rain fell on the windshield. The wipers smeared and squealed in measured arcs. We just sat. It was getting cold. The heater puffed inadequately from the corners of the windshield. We sat. Grandpa Dunny's hands shook. His whole body shivered.

"Grandpa, are you all right?" I asked. I was worried listening to his faltering breaths.

"I suppose it was more than I imagined," he said. "I've piped many a service. Every song than can be heard. *Danny Boy, Scotland the Brave.* All of them. Made a fine spectacle for the families. But this wasn't just playing the pipes today, lad. No, I was the piper and I was the pipes. I could feel my blood rising in the drones. I just need a wee bit of a rest."

"What's going to happen now, Grandpa?" I asked, sensing he wasn't about to move.

"Oh, there's a plot in Ross Bay Cemetery," he said. "She'll be buried there. We can visit when the gravestone's in its place. In a few days."

"Can I see it, Grandpa Dunny?"

"Now, lad?"

"Yeah," I insisted. I wanted to see where she was going to be, to have a picture of the place in my mind. Was it a good place?

"It's been a trying day, Calan – for us all. I think it might be best to get on home."

"I just want to see, Grandpa."

He looked straight ahead, unblinking. Then he turned to me. "All right now," he said, "it's not so far." I don't think he had the energy to resist me just then.

Soon we pulled into the parking lot at the Ross Bay Cemetery. At first glance it seemed a park of broad sweeping trees full of colour in the dripping leaves. I followed Grandpa Dunny out of the car. In the distance where the cemetery seemed to end, shone the brightness of the sea. The ocean smell was not so noticeable now. It felt more like a fleeting re-acquaintance. All around us gravestones rose from the lawn, neutral tones of tribute against a green light that seemed to be ever present on the west coast – a lighted fuse that ran through the greyest of days.

We walked through the wet grass. Grandpa Dunny pointed ahead to a pile of excavated earth covered with a canvas tarp. We followed a path between the rows of grave-stones and wilting flowers while crows strutted away from us like kings. One landed close to me and I saw its blinking eye. A man by himself huddled before a grave with his back to us. In the distance, people were gathered under umbrellas around an open grave. There was a row of black cars, and everywhere the graves.

I imagined the dead bodies in their favoured suits and dresses, their hands clasped like my mother's, looking up with their sightless eyes into the unthinkable dark, a thousand un-breathing mouths, side by side, interned in captive isolation. They were all gone. As we came up to my mother's plot, I sensed that something or someone was near. Was it in the fine trees, the arbutus slick and bright near her grave? I wondered if she was waiting there for me. But I felt fear and that confused me.

"Why do I look so, Grandpa?" We stood at the edge of the grave in the dimming green light.

"You are listening, lad."

"I don't hear sometimes. What they are saying."

Grandpa Dunny stared down into the hole that would hold my mother. The rain now slanted down in sheets. "If someone came to you and spoke in a language that was not your own," he said in a listless narrative, "you wouldn't understand the words, but you would know what was being said. It would be in their faces, their posture. Anger. Joy. Sadness. You would know, Calan. The language of trees is the same. If the world shimmered as one whole and you were a part of that shimmering, then why wouldn't you be able to understand the many parts of yourself?"

"There is something here, Grandpa."

"Sadness, I suppose."

"I know what that feeling is. It's not that."

"Come, Calan, we're getting soaked as rats." All at once we looked out across the graves. A solitary figure approached us.

Grandpa Dunny took hold of my arm without taking his eyes off him. He looked like a faceless shadow, a man in a black suit. He came on purposefully. Then he was on us and showed his face, his cold familiarity.

"I loved her, old man!" he said. "You don't know how I loved her. You took her away, the both of you. I could throw you down that hole, cover you plenty. They would never find you under her coffin. But you might like that. So I won't do it. But I could, the worthless pair of you. You have a sickness that is not with the Grays!"

Grandpa Dunny let go of my arm and hurled himself across the grave as a panther might do, but he fell short. His foot caught and twisted. Mud streaked down his legs and kilt. My father stepped aside and laughed, a mad cackling. He knelt down beside Grandpa Dunny.

"A man in a dress," he said. "A pitiful excuse, you are."

"Leave him alone," I said.

"Shut up, boy!" he snarled.

Then something desperate but true came out of my mouth. A part of me had had enough. I felt like a McLeod, not a tragic Gray. "Leave him be or I'll kill you," I said. I put my head down and looked as fierce as I could, called to the trees, petitioned the world, my mother. "My Uncle Reggie has a gun. I will kill you."

He stood up and looked at me in that way of his, as if I were nothing to him. I saw his hollowness, his heartlessness. Yet I saw something else in his eyes. He feared me. He turned and disappeared, dissolved into the insistent rain. The mourners across the way remained at the grave while Grandpa Dunny lifted himself up. He was a mess, his fine piper's dress muddied, his long hair curled wetly across his wounded face.

"Let it go, lad," he said. "Let it go."

And the sea moved like mercury. It touched something latent inside me. I could smell it fully now. She is home, I thought.

CHAPTER EIGHTEEN

The empathy of my cousins soon ebbed. They had me figured out, so they thought – an oddball cousin, a chip off their eccentric Grandpa's block. I could hear them through the basement window, tapping, laughing, when each morning I stood by the arbutus. Unwittingly I entertained them, lent them fuel for their devilry. I stayed near the tree hoping that my mother would drop by. I lingered there until they all left for school, until it was safe to go back into the house.

Another week and I would be back in school. It terrified me to wonder what it would be like – the new kids, what kind of class I would be assigned to. I couldn't think of it without wanting to throw up. But there was Grandpa Dunny's *wee house by the sea*. It was nearly ready. He was at the house helping the carpenter so we could move in before my first day at Oaklands Elementary. I was sure he must have recognized my limitations, my lack of initiative and skills. I would only get in the way. But, I suppose even Grandpa Dunny needed to be by himself, to sort out his own world. And soon I would be there, too.

I waited by the tree. The sun was out and the neighbour-hood had that new-penny look, polished and made clean by the rain. Steam rose from the rooftops. The world glistened, dripped. I listened for the close of the door and the rattle of my cousins' bikes when Kenny leaned over the fence.

"You're weird," he called out to me. Then he pedaled away.

I *was* weird. I talked to trees, but I didn't hate Kenny. I had someone else to hate. My hatred burned away inside me. I suppose it was always there, simmering. I never knew what to do with it, or why *he* visited my dreams. Our antipathy to each other was all acted out, so many nights, in so many ways. In the morning there was no resolution, nothing in a dream that could make things right, no correction in a haunting fantasy, only a growing bitterness, knowing that I could not escape him, that he lived inside me.

Auntie Netty had my porridge ready for me at the kitchen table. She was busy over the sink. So many mothers stood at that same place it seemed to me. My mother did, her hands occupied with the dishes while she watched out the window, wanting to know where *he* was. Auntie Netty did that very same thing, looking out into the street. Then a car door closed. She undid her apron and dried her hands on a tea towel. She opened the fridge, removed sandwiches wrapped in wax paper and placed them in a lunch box.

"Uncle Reggie forgot his lunch," she said.

The front door opened and Uncle Reggie came into the kitchen, his feet heavy on the linoleum. He was in his uniform. He dropped the mail on the table.

"Must be losing my mind," he said. "I keep forgetting my lunch." He laughed and my porridge shook.

"You just miss me, Reg," Auntie Netty said playfully. She gave me a wink.

Their effortless mingling was without fear, an easiness that I could have watched all morning. Perhaps it was all for me, roles they played. But I didn't care. Then Uncle Reggie turned to me. I saw hurt in his eyes as if he didn't know what to do with me, this man whose job it was to protect.

"How are you today, Calan?"

"Fine," I said. A word to satisfy his worries.

He kissed Auntie Netty on the cheek and turned to leave the kitchen. As he brushed by me, I saw, tucked into his holster, the walnut checkering of a revolver handle. I had never seen anything like it, a gun you could hold in your hand. The heavy look of the metal seemed dangerous, and not at all like *Marshal Dillon's* Colt, bigger than *Bat Masterson's* derringer. The gun was so close, I could have touched it.

Uncle Reggie went back to work and I finished my breakfast. There was a talk show on the radio where people had opinions about things that I didn't understand. A host had a loud, blathering narrative that seemed similar to Grandpa Dunny's when his emotions were up. Auntie Netty seemed to be listening. She sat with a cup of coffee. Then she picked up the mail.

"Look at that," she said, "a letter for you, Calan." She handed me an envelope.

I took it and looked at it. It had my name on it.

"Go on, open it," she said.

I opened it. There was a card inside. On the front there was a painting of several white-trunked trees near a pond and on the pond two white swans swam together, and from them, ripples across the water. Inside, the card read:

> *Dear Calan,*
> *Sorry about your mom.*
> *From Janet*

Later I hurried downstairs to the basement before the eruption of cousins, to look at the card once again, to read it over and over. Did she paint it herself? I wondered about her, the prairies and their dry flatness and the sky that didn't hide anything. I sat on my cot with the card and ran my fingers over the painting. It seemed familiar somehow and Janet's words, so spare and innocent. It was just like Janet to take me away from darkness, from a stream of thoughts, and images of that gun in my hand, steady, waiting for the Country Squire to show itself. I tucked the card into *Trees of the World.* I wouldn't show it to the cousins. I would have never heard the end of it. I was relieved when Auntie Netty said nothing about it at supper. I braced myself when the cousins poured down the stairs with their brazen unpredictability. Kenny had an announcement that made him animated and giddy, and doubled him over.

"The fight's on," he said, "tomorrow after school, at the paper shack. Buddy's going to pound that Butchie!"

"You have to come, Calan," Jimmy said.

"There'll be lots of blood," Kenny said.

"That Butchie will kick you in the nuts when you're not lookin'," Jimmy warned Buddy.

"He won't," Buddy said confidently.

"I've seen him do it," Jimmy said.

"It was you, Jimmy," Kenny laughed. "You held onto your balls for a week."

"Shut up, twerp," Jimmy said. He swiped at Kenny's head.

"It'll be one punch," Buddy said. He jabbed at the light bulb hanging from the ceiling.

"Buddy's got moves like Cassius Clay," Kenny said. "Dad said so. Show him how your feet can move, Buddy. Show Calan how you can fight."

"He'll have to wait," he said.

"Have you been in a fight, Calan?" Kenny asked me.

"No," I told him. They all stood around me like the Bratt inquisition.

"You've never been in a fight?"

"Hey, you tools," Larry said, "enough of that stuff."

That tempered them. They knew what Larry meant. It seemed that they just wanted me to be a certain way, to walk among them with their same pride and daring, a Bratt initiate. I suppose they thought I was in need of an education that was not afforded a prairie kid. But the quiet never lasted long. I don't think Kenny Bratt could go a minute without something jumping out of his mouth. I expected his reckless observations now. And I learned there in the dim vaults of Cedar Hill Road, that there was no limitation to where his mind would venture next.

"Show him, Larry," he said.

"Show him what?" Larry said.

"You know, the thing you do with your dink."

"You show him, Kenny," Jimmy said. "I saw you beat off into the laundry tub with Dad's *Playboy*."

"Did not, Jimmy!" Kenny's cheeks turned red.

"Saw you pulling on it."

"Jimmy's got a foreskin."

"Oh, you're going to get it now, twerp, " Jimmy said. He grabbed Kenny by his arm, gripped him in a headlock.

"Let him go, Jimmy," Larry said. "All right come on you guys. This is the last time I'm going to show you."

What does a boy know of such things? How does knowledge enter him? We gathered around Larry like disciples.

"Get the flashlight and cut the lights, Buddy," Larry said.

"Mom caught him once," Kenny said.

"Jimmy, shut him up," Buddy said.

The flashlight beamed like a spotlight on the stage of boys. The light found Larry and his privates held in his hand. Privates, something to hide. Larry began to rub it for us to see. His penis was like a lantern, and Larry was urging the genie out of the spout. There were no words, only graphic instructions for adolescent apprentices. It was a trick of the body, a feat of form and function, a study of pearly spit that soon began to burp from Larry's boner. That's what the boys called it. Every boy gets a boner Kenny declared. I was glad that he never asked me, and if he had, I would have lied and told him that I did.

I was sure that those cousins were a lost breed of boys, a species confined to west coast basements. They played with the posturing of apes, a loose band of brothers held together with a common name and a keen deference for their oldest brother who showed no shame for his hands-on demonstration. That was a definable moment in my life when education was freely granted, had no curriculum other than hotwired self-exploration. It belonged to me now. There was nothing left for me to do but practice when the age of urges arrived in its own time.

CHAPTER NINETEEN

I waited in the lane watching a robin on a fence post. The bird cocked its tail as I stepped toward it. I liked its shape, the perfect curve of its head and nape, and its breast, the colour of a clay pipe. Rain ran off its back. It comforted me to see it there, sublime and circumspect, daring me to take another step. There was nothing else in the world just then, only a boy and a robin each reflected in the eye of the other. I would paint it someday, along with gravel bars, eagles and forests. I would paint it in a maple tree, or perhaps an arbutus whose colours would complement the robin's tones. My mother would have liked that. She would have been pleased with the soft and harmless beauty.

But I didn't get to take another step as the robin suddenly flew from the fence in a swift burst and blur of feathers. It was gone as Kenny Bratt came rocketing down the lane and skidded to a stop in front of me, spraying gravel on my running shoes.

"Get on, Calan!" he said excitedly.

I stood there before him not sure what to do.

"You never doubled?"

"No," I said.

"You're so stupid. Buddy and Butchie are at it. We can't miss it. Get on!"

Like the robin, I moved. I climbed onto the crossbar and Kenny pushed the bike, running alongside it. Then he jumped on and stood up on the pedals. I could hear his frantic breathing in my ear and felt his knees banging against my ribs. I wobbled and grabbed his arm.

"Just hang on to the handlebars," Kenny said, "and keep your feet out of the spokes!"

I took no offense from Kenny. It seemed that he was always corrected. He was an easy target for his brothers on the bottom of the heap. Cuffed and slapped and mocked. I was amused at the way he talked to me. I suppose he needed to pick on someone to balance out his life. He rode as if a firestorm licked at our backs. The world fell away behind us. I held on to the CCM Golden Hawk with its three speeds, its chrome fenders and gold trim. It was a fine bike, left out in the rain by the garage with the rusted frames of former glories.

We swung wildly onto Bay Street. All at once Kenny veered recklessly across the road in front of cars sounding their horns, making for the sidewalk on the far side. He raced on and at last turned off where the boughs of great evergreens swept down in skirts and shrouds – a hidden place for pugilists. I jumped off and Kenny threw down his bike. A crowd of boys jostled and swayed at the side of a paper shack where paper-boys hurriedly stuffed newspapers into their delivery bags and carriers so they, too, could join the circle of beaten ground.

I lost Kenny in the crowd of boys' backs. Somewhere beyond them were Buddy and Butchie. I didn't want to see them fight. It made little sense to me. But a part of me moved me closer and soon I was at the edge of the pit. They were on the ground, beneath the dripping tent of firs, their arms and legs gripped and tangled in some ritualistic battle of honour. The cheers that rose up were for Buddy. The boys were angry, a palpable heat blared from their faces.

"Get him, Buddy!" one shouted.

"Don't let him pin you, Buddy!" said another.

It wasn't fighting in the way that I had imagined, like the sparring in the basement, a toe-to-toe match of skill and mettle. I could hear Buddy's grunts as he strained against Butchie, the two of them wet and muddy, their teeth spitting fury. Then Butchie heaved Buddy all at once, tried to flip him over on his back, to hold him down, to make him give in. But as he struggled with Buddy's arm, slick as a fish, Buddy rolled clear. He sprang to his feet and drove his fist into the side of Butchie's jaw. There was a cold meaty thump. Butchie was stunned by the blow. He winced and shook his head, but he got to his feet. The boys cheered, and there, at the back, I could see Larry Bratt.

Now the two boys were apart. They had a moment to measure each other. A bright welt showed on Butchie's cheek. They crouched and moved in a circle, round and round, their arms outstretched, pawing, tempting each other, menace in their savage faces, a union of violent intent. They were covered in needles and sticks, doused in a slurry of earth. I could see Butchie now. He was bigger than Buddy, thick around the middle. His black hair was combed back in ripples. It lay stiff and wiry even in the sopping afternoon. He was big boned and strong. The crowd of boys shouted at him, emboldened by their number.

"Cock hair!" they called. They had come to see the bully fall.

Buddy put up his fists now, raised them like Cassius Clay in the way that he practiced. He moved his feet for the crowd, confident and inspired by his favourable blow. His agility seemed to confuse Butchie. Buddy jabbed him in the belly. Butchie backed off and I could hear Larry urging his brother on.

"That a boy, Buddy!" he cheered with the rest of them.

Then Buddy advanced, moved in on Butchie and struck him on the chin with a solid left fist, followed by a straight out jab and then another. He moved in close and threw a mighty punch with his right hand, but it was reckless. It shot past Butchie's ear. Butchie stepped aside and drove his fist square into Buddy's nose, slammed it good. Buddy's nose seemed to explode. Blood sprayed and ran into his mouth. He spit and swiped at the gore and fell to his knees.

Butchie hit him again in the eye, a flat thud, and Buddy went slack and his shoulders folded. Then Butchie stepped back. A hush fell over the boys. He wore black shoes, points they called them. It seemed that Butchie was about to kick Buddy in the head, while he was down, with his eyes white and rolling senseless. It wasn't a fair fight now. I could see Larry pushing through the crowd cussing and swearing at Butchie. I moved into the ring of fighters, to Butchie with his cocked leg, and I placed my hand on his shoulder. He turned with swift rage in his eyes and a hate that was destroying him.

"Butchie," I said to him, "don't be like your father." That stopped him cold. "Don't do it, just walk away."

I don't know why I said that. I knew nothing of his family, of his father, but I could feel the cause of his struggles. His mean and threatening posture was the only way he knew to protect himself. I saw it all in that collapsing moment before he could kick Buddy's bloodied face. I did it for Buddy, but more than that, I did it for Butchie. Butchie Burnum started to cry. He swiped at his tears. He couldn't understand what had happened. He looked at me, backed away in confusion. The boys parted and let him leave. Buddy didn't move. Larry helped him to his feet. The rain fell in sheets and washed the blood from Buddy's face.

How I managed to tell Butchie to walk away, that there was indeed another road possible, I didn't know. I could feel things. I could hear the language of trees and I knew the heart of a boy. But I wondered if it would be enough to save me from the shadow that I could feel approaching.

CHAPTER TWENTY

Grandpa Dunny's *wee house by the sea* was just that. I could see it through the forest. The sun illuminated its wood, a fresh russet against the brilliant waters of Parry Bay. He parked his Bug by the road. He wanted us to walk down the driveway to show me his domain from where it started – the rock, the trees and the entire understory in the shadows where the sun touched the earth with its disconnected shafts. He had his cane now, going down the grade.

"There," he said pointing to trees, their slow swaying in the good breeze. "Hemlock and cedar and spruce, and the mighty Douglas fir, all of them here, Calan. The grand firs with their upright cones and in the glades of fallen trees, the dogwood. A sight to see in the spring with their white blooms. And down below the huckleberries that will make a summer feast. Salal and Oregon grape and plenty of ferns and mosses. I walked about with a book of such things, studied their names and habits. My glorious living things. You'll love it here, Calan, a place to excite a boy. Full of life. And you'll hear the winter wrens, their songs like a bubbling brook and the thrush that hide about with their secrets and mysteries, their melancholy song like a rusty hinge.

"Come now, Calan, down to the beach. We'll see the house when our looking is done. We'll get a fix on where we are. A man can breathe here and a boy can grow."

The driveway curved down to the house. Sunlight splashed on the cedar shake roof and siding. There was another building, lower down on a bench of rock. We passed the house. All was bright now. The trees ended where slabs of rock fell to the water, where waves burst onto the broken shore. Grandpa Dunny was careful now, picking down a stone stairway to the rocks and pools. At the shore he stood and gazed to the east. The sun's rays reflected in the water and on a slow ship passing by. He didn't speak. I looked out to the islands and across the strait to the Olympic Peninsula. I felt the wet brine against my skin.

I looked down at the pools, in the crusty rocks at barnacles and mussels. A starfish lay like a purple abstraction. Submerged crabs waved their white-toothed arms. Seaweed and logs hoisted up on the rocks by storms. Out in the water, a forest of kelp rose and dipped like a slow pulse. Gulls arced and cried. There was such richness – a lost world, astounding in its form and rhythm. It lived and breathed abundance and was as wild as anything I had ever seen.

"We'll bring our sketch books," Grandpa Dunny said after a time, "our paints and canvas, down here when the light suits us. We'll paint the morning with blazing pink. We'll paint the creatures, the rocky shore and shadows. And we'll paint the great trees. This is the place for you, Calan. How does this fancy you, lad?"

It was all a miraculous place for sure, but I had landed on an alien shore. I could feel no excitement now to paint or sketch such scenes, only my brooding and sadness. I looked out at the sea with a measured scrutiny. Too young to know, I found it cold and seductive. It was more than my senses could bear. There was beauty everywhere, but it had no chance against my pain. I could put my sense of loss and outrage in words now. Someone watched us from down the beach, a tall willowy man with a dog.

"I like it, Grandpa," I said.

"Aye, it's a thing to like," he said. "Come now, I'll show you your new home. And pay no attention to old Percy Croft. He's a gardener for a wealthy estate in Oak Bay. He's a bit sour. I suppose it's his skin condition. Awful to have such a raw peeling face. Pay him no mind."

The house was wood inside and out, carved out of the forest with timbered beams and plank floor. It smelled of cut wood and pitch. There were four rooms, a kitchen looking out over the bay, a room with a bookcase from floor to ceiling, a stone fireplace for the winter and two bedrooms. It was a tiny house, but the picture windows facing the beach made it seem larger than it was. It was warm and inviting, a sanctuary for my grandpa. He had hung on the walls photographs of my grandmother, my mother and her sisters, and a painting of the wind swept heather in Scotland. Colourful tartan blankets were draped over a chair and couch. There was a barometer in a sailor's wheel and lamps made of driftwood with shades like parchment. I saw how a man could make a world of his liking. I loved the *wee house* at once. The building built into the rock below the house was a studio. It was also built of wood and had the same charm as grandpa's house. I would go there to dream, to view the water, to watch the eagles in the trees and the herons in the pools. The arbutus fastened to the rock beside the studio flared like a beacon in the morning hours when the sun found its trunk and limbs.

All was set for me, made for me – even the death of my mother was shaping me in ways that I did not know then, as if it were all designed to be just so – what I needed and where I needed to be. I began to settle into the west coast, its moods and mysteries. It worked its way inside me, day by day, bore into my bones, purged the prairies from my eyes.

My cousins, the shameless Bratts' made a difference to my

life in ways they would never know. They didn't really like me, didn't know me. There were times when they didn't want to know me. I was the unalterable, odd cousin that no one spoke to at school. I was a boy in the special class where everyone was cruelly teased. I could only watch during marble season when the boys pitched their cat's eyes and crystals against cobs and king cobs. Kenny had a coveted *Crown Royal* liquor bag of purple velvet filled with marbles. When baseball card season arrived the boys clapped their cards in games of odd and even and flicked them against the school wall, closest takes all, while I stood dreaming of my own Mickey Mantle and Roger Maris, team cards and checklists. I loved the *Indians* because of Jules Bear. I never got to participate. I was an embarrassment.

One day I was out near the edge of the school ground, wondering about the horse chestnut tree and its curious flowers, by myself as always, when I turned to see the cousins watching me. They laughed and waved their ridiculous hands, but suddenly stopped when Butchie Burnum approached me. He came across the field with apparently something on his mind. I watched Butchie and I watched the cousins. I supposed they were waiting for him to knock me flat. They never moved. They had no rescue plan that I could see. They just watched their dumb cousin and they watched Butchie Burnum. I prepared myself for a punch or a kick. But Butchie held out his hand until I took it, and shook it like Grandpa Dunny. Butchie never picked on anyone ever again.

On another day a few months later when I was out with Grandpa, I saw Larry Bratt and Butchie sharing cokes at a corner store. No one in the world could have seen my smile just then, but I believe that my mother did and perhaps smiled along with me. I was never teased again. The Bratts' became my protectors. They made room for me. I was a Bratt more or less. I had gained some status for taming Butchie Burnum, found a place in their feral hearts.

Grandpa Dunny took me to Auntie Netty's for Sunday

dinners and birthdays. He drove me to Oaklands Elementary School every day. He met my teachers. Later he drove me to Victoria High when I allowed it, dropping me off a few blocks away at a time when I grew self-conscious of such things. He understood. We painted and we sketched in the studio and along the changeable shore. We painted what we saw, what we felt. One day he took me to see my mother's grave. We stayed a few minutes to be with her, to remember, until it became too sad. Then I followed him to another grave that he wished to show me, the grave of Emily Carr. Then he drove me downtown, to a fine Victoria gallery, to see her paintings – the great overstated trees, the daring strokes and glimpses of dreams in clouds and limbs, places inside me. It changed me. It was a time of reshaping, of creation and peace.

There was no room in my life for darkness. It seemed to fade away. In part I credit my grandpa. He could tell the change in weather, the fortunes of tides and seasons, and he knew my ways as he knew his own. In the early spring he introduced me to the first flowers of Indian Plum, crushed the fresh green leaves in his fingers and shared its sweet, earthy aroma, and salmonberry blossoms, magenta suns on naked canes along roadsides and ditches, red flowering current, and trillium, a sublime, religious wonder in the woods at Easter. We grew closer and closer.

At times I would retreat to my room, turn on my radio and wait for my favourite song, Brian Hyland's *Joker Went Wild*. For the first time I recognized that I could have something meaningful and personal – that there could be a song for me. Later I was stunned and mesmerized when I heard Jimi Hendrix and his visceral guitar. The first driving riffs of Led Zeppelin made me euphoric. I found music, the electric temple. And I had my things. My favourite shells and bits of wood were all comforts to me. The *Trees of the World* was always present for me to study, to stimulate my imagination and cause me to open my paints. But my most precious possession, which I kept on the dresser so that I could see it before falling asleep, was the card from Janet. I imagined her growing older, what she looked like. And I wondered: did she still love me?

The trees of the forest spoke a language of endurance and wisdom. I felt it often, so familiar that it became a background murmur, like grandpa's classical music playing softly in subdued accompaniment. They were my true friends, living entities of wonderful strength. They were everywhere. When one fell from a storm or a woodsman's axe, I grieved. I grew tall through my teens, a miracle, and I grew in compassion for the living things around me. My past faded into the distance. I never imagined that they might be linked somehow. It was a glorious life in Parry Bay.

On my sixteenth birthday, May 4th, 1970, a letter arrived for me. It came on the same day as the Kent State shootings, the day of my undoing.

Calan;
You know nothing of me. Stay away for your own
good.
Gray Farm

I didn't know what the words meant, or why my father signed it the way he did. Gray Farm, as if his growing menace had claimed it. Grandpa Dunny was silent for weeks after that. The subject of my paintings began to change. Then he found the cigarettes I had hidden in the studio. He found the jar of homemade wine that I had bought off of Jimmy Bratt for fifty cents. When he saw what I drew in my sketchbook, the Smith and Wesson .38, a bullet exploding from the muzzle, MG plainly etched, he looked at me for a long time. He seemed to know my inner-world more than myself, my obsessive gloom hungry now. Its chilling return always worried him. He took my shoulders in his firm hands.

"Let it go," he said, "for the love of your mother, let it go."

He said this as if I could just open my hand and all that was wrong in the world would fall away. When the second letter came on my seventeenth birthday, the trees quit speaking to me.

Calan;
Time is running out. You don't have the guts.
Gray Farm

THE MORALITY OF TREES

CEDAR

CHAPTER TWENTY-ONE

I slept in on weekends, at the cusp of summer, into the afternoon as if sleep had an endless quality I could exploit, buried under another clan's tartan. *Hudson's Bay* is not a clan Grandpa Dunny would affirm. Now he resorted to a dinner bell he had picked up at a Victoria second hand store. He complained to Delbert Crane that it was the only way to get me out of bed, to ring it until my head throbbed.

"Come on, time to get up, Calan," he said poking into my bedroom. "You can't sleep your whole life away. Lord, its smells like a brewery in here." He came in and threw open the curtains. Fresh air rushed in. "Delbert is waiting for you."

I had forgotten about Delbert. He lived down the beach in a rented shack. He was a carpenter who worked at odd jobs in the bay. When he wasn't working he chiselled away at a cedar log that he salvaged after a storm. Then one day the log had become a canoe.

"All right, all right, I'm up," I said. My eyes stung and there was a woeful groan in my belly.

"There's your porridge in the kitchen."

"Don't you ever get tired of that stuff? Why can't we ever have bacon and eggs or something?"

"I doubt you could stomach it, lad. The mush is good for the heart and the bowels. Up you get."

"Great, I'll try to remember that."

"And where are you getting your liquor? It's not Jimmy still?"

"No, not Jimmy. Uncle Reggie kicked his ass pretty good."

"Then where?"

"Who cares?"

"I care, Calan. The way you've been. Sulking all the time. I'm worried about your wild drawings, your fantasies. You're obsessed with him. Those blasted letters. I know it is. It's got you all mixed up inside. I promised Delbert that you would help him. Get your hands into the wood. It's what you need. Now get dressed and out you go!"

He was upset with me. He didn't like the changes that he saw, my moody *don't give a shit* attitude. I was sorry when I disappointed him. He had done so much for me. He didn't deserve any of it. I suppose he was thinking of a career for me, something I could do with my life. I never thought of such things. High school was preparing me for an occupational life. I was an *Oc,* like the seabird. I was one of the boys filling the woodworking classes where I learned how to make hockey sticks and wooden pucks when the instructor wasn't looking. And I learned that the painting room wasn't just for painting on the day that I found Jimmy Bratt sniffing glue. My report cards were always full of Cs, but I could paint and I could draw. That was something. However, my art was becoming an expression of my anger and darkness, a tunnel into desperation and ruin. Grandpa Dunny couldn't see the good in it. The images frightened him. I drew pages of handguns, rifles and hollow-eyed targets, fanged, clawed and recoiling. I didn't seem to have any control in the matter. The mad images rushed into my mind and I drew them. Delbert Crane was just another of Grandpa Dunny's diversions, to steer me away from *him.*

The canoe was sitting on wooden blocks above the high-water mark. Delbert was working with an odd looking axe. Curls of wood gathered around his feet. The sun was full in the bay. The breeze was warm and the tide had turned. A harbour seal turned toward the beach, curious. The sun glanced off its slick back. Then the seal was gone. It was a good day to be out along the ocean. Every day was different. Something new was always washing up, exposed by the retreating water – bottles, Japanese glass floats, the dismembered limbs of crabs in mats of sea grass, feathers, bits of blue, green and red glass like jewels – a line of debris like a thousand miles of changing scenery in that bay.

I never talked to Delbert much. It was Grandpa Dunny who always stopped to talk to him when he was working on his canoe. Grandpa told me that his carving was not the ambition of an idle man. I think he liked Delbert's sense of commitment to such a project. I'm sure that he hoped that his determination would rub off on me.

Delbert looked up as I approached him. I sauntered, a tentative, slouchy walk that signalled my disinterest. He had the look of some of the young guys I had seen on Douglas Street and in the parks with their guitars. They had an air of freedom about them with their thin, angular, long faces and hair down to their shoulders. They had unkempt beards and were always eager to flash a peace sign. Delbert's hair hung straight. He wore a red checked handkerchief as a headband, a white t-shirt with bursts of orange like suns and jeans cut above the knees. His sandals were cut from a car tire and fitted with a lattice of leather. His fine beard made me self-conscious of the few hairs on my chin. I wore my own hair long. I dressed in jeans and liked the psychedelic scene well enough but Delbert Crane was the first hippie I ever knew.

"Hey, man," Delbert said. He went on working.

I stood and watched him. He was working up a pretty good sweat. Drawing the heavy handled chisel looked like hard work.

"What is that?" I asked him.

He never faltered and leaned into his work. After a few more draws he paused, removed his headband and wiped his face. "It's an adze," he said. He held it out to me.

I stepped up and took it. Now I could see the belly of the canoe, a hollow taking shape and I noticed the sharp cuts where the adze bit into the wood. They looked like the markings left by a beaver.

"Try it," he said.

"Are you sure?" I was a little hung over and didn't feel like doing much of anything.

"Why not? Looks like you could use a work out."

I gripped the adze in both hands. I didn't like his comment about my skinny arms. I was taller than Delbert. He was lean, his arms well muscled, but I suppose to him I didn't look like much. He caught my hurt.

"Just kidding, man," he said with a big grin. "Calan, right?"

"Yeah."

"Just try it. Give it a few strokes to get the feel of it. You saw how I did it. Go on. You're not going to break anything."

I came alongside the canoe, raised the adze and let it come down into the wood. It bounced off. I tried again with more effort. The steel struck hard and I pulled it back. I was glad to see a short curled shaving.

"Now," he said, reaching for the adze, "take a handful of chips and smell them."

"What for?"

"Just do it, man. I'm not trying to fuck with you."

I leaned over the canoe, took a handful of woodchips and brought them up to my nose. The scent was wonderful. I could smell more than the shavings. I could sense the wood of the canoe itself, aromatic and sweet, rising and warming in the sun. "Cool," I said.

"Western red cedar," Delbert said, "the favoured wood

of the Nootka. They used to build whaling canoes over sixty feet long. This one's not going to be that long, maybe twenty-five."

"Why are you building it?"

"Man, you ask a lot of questions. Here's one. Why do you draw? I see you and your grandpa out on the beach. It's a hard thing to answer. It's something you just feel like doing. You know what I mean?"

"Yeah."

"Yeah, maybe I'll go up the coast." He turned and looked toward the north as if something had meaning there.

I saw a wistful look come into his eyes and he went quiet. I thought that perhaps we were done, that I had given Delbert Crane all the help he needed from me. I waited a minute and studied the boat. It had the shape of a canoe. The hull was hewn with pegs drilled into the sides.

"What are the pegs for?" I asked him.

He turned back to the canoe. His eyes hesitated, and mapped me briefly as if he were trying to remember who I was. "So I know how much to take out of the interior," he said.

"How do you know all that?"

"Well I had a log and an idea. I visited the provincial museum and told them what I wanted to do. The curator explained to me how the Nootka used to build them. He gave me some literature. So I started. Pretty simple. And hey, man, I don't have a fuckin' clue if it'll float."

"It's a little narrow."

"You know, you're a fuckin' genius."

"Why?"

"Because that's what I have to do next. After I take the belly down to the pegs, I need to fill it with water, let it soak, then fill it with hot stones. That'll soften the wood and let me install the crosspieces that'll spread it to the width I want. Not too much or it'll split the fuckin' thing. I'm going to build a big fire and heat up some stones. Hey, you and your grandpa can help me. We can cook fucking hotdogs. What do you think?"

"I guess." There was something about Delbert that wasn't quite right. Something in his speech and the dart of his eyes. He was always looking off somewhere. I liked to gaze out over the water myself. There was always something to see – clouds and boats, rafts of sea ducks and a bald eagle in the crown of every tree. But I wasn't nervous about it. When I looked away I felt him watching me.

"Cigarette?" he said plucking one from a pack of *Players*.

"No, my grandpa might be watching."

"Do you smoke grass?" He lit his cigarette and took up the adze again.

"Not much," I said.

"No?"

"I'm more into beer and wine," I said realizing that Delbert was fishing, to find out who it was that was standing there before him. But he seemed to like my answer.

"A little grass and a little wine and Cat Stevens," he said in good humour. "It keeps you calm, you know, when things get too heavy. There's lot's of shit in the world. But I wouldn't recommend working on a roof when you're high. Not good, man." He laughed.

I sensed that Delbert wanted a prompt from me before continued. He was a funny guy even if he seemed suspicious with that odd inflection to some of his words. But I supposed that it wouldn't hurt to hear the rest of it. "What happened up on the roof?"

He stepped back with the adze in his hand. "I was roofing for a guy once," he went on. "You know, cedar shakes like your grandpa's house. Well, at lunch I had a few tokes of some good weed and a thermos of wine. It was all cool. But I got near the edge of the roof and looked down. The owner was a rich dude and was wheeling out his Jag convertible with the top up. I leaned over for a look, but I kept on going, man. I did a complete somersault and went right through the fucking roof. Shit, he was a bit freaked out when he turned and saw me in his back seat. I just said, 'hey man, I guess I should have used the ladder.'"

Delbert and I laughed together and then he went back to work on his cedar canoe, working the adze with a hollow, knocking rhythm. He seemed satisfied that I was a good enough kid. Before I left he reminded me to ask Grandpa Dunny if we could help him with the steaming of his canoe. As I walked back home along the beach, I wondered about Delbert. He hadn't said much about himself other than he liked to smoke marijuana and drink wine, but that could be said about any young guy. He also liked to tell stories when the moment was right for it. But more than that, he looked almost dangerous as he stood with the adze in his hand when he told his funny story. There was something intimidating in his posture. And that's when I wondered what he knew about guns.

CHAPTER TWENTY-TWO

Down the beach Delbert's fire had been burning most of the afternoon. White smoke drifted over Parry Bay and caught in the trees like flung sheets. The acrid, punky smoke filled the house with the smell of salt and damp wood. The flames continued to lick up into the falling light. The water in the bay was flat and bright. It was high tide and time to go.

"This'll be a time," Grandpa Dunny said as we headed up the beach. "Hot dogs over a fire. It's the thing of legends. A queer custom to be sure, but I dare say, it'll be a memorable night. The way the natives used to build their boats. I knew that you'd take to him, Calan."

"Yeah, he seems all right," I said. I helped Grandpa along the uneven shoreline.

"Well, you don't sound too enthusiastic. What is it?"

"I just felt something that's all," I said.

"That's a wonder, lad. You haven't been feeling much of anything of late. Spending too much time hanging about. Can't you see that it's out here where you'll find your way? I believe you know that. I don't have to tell you. Keep your mind active. That's the answer, Calan. We'll see how we make out with the canoe. I think that it will please you. You'll see. Delbert is a fine young man. I'm sure of it."

"Where's he from? He doesn't seem to be from around here."

"Glory be, we're all from somewhere. Now isn't that the truth?"

Grandpa Dunny so desperately wanted a friend for me. I knew he was getting older, slowing down. His old bones troubled him in the early morning and when the weather changed. He hobbled now, painfully. I was certain he was preparing me, in the best way he could, for my life without him. I couldn't imagine the world without him, without his wisdom, without the acumen he brought to the intricacies of life.

The cousins rarely came to the house. Mostly we visited Cedar Hill Road for Sunday dinners when Grandpa and the aunts would have a time of it. The Bratt boys would usually be out with their friends. And when they were at home they gave me my own space. They had learned how different I was. How reclusive and silent. I didn't mind their exclusion. I still remembered the early days when they accepted me after all.

I never expected to find a friend, never sought one out. I would even walk away from the seduction of dancing girls and their flower-child incense. They were not friends to be had, no matter what Grandpa Dunny's intention, when he took me downtown once a week for a cup of coffee in a nice shop full of young girls. But I was all eyes. I never recalled a face, but I recalled jiggling breasts and eager nipples. I remember well the hippie chicks with their free love mantra that moved Grandpa to eye me queerly then laugh as heartily as ever a man could.

It was my relationship with Janet that gave me a measure of my own sexuality when I was alone. I knew our love was a fantasy, a release, a construction from memory, but it sustained me. She would never know. I suppose she was a friend. And the trees that I could no longer hear were the most unusual of friends, if they were friends and not some indication of my sanity. But I wondered, what is a friend? Who made up such definitions? My only friend, if I had one at all, was my grandpa.

"Why are you so eager to find a friend for me?" I asked him as we walked along the beach to Delbert's fire. "Are you planning to go somewhere?"

He stopped there in the afterglow. The lights of Victoria reflected on the water. "We'll all pass on in this life, Calan," he said looking up at the blue-black sky. "One day I will join your grandmother and your mother. That's a fact. What will happen when I'm gone? I fear that you'll go after him. I'm afraid you'll go back to Gray Farm. That's what he wants. He wants you back. He's a dangerous man, Calan. I heard the threats you made to him on the day of your mother's service. He wants something. It's an evil thing to be sure. Don't you see?"

"I can't leave it alone, Grandpa. I just can't." Finally the truth could not be averted, weakened or denied. Grandpa Dunny was right to be afraid.

"I'm not a man to pray to the almighty, but I pray that you'll shake off whatever it is that has a hold of you. The trees are still there, you know. They speak their language. I hear them everyday. You're not listening, Calan. They're whispering a warning to you. They know you. They know your goodness, but you've stopped listening."

"Any chance that we're both crazy, Grandpa?"

"Oh, Calan, what will you do when I'm gone? What will you do?"

Why did I harbour such thoughts of vengeance? Was I two people? Did they fight for the trigger, a struggle for justice or retribution? Grandpa Dunny feared what blind rage could do in an instant, how it could alter the course of my life forever.

Yet I had set the timer, the clock, the ticking toward the end that I chose. I was the keeper of it all, but I couldn't stop. Perhaps it was my destiny. I would correct the wrong, all the things that *he* stole, that *he* hurt. *He* would pay for it.

"Grab a bucket," Delbert said as Grandpa Dunny and I emerged from the dusk.

We took our buckets, walked out into the surf in our sneakers and dipped our buckets. In the firelight, our long shadows looked like humped toilers in some forgotten pagan ritual. We spilled cold seawater into the belly of the canoe over and over until the water sloshed below the gunwales. Then Delbert took a shovel and scooped the stones from the fire. They had been baking like loaves in a kiln. He slipped them one by one into the canoe and the water hissed and steamed. I helped Grandpa Dunny gather more stones and we added them to the fire as Delbert removed the ready ones and dropped them into the boat. Soon the water boiled. Delbert unfolded a great tarp. We draped it over the canoe and weighted the corners with heavy beach rocks. The canoe was sealed and the steam would make the wood pliable by morning and ready for the crosspieces and thwarts.

We sat around the fire on beached logs cooking hotdogs skewered on sticks of Indian plum. We roasted them until they blistered black and grease shone in the firelight. Delbert had made a table of flat stones that held a jar of mustard, a bag of buns and a gallon of *Double Jack* wine. Three ceramic mugs were festooned with peace symbols. We ate and drank our fill, burping our contentment. We sat lost in another time watching sparks ascending until their flare gave out. I felt a certain satisfaction in helping Delbert with his project. Grandpa Dunny knew that I would like it, creating a boat from a tree as the Nootka may have done when they were a free people. They would have celebrated such an accomplishment.

Percy Croft entered the peripheral light as he was passing by with his spaniel dripping with seawater. He stopped to raise an accusing finger as his dog shook itself. "I know who you are," he shouted at Delbert, "I know you!"

Delbert jumped to his feet and leaned over the lick of flames. "Don't you point your finger at me, you scabby old man," he countered, "just fuck off!"

Percy Croft's eyes, red in their sockets, settled on Grandpa Dunny as if marking him, too, as a deviate. The hate in him plain.

"Come on now, Percy," Grandpa said still sitting on his log. "There's no need for that nonsense. Get on home. I can see that your good dog can shake itself from arse to snout and spray us plenty. I don't imagine that you'd like to be tossed into the sea so that you might try it yourself. Do you hear me, Percy?"

Percy glared, huffed, then moved on down the beach vanishing like a phantom into the advancing night.

Delbert returned to his place around the fire. "You sure have a way about you, Dunmore," he said. "Keeping your cool like that. That old bastard has it out for me. He hates long hairs. And he's got you pegged for one."

"I see that, Delbert," Grandpa Dunny said, "but you must know that McLeod men have favoured their locks since we fought for Bruce at Bannockburn over six hundred years ago. There's no shame in the length of a man's hair."

"And to think I thought you just an old hippie," Delbert said. The wine was working him over now.

"Call me what you like," Grandpa said, equally intoxicated. "Labels are nothing but another's man assumptions. They do nothing to define a man or rid him of his faults. In fact, they only show the man who uses them to be one ignorant son of a bitch."

"Wow man, that's heavy shit. You can't tell me, Dunmore, that you like what's going on in this world."

"The truth is, I don't nor should I. You hippies have no monopoly on injustice."

"Injustice, you don't know injustice!" Delbert declared, tossing his hands. He was plainly aggrieved.

"Is that so now? You seem to be of a mind with some experience."

"Look around you," Delbert said. "The straights want us all to conform. You know, the status quo. Stand in line and shut your fucking mouth."

"Aye, you're right about that," Grandpa Dunny said. He raised his drink in a toast.

"I saw one suit kicking one of those Hari Krishna dudes. Just for standing on a street corner chanting in his robes. Everyone is so uptight. Hey, man, he wasn't hurting anyone. He just took it. Never did anything."

"Aye, if I was out in my kilt and such a man was set to give me trouble for my dress, I'll admit to you here and now, that I wouldn't take it. Not for a minute. I would shove his briefcase up his arse."

They laughed and slapped their thighs. They rocked and howled. I thought their banter was a curious thing, swilling their wine with the sting of smoke in their eyes. Grandpa allowed me only a dribble of wine, but now I held out my mug and Delbert filled it. He passed me a cigarette, took one for himself and lit them both with a burning stick. And still they went on as if there were just two opinions worthy of men, some rite lost to me in Parry Bay. What did I know? I could only speak of one man's injustice – the severity of what *he* dealt, the violent injustice that I met with the justice steeping in my gut.

Old Percy Croft, with his outburst, made me wonder more about Delbert, made me listen. I watched his jaw slowly unhinge, giving up bits of himself. What did Percy Croft know? I had an idea. There had been something cryptic in what he said. A word had stuck in my head from the story that Delbert had told me.

I poked at the fire with my own stick and waited for an

opportunity to speak. When their laughter faded I sat up, and with a grin of inebriated pleasure and my sad pretense, I said it: "Tell my grandpa about the time when you were working on the *roof*." I stumbled over the word and Delbert jerked toward me. The muscles in his neck tightened. A shadow seeped into his eyes.

"Why the fuck did you just say that?" he snapped. His uneven teeth showed in the firelight.

"What?" I said dumbly.

"You little shit. You're fucking with me!"

"No, I wanted my grandpa to hear the story. It's really funny."

"What's this all about?" Grandpa Dunny said. He stood and wobbled. All the fun had drained from him. He stood flushed and sensible.

"Nothing," Delbert said.

I was surprised by his reaction, but I wasn't afraid of him. I had seen anger like that, the flash of it, so swift. He was hiding something and I wasn't going to leave it alone. I had to prove my mettle. "You said *ruff* instead of roof," I said. "Who talks like that?"

"You prick. I knew there was something funny about you."

"Stop it, the both of you," Grandpa Dunny intervened. "I don't know what this all about, but whatever it is you need to get it out. Now what is it?"

"He's not telling the truth."

"Fuck you!"

"You're not from around here, are you Delbert?"

A sobering pall fell around the fire as Delbert took stock. Alcohol had made me bold and foolish, and provoked my own clumsy tongue. It had drawn out a certain cruelty in me. I wanted to make him wrong. I wanted Grandpa Dunny to see who it was there before him. I didn't want him to admire Delbert. I didn't want them to laugh together exposing my flat and dull personality, my defects.

"Delbert, do you have something to say?" Grandpa asked him. "If not, the night is done. I'm getting a wee bit drunk. And the both of you have had enough."

Delbert turned away from me now. I had upset him to be sure. He didn't quite know how to answer Grandpa Dunny's question. He was thinking, giving it a great deal of consideration. Then the firelight seemed to soften. The covert shadows fell like ash from his face. There was something of ablution and disclosure. He looked up.

"Sit down, Dunmore," he said.

The waves lapped easily on the beach. A blue heron *gronked* and lifted from its secret place.

CHAPTER TWENTY-THREE

That jug of cheap wine seemed bottomless. We drank and it went down well as we sat around the fire of bleached-white driftwood. Grandpa Dunny and I waited confused and curious while Delbert finally admitted a truth to us and himself.

"Some things you just don't want to talk about," Delbert said. His slurred words betrayed the full measure of his drunkenness. "Like, hey, man, most of us have some shit. You know what I mean? So we just go about our fuckin' business. That's it. I don't need to know your shit and you don't need to know my shit. Simple right? Yeah, until some fuckin' kid catches you on a word. A word!"

He pointed his finger at my face while speaking only to Grandpa Dunny.

"So, look, man," he said to me, "how did you know?"

"It wasn't just the word," I said.

"You could tell."

"Yeah."

"What the devil are you two talking about?" Grandpa Dunny asked.

"He's an American," I said.

"Yeah," Delbert said, "born in Peoria, Illinois, one hot as hell day, so my mother said, in August, 1950."

"Aye, then you're on the run," Grandpa said.

"You win the fucking prize, Dunmore. I'm your one hundred percent, certified, bona fide, fortified and electrified draft dodger."

"You're a long way from home, lad."

"Don't I know it," Delbert said.

"Why did you leave?" I asked him. It could have been a stupid question, my grip on the obvious, but Delbert seemed to understand the relevance of it.

He lit a cigarette. "I love Canadian smokes," he said. Then he looked into our faces and smiled. "There was this kid who lived on our street," he went on. "I went to school with him. His name was Walter Bates. We called him Wally. You know, like in *Leave it to Beaver*. Anyway, in the eighth grade there was this spelling chart on the blackboard. And there was Walter Bates with no stars beside his name. He wasn't that smart but everyone would remember him. Our teacher was kind of formal so one day I erased Walter and wrote Master in its place. Yeah, Master Bates. Everyone doubled over. Man was that fuckin' funny. I got the strap, but it was worth it. The girls never looked at Wally the same after that.

"Wally was killed at the Battle of Hue City in 1968. It was his first tour in Viet Nam. He caught an enemy B-40 rocket. They sent home what they could find. There were a lot of young guys being shipped out. My mom and dad were afraid. They didn't believe in the war. And the thing is, my dad was in the navy. He served under U.S. Navy Commander Albert Bigelow. Well, that changed his life and it changed mine. He was on the bridge of the destroyer escort *Peterson* in Pearl Harbour on August 6th, 1945, when the atomic bomb was dropped on Hiroshima. That was it for Bigelow. He left the navy. What kind of fucked up country does that?

"Bigelow and his wife went on to look after two women

from Hiroshima. They called the young Japanese women who were burnt and disfigured from the bomb Hiroshima Maidens. They were brought to the U.S. for plastic surgery. When the government continued with nuclear testing, Bigelow decided to do something to stop it. In 1958 he took a crew aboard the *Golden Rule*, a thirty-foot ketch, and set sail for the Marshall Islands to protest nuclear testing. No more bombs, man. But the U.S. Coast Guard arrested him. There was a lot of shit back then. But he made a difference. He wrote a book about it, *Voyage of the Golden Rule*. I still have the copy my dad gave me.

"My parents drove across the border from Detroit and left me in Windsor. I was in Canada. Came all the way out here, stayed in the Slocan Valley with some other Dodgers. But I couldn't stay. I had a plan."

Delbert got up and walked to the edge of the firelight. He planted his feet and he pissed into the pitch black for what seemed five minutes.

"What kind of plan?" Grandpa Dunny called out to him.

Delbert returned to the fire.

"You can't tell anyone this," he said in a stark even timbre. "I mean it. I'd be in some serious shit. I've something important to do. I have a boat in Sidney. The Americans plan to detonate a nuclear bomb at Amchitka Island in Alaska this fall. Bastards. There's talk of a protest. A group from Vancouver, *Don't Make a Wave Committee*, want to take a boat up there to protest the test. My old lady, Gloria, is working on a fish packer in Port Renfrew for the summer. We're going to take my boat, *Albert Bigelow*, and join them. If we're stopped, we'll paint our faces red and black, knot our hair on the top of our heads and take to the war canoe. We'll be fierce but it's not a war, man. It's a protest. Fuck, man, we're killing the planet. You know what I mean? They're fuckin' takin' down these huge trees up the coast. There's big fuckers that are a thousand years old and over three hundred feet high. Gloria took me there. It'll make you weep, man. I'm going up to see her in a few days. You should come along, Dunmore, take the boy here. We'll take the *Albert Bigelow* and see some great shit. I'll take you to an old tree, the Red Creek Fir. It's big, man. Fuck, am I drunk."

We sat around the fire and peered into the coals. The fire was dying down but no one was up to dragging more wood from the pooling dark. Then Grandpa Dunny fell over backwards off his log. I stared at his feet before I picked him up. We left Delbert sitting there and stumbled down the beach until I had to stop. I sat Grandpa down on a log while I lost my hotdogs. He sang some Scottish ballad into the spinning night. Somehow we managed to find the house where I put him into bed, shoes and all. Then I fell into my own bed, asleep before my head bounced on the soft quilt.

In the morning Grandpa Dunny had a cup of coffee waiting for me on the deck.

"Good morning, Calan," he said a bit too chipper.

"What's good about it?" I sat down, poured cream and sugar into my coffee and stirred. The spoon made a dreadful clang.

"Well, look a that," Grandpa said. "The crows have found some breakfast. Something dead washed up, I dare say."

I looked hard at the crows picking at the beach. "Yeah, something dead," I agreed.

"Delbert's back at work on his canoe," Grandpa said.

"Do you remember what he said last night?" I asked him. In the distance Delbert was folding his tarp, preparing the crosspieces.

"I remember."

"He wants to take us up the coast in his boat."

"Aye."

"Do you think that he'll remember?"

"I've been thinking on that all morning. He'll remember all right. But will he regret it?"

"He might not have a boat at all, you know."

"He has a boat," Grandpa said. "A man cannot make up a story like that when he's drunk."

"If he's telling the truth, it's not wrong, is it?"

"No, Calan, it's not wrong."

"You fell over backwards last night."

"I decided to look at the stars is all. It happens to the best of drinkers. It's a shame about your supper, though."

We laughed. "He doesn't like me much."

"Well now, you found out his secret. That's not an easy thing for a man to accept. I think that perhaps he'll be better for it. Time will tell."

"We can go over there."

"No, I think we'll let him be. I've heard of those great trees and they're a mystery to be sure. No, if we're to go, he'll come to us."

Grandpa sipped his coffee and watched the crows and Delbert. He was always hoping for some great thing for me. It was the giants of the old forests now. I knew he wanted me to see them. I looked at his hand beside mine, holding our coffee cups, and compared the two of them. His skin was rough, his knuckles thick, a pair of ski-jump thumbs. My own hands had done nothing yet. The sun was warm on my face. Everything seemed to have slowed. The world was reduced to the bright rolling skin on the bay. A hummingbird came to the feeder. I heard the whirr of wings before I saw it. I lit a cigarette. Grandpa said nothing. I couldn't watch the crows.

CHAPTER TWENTY-FOUR

Grandpa Dunny, Delbert and I passed Discovery Island rounding the bluffs of Victoria. The sea was fair and a good July sun shone upon us. Expectant gulls followed our wake of roiling milk. Everything seemed unnatural to me. The land was so far away and the water was all about us, gaping green and deep. A flimsy length of rotting wood was all that kept us from a cold and certain death. A Saskatchewan boy plying the main. Could Janet have imagined it?

Delbert was at the wheel at mid-ship and he wore a white captain's hat with gold braid trim. I leaned against the rail and held tight to the ropes and wires. The sea hissed against the hull and the *Albert Bigelow* rose and fell in slow undulations, bearing north to Port Renfrew. Grandpa Dunny, with a foot up on the hold and his chin hoisted proud, looked a mariner through and through. His fine eye took in the boat. He moved up and down the deck, looking down at his feet, up to the spar and out over the water, as if remembering a bygone life aboard those very planks and timbers. The wind in his hair the way he liked it and I could see, too, the hump growing in his old back. He turned to Delbert.

"Delbert," he said, "you haven't told us how you came

about this ship of yours. There's an odd bit of rigging hanging here."

Delbert tossed me his pack of Players. "Light me a smoke," he said.

I wondered why he treated me so curtly. At the wharf in Sidney he was rough with his orders as I fought with the knots and cleats. I didn't understand ropes. There was another story coming and I was made to feel like a peon to assist in its telling. There was something about me he despised. And there was resentment in me now. My blood surged at his every unkind and condescending word. I decided to confront him when the time was right. I ducked down from the wind, struck a wooden match, lit his cigarette and handed it back to him.

"I had a job as a deck hand last summer," Delbert said. "It didn't last long. An old-timer named Hoot Larsen hired me in Ucluelet. I had no experience but it didn't matter to him. His boat was called the *Miss Direction* – a thirty-two-foot salmon troller built in the '30s. Hoot fished the west coast all his life. He knew his business and he knew the water. He taught me how to work the girdies and winches, snap the hootchies and spoons to the lines, set the stabilizers and drop the cannon balls. He showed me how to dress the fish, avoid belly burn and ice them away in the hold. Hoot was a good man but he had one bad habit. He loved his whiskey.

"We were long lining for halibut a few miles out and caught a big son of a bitch about two hundred pounds. Hoot had an old Colt .22 and shot it in its flat fucking head so we could gaff it over the stern. He was feeling pretty good about his big catch so he decided to set the lines for salmon as we worked our way back. It had been a good day. It was raining and there were good swells. I was working the trolling pit bringing in cohos and a few good springs when Hoot dis-appeared into the wheelhouse. I think the bottle was calling him. About that time I felt sick. It was my first time at sea.

I didn't notice how close we were drifting toward the rocks as I was just trying to stay on my feet. Seasickness is nasty shit. Then the boat jerked. We hit something, not hard, but whatever it was broke the stabilizers clean off their stays. Hoot came out to have a look. He was a sight. His eyes were like boiled eggs. He looked about fucking dead. We lost everything, all the rigging.

"Poor Hoot limped into Ucluelet. He was ruined. He was too old to fish. He apologized to me. His boat was about done and he offered it to me for five hundred bucks. So I bought it. He died that winter in his cedar shack. He drank himself to death. Sad fucking story. So now I'm the captain of the *Albert Bigelow,* and it *will* make history."

Grandpa thought this was a great story, but I had doubts. How could Delbert have done all that at his age? Perhaps he thought Grandpa Dunny just an old fool who would listen to anything, while it seemed he thought me useless and simple, not worthy to be his friend. I didn't want to be Delbert's friend. He made me feel like a retard, which was the worst thing he could do. I had to turn away from him, push my anger down into my guts, push it all the way down before I saw my father standing there in his place. I closed my eyes against the forests and sea, gripped my hands hard to the railing to keep them there.

The day wore on. The *Albert Bigelow* was true and trim. Delbert had his transistor radio playing, some rock station from Bellingham that had a preference for The Doors it seemed, playing: "Unknown Soldier," "Break on Through" and "Light My Fire" in succession. I didn't mind the music, but Grandpa Dunny only tolerated it. Yet music seemed to fit life on a boat with its free and constant movement, the boat shifting to the ceaseless rhythm of water. Delbert pointed to a blow of water off the port side. There we watched the arc of a long back and tail flukes rising from the water, dripping, halting, suspended, before slipping under the dark sea.

"Grey whale," he said.

Grandpa was pleased by the sighting as he looked hard over the water, expectant as a young boy waiting for it to resurface. "I'll wager that you've never seen such beast on the prairie, lad," he said to me.

He wanted me to be awed and staggered by the beauty of the coast as if the raw and rugged spectacle of it could purge and heal me. How unswerving he was with his beliefs, in the curative powers of the natural world. It was his purpose now to lay it all out for me, point the way for a man to find himself, to know himself. My indifference seemed a mean and callous thing. It hurt him.

We were a pair. He understood me when others dismissed me. And he paid a price for it. The cousins developed an aversion to the *wee house by the sea* and the aunts had come to enjoy a certain distance from him. Oh, they loved him dearly. I suppose they had just grown used to Grandpa always being there for them, on the telephone, stopping by for tea with his carnival handshake. It seemed to me that he was the initiator, the one to reach out and never the receiver. We were alike in many ways and found comfort in our eccentricities, but still we owned our own solitudes. He was a talker and I was a listener – what two better souls to share the world.

Grandpa was snoozing when the news came on the radio. The sun fell full on his face as he lay on the cover over the hold, his hands clasped behind his head, lazy, relaxed and blissful. The breezes played in the wiry strands of his beard and hair, which were like sprays of sea grass. Jim Morrison had died from a drug overdose in Paris. He was twenty-seven years old. Delbert was anguished, beside himself.

"What the fuck?" he said. "No way, man. No fucking way. Did you hear that?"

He turned to me, his long face twisted, distorted. He was distressed and shook his head from side to side, unwilling to accept the news that had come around the world to find the *Albert Bigelow*. I looked at him. People die, I thought.

"That's a drag," I said.

"That's a drag? What the fuck's wrong with you, don't you care?"

"Not that much."

"You have no fucking heart, man. You don't do anything. You don't fucking talk. You never laugh. You're a fuckin' zombie, man!"

I looked at Grandpa Dunny. He was asleep. I cared about life, but I didn't know Jim Morrison. Why should I carry on as if he meant something to me? He was a poet, a lead singer in a rock band. I cared about my mother, my grandpa. But more than that, I wanted Delbert to think that I didn't care. It was the only way I knew to strike back at him. Jim Morrison was not much older than Delbert. He could die, too, I thought. I could stand up and bowl him over the side. Just like that. I wouldn't look back as he fought the cold shock of the sea and thrashed about, his stiff hands useless against the passing hull. The drone of the diesel engine would drown out his futile screams. Then I would be at the wheel and somewhere in the wake there would be Delbert's stupid captain's hat floating above his slow descent. The last thing he would see in his short life would be my back.

"You don't know me," I said.

"What is there to know?" he asked.

I just stared at him and that bothered him. He turned away. He left the deck and navigated from the wheelhouse. He wanted to be alone to mourn the loss of his idol.

On that confined and bankrupt vessel there was no where to run, no aspen gully to hold me. At sea there was a vastness that matched the prairies, a sky that had no end and clouds unlimited in form, rushing endlessly to the meet the forested mountains. Yet there was nothing under my feet. My sense of the earth shifted. It seemed like an error to have come, an impossible circumstance to undo. Then I found an unlikely place on the starboard foredeck. I lay down flat on my belly and watched dolphins riding the bow waves. The sea bubbled over their rubber faces and one tilted an eye to me. For a moment I remembered reverence and I thought of Jules Bear. Then I forgot everything as I reached down when the bow settled low in a deep green trough and I touched a dolphin's beautiful back.

CHAPTER TWENTY-FIVE

In the late afternoon the *Albert Bigelow* turned away from the open sea and entered a deep bay where the fingers of the San Juan River spilled its sweet mountain water. Sea ducks skittered and a bald eagle wheeled overhead as Delbert eased his boat alongside the government wharf in Port Renfrew. I threw bumpers over the starboard side while Grandpa Dunny took the stern rope. I sidled along the wheelhouse, grabbed the bow rope and we both jumped onto the wharf. I reeled as my sea legs folded under me. I stared down where the rope needed to be and could feel Delbert watching. Grandpa knew my trouble with knots and shouted his encouragement.

"Twice around the cleat and then a half-hitch, lad."

Soon the boat was snug. It had come a long way around the southern tip of Vancouver Island, not a boat to be coveted by discriminating sailors but a capable ship after all. As Delbert made his checks after a long day on the water, Grandpa came up to me, pretending to inspect my hitches.

"Now you just keep your counsel, Calan," he said in a guarded voice. "Delbert has his ways, I can see that. But there's no need to make him wrong."

"You heard him then?"

"Aye, a sailor never sleeps, you know."

"He's getting to me, Grandpa."

"Well, just do what you've been doing. It takes a man to turn away. It's not a weakness but a strength he has. It's nothing you've done, lad. Sometimes there's a clash of souls. No real explanation. But you must take heed now."

He gripped my shoulders and I felt the dig of his fingers. I was sure now that he had heard my thoughts as well.

The fish packer Gloria worked on was docked nearby and Delbert left us on the boat to fend for ourselves. "I have a date," he said. "Don't wait up for me. There's food in the cupboard." Then he was gone, to see his old lady. G L O R I A, he sang with a renewed levity as he skipped down the pier.

Grandpa Dunny had been watching the activity around the boat ever since we docked. I could tell he wanted to saunter about, perhaps take up a conversation or two with the fishermen. It was one of his joys to seek out a story and to add his own. With his ready storehouse of Scot lore to prime a listener's ear, he would have them spellbound or mutinous before his handshake gave out.

"Go on," I said, "I'll cook you some supper."

"Now that's a might worrisome."

"Don't you worry, Grandpa."

He smiled, slapped my back and stepped over the rail. With a hand behind his back and his cane in the other in that jaunty and expectant way of his he made his way down the wharf among the boats.

So now I had the wheelhouse to myself, without the distraction of Delbert. I always felt a tension around others who I didn't know well, an alertness that made me cautious of what I said. It was exhausting to be constantly on guard, vigilant against certain rejection, my Gray Farm legacy. To be alone was satisfying. I had no one to please, no arguments or fires of retribution stirring in the dark folds of my brain.

Old cedar panels walled the wheelhouse above and below the windows. Delbert had boasted about his restoration in progress. The wood was all lacquered. A brass compass and gauges were highly polished. Maps and charts ringed with coffee from slopping cups sat on a table with a bench for two on each side. There was a fine wheel, worn on the spindles I imagined, from the meaty palms of Hoot Larsen. Kitchen things stuffed the shelves and above the wheel a two-way radio crackled now and then with a message or a weather report. The galley was down below with a diesel stove and beyond it, up in the bow, were our sleeping bags jammed into narrow bunks.

I began to look through the cupboards for something to make for our supper. I had no idea what possibilities I could create. I was hungry. I was sure that Grandpa Dunny was the same. I found a can of corned beef and set it on the table. Next I placed a can of peas and creamed corn and a loaf of white bread beside it.

Then I turned back to the cupboard to close it and there at the back in the unlit void was Hoot Larsen's .22-Colt pistol. I reached for it, over spilled bullets, and touched the cold barrel. I pulled back, jolted by a current of fear arcing from my fingertips. I wondered if Delbert knew it was there. I looked out the windows to the marina thick with spars and masts. I could see Grandpa Dunny with a group of men, his arms flinging to the heavens.

I had to think. I could just look at it. My hand found the handle and my fingers crept over it, tentative and unsure. Then I gripped the gun and removed it from the cupboard. The wooden handle was split and wrapped with electrician's tape. The pistol was heavy in my hand. I studied how it looked and how my thumb felt against the hammer. I took a rag and rubbed the barrel until it shone blue, that gunmetal gleam I remembered. I stroked it the way Larry Bratt had loved himself for us so long ago.

I felt its energy shoot up my arm. A chill ran right through me until I could taste metal on my tongue. I felt confident with a sudden power that scared me. I put the pistol down on the table and stared at it as if it were a new species waiting to be discovered. By itself it was nothing but a companion to the corned beef and canned peas, inanimate objects waiting for what a hand might do with them – make a dinner or a killing. I picked the gun up again and thumbed back the hammer. There was a shell in the breech. I panicked. What if the gun went off? My heart pounded like a maul in my chest, chiselling against my ribs. Then I remembered a library book that I used for my drawings. I recalled some of the illustrations and descriptions. I held the hammer back, squeezed the trigger and then released the hammer. The careless and frightening moment passed. I opened the gate to the cylinder and emptied the chambers. There were two spent casings – one shot for that great halibut, and another for the old fisherman. I was sure then that Delbert had shot Hoot Larsen in the back of the head and stolen his boat.

The gun in my hand gave me crazy thoughts and a wicked temptation to aim it, to shoot something. I felt an urgency rising in me, but I knew that I couldn't give in to it. I sat down with the cans and the gun in the gold light of the sun shining through the wheelhouse windows. How it changed me to see a gun and hold it. When Uncle Reggie brushed by me in the kitchen on Cedar Hill Road, I had seen the hard leather of his holster and smelled the same gun oil.

The *Albert Bigelow* had its subtleties – the imperceptible movement against the wharf, old wood sounds stretching and shrinking, the sudden sawing of the bilge pump – all sounds of a living thing. Outside, beyond the fishing boats, the steep forests overpowered the reach of the sea. The verdant textures and clinging mists filled the distance with mystery. These things could arise in me now, alone in an unmoving world where time was marked by the setting sun. But the Colt still rested in my hand, unresponsive to my stroking thumb. I wanted it to be mine, to urge it to the life I wanted for it, but it didn't belong to me. Quickly I realized I had to get it out of my mind before Grandpa came back. He would know. I felt a tremor break cold in my gut. Oh, he would know. I returned the gun to the cupboard and started on our supper.

I began with the corned beef and removed the key from the side of the can. When I applied it to the tab it broke off after two turns. I stared at it in disbelief, then I took a fork and pried the ribbon of metal around the can until I could remove the top. I dumped the corned beef into a frying pan and chopped it up into fatty cubes with a butter knife. It vaguely smelled of meat and masked the gagging fumes from the diesel stove. I opened the can of creamed corn, covered the cubes of corned beef and added the peas. It was a curious banquet but it was food. I took the frying pan down into the galley and set it on the stove. It took a while before the mash began to steam and burp. I set the table and stacked slices of bread on a plate. Grandpa Dunny was coming down the wharf. I could hear him whistling one of his tunes. I heaped our plates, sat down and waited for him.

"Look at that," he said, shoving through the door, "food fit for a king. And we are kings, lad. And all about you is our kingdom. Everything a man could want, right here. A glorious place indeed. And those salty boys have their tales, glorious stories of storms and wrecks and packs of killer whales and more. Now, let's eat."

I waited for Grandpa Dunny to begin. His spoon plunged into his food and came up with a square of meat dripping with creamed corn. He leaned over his plate and gobbled it down as a starving man might. Then he noticed I was watching him. He smiled and I knew he was pleased with the meal. We ate with the afterglow bright on our greasy lips and cleaned our plates with slices of bread.

Grandpa pushed back his plate after he was done, took

up his napkin, wiped his mouth and sopped up the spilled corn from his beard. He had been quiet while we were eating. I knew he had something to tell me, but I let him rest a while. Then I realized his hair and beard were nearly all white now. They glowed like a lamp in the setting sun. I supposed it was the light that illuminated him like that. But perhaps it was something else that wanted my attention. Perhaps it was life showing me a thing that won't last. Then he sat forward.

"One of the fishermen," he began, "a friendly chap, was telling me about this old boat. *Miss Direction*, he told me, was not such a doomed name as it would appear. He said that a young Hoot Larsen was outfitting his new boat in Ucluelet when a British girl arrived on the dock looking for the *Salmon Queen*. She was hired by the local paper to write a piece about the new boat, the jewel of the fleet. But she had her directions mixed up. Story has it that Hoot fell in love with her on the spot. Well, they married and fished together for years up and down the coast until she died unexpectedly of some rare disorder. Hoot never recovered from his loss. But it gets more interesting, lad.

"The fisherman went on to say how Delbert came to own the *Miss Direction*. He bought it from Hoot, that's the truth. And when Hoot passed away that winter, it was Delbert who came up from Sidney in rough seas to give Hoot a proper burial – a nice coffin and tombstone. Wrote the inscription himself. If I can remember correctly, he said that it read: *He loved the sea and every missed direction.* He said that Delbert paid for it all. Oh, we can never know much about anyone. But I must say, Calan, I do like that story a lot. My, my, the weather's changing. I just got a good burn in my hips."

I had to go for a walk. Grandpa's story was counter to what I thought. I was confused and angry at being wrong. Delbert wasn't the villain that I thought. In my mind I had pitched an innocent man into the sea and let him drown cold and alone. Grandpa Dunny made no judgments, no moral proclamations when he recounted the story of the *Miss Direction*. He let it rest with me. And when I slipped out of the wheelhouse door, he simply went about cleaning up the dishes.

The sky was still bright above the pier that led to the solid ground of the Port Renfrew Hotel in the distance. I took my time, leaning on the railing, looking out over the fishing fleet that was tied up for the night. Squares of light framed whiskered men at their cluttered tables. I lit a cigarette to calm me, to settle my demons. I continued along, unhurried, and listened to the falling birdsong of a thrush answering from the dark halls of cedar surrounding the hotel. Then all was hushed and the night stars broke through the firmament, one by one in their infinite order. How was it possible to know the stars, the boundless and unreachable sweep of them and yet never really know oneself?

Then something disturbed the dusk. Footfalls drummed on the pier and a form emerged. Someone ran toward me, nearer and nearer. I stopped. It was a girl. She was frantic.

"Calan, Calan!" she called out, approaching fast.

"Yeah," I answered back for her to hear. It had to be Gloria.

She reached me and grabbed hold of my arm, breathing in great gulps. "It's Delbert," she managed to say. "They have him behind the hotel. Two loggers. They're going to kill him. He shouldn't have opened his mouth. I told him. Oh, my God, help him!"

"Wait here," I told her, oddly calm, my reaction involuntary and swift. I spun around and tore down the pier to the *Albert Bigelow*, as fast as I had ever run in my life. I leapt over the rail and burst into the wheelhouse. Grandpa Dunny jerked around, startled by the look of me.

"What is it, Calan?" he said.

"Delbert's in trouble," I said as I opened the cupboard and took out the Colt. I never looked at him, never said another word. Then I was running again, the gun pumping in my hand like a baton with Gloria shouting *hurry, hurry* and Grandpa behind me, his crackling voice breaking over my back, *No, Calan, no.*

But he could do nothing to stop me now with an old man's fears, his nightmare gripped in my hand. I caught up to Gloria. She gasped when she saw the gun. We ran toward the hotel. The forest filled the night sky and I lost my bearings. And then she pulled my arm and we veered away from the pier and ran behind the hotel. There, in the dull lamplight of the parking lot, two men stood above another and kicked him as he lay prone and foetal. Delbert moaned and jerked in the dirt.

They never heard me coming or knew what it was that met them so fiercely. I whacked the first one on the side of his head, above his eye, with the butt of the Colt. He stood back dazed and bleeding. The other one started to turn to me but I took the pistol and held the barrel against his temple.

"He's got a fucking gun!" the dazed one said.

I held the pistol against his head and cocked the hammer. The man didn't move. The solid click froze him. "You two fucking apes better leave before this thing goes off," I said.

"Okay, man," said the one behind the cold steel.

"Just a misunderstanding," the other said.

Gloria went to Delbert as the loggers backed away from him. I aimed the gun at them. Then I released the hammer and lowered the pistol. They turned and hurried away and were soon lost in the shadows.

I lifted my head. The moths in the lamplight brought me back to earth, returned me to the movement of time. I looked over my shoulder because I could feel him. He was standing there motionless and unable to speak in response to what he had just witnessed, a heroic act worthy of his lore or a boy corrupted by his first taste of blood.

The next morning Grandpa Dunny and I sat in the wheelhouse drinking our coffee. He wouldn't look at me and

I couldn't find a useful word for him. The rain was falling in dismal sheets as Gloria helped Delbert onto the *Albert Bigelow*. He was holding his ribs.

"I'm sorry boys," he said, "but I think we better get our asses out of here." He looked at me queerly, remembering I suppose what I had done the night before, amazed, perhaps, by the skinny kid who rescued him.

We left Gloria on the dock with her umbrella, in her granny dress and hiking boots, a kerchief over her frizzy hair. She seemed a good person. She was sad to see us go. Then she turned and walked away.

The *Albert Bigelow* was going home. Delbert pointed out the window to the rising forest. "They're up there," he said, "up the San Juan River, biggest trees in the world. If the fucking loggers haven't got them. I wish I'd been able to show them to you."

The rain beat against the window panes. It seemed urgent to find me out, to gather me in its liquid arms and soak me with a certain death. Outside the rolling sea and the grey wall of the unreachable horizon surrounded us. I looked down at my hand, the fleshy palm, unmarked, a boy hand. And I thought about how I destroyed *them* with an empty gun.

CHAPTER TWENTY-SIX

Back home we returned to a familiar routine. Each day was renewed by the tide. I liked the succession of motion that always left a new offering at our feet. I enjoyed the resumption of our ritual of coffee on the deck overlooking the beach where crows entrusted their lives to death and decomposition. The sun was like a warm sweater and steam rose from the mossy rooftops. On our first morning back in the *wee house* Grandpa Dunny had been sitting on a beached log near low tide. He seemed to have found a measure of peace there. He sat so still that the crows scavenged very near to him. I had learned to leave him alone at such times. He was working things out in his mind, looking for the good in people, in life. He always seemed to find it.

The night in Port Renfrew had left him shaken and defeated. I was sorry for it, but Delbert could have been killed if I hadn't stepped in. Now it seemed he wouldn't be able to finish his canoe, the prow and stern pieces. Instead he would be mending his bruises for the rest of the summer. When I saw him on the beach he had a different look, a smile I knew expressed his gratitude, his respect. Grandpa couldn't see it that way. He knew the temptations that courted young men, the fear and rage that called them to war. When conditions were right, a man will take up arms. I knew that Grandpa would honour such courage in the face of injustice, but he didn't believe in the war against my father.

The tide turned and the sea was at Grandpa's feet. I stood up to look more closely at the unmoving shape of him. Perhaps he had fallen asleep and didn't notice the waves washing up around him, but I was alarmed now. Something wasn't right. I hurried from the deck to the beach and down the pebbled shore, skirting the salty pools. The crows stepped away as I approached him. Their black watching eyes chilled me through and through. It was all so ordinary – the breeze in his hair, his shirt sleeves billowing ever so slightly. I called out to him but he didn't answer. Then I stepped in front of him. The water rose over my shoes. His eyes were closed, his jaw shut and his chin resting on his woolly beard. His cane propped against him. My poor grandpa, dead on a log.

I sat down beside him and cried. I took his cold hand in mine as the sea rose up our shins. I cried like the gulls and eagles and I cried out to Delbert to help me carry him. Then I noticed a sheet of paper tight in his other hand and I pulled it free. Just a piece of paper for a sketch, I thought, but there was handwriting on it. My tears fell hot. The ink swelled purple and bruised. It was another letter for me.

Calan,
You have the old man's sickness. All is dead spineless
boy.
Gray Farm

My savage cry erupted across the bay for all the world to hear. It came snake-cold and wild from my very core. My life was reduced to a fine blue flame of rancour and retribution. *He* would pay for what he stole from me. Delbert heard my wounded bawl and came running down the beach, his hand clutched to his side as the log moved, buoyed by the tide. The letter fell from my hand into the surge. The words dissolved and were lost. Grandpa Dunny fell against me. Delbert saw this and took him under his arms.

"Oh, God, Dunmore," he said.

I held Grandpa's feet and we carried him over the crusted rocks to the finer pebbles of the elevated shore. We laid him down on his back and I folded his arms over his chest. Then I hurried down to the water's edge to get his cane. When I returned I dropped to my knees before him, my grandpa asleep in the sun. Delbert knelt down beside me, his face raw with the pain in his ribs.

"What happened?" he said.

"I don't know. He was just sitting there and died."

"He wasn't sick or something?"

"No," I said, but my mind seethed. The bastard had killed him.

"God damn, Calan, you have to call someone."

"I'll call my aunt. I don't want to. But I guess I have to."

"We just can't sit here with him."

"For a little while."

"I haven't been this close to a dead person before."

"He's still around here."

"I wouldn't be surprised."

"Yeah, he's here."

"I'm sorry. I really liked your grandpa."

"Yeah." I sat there on the beach with Delbert, our arms resting on our drawn up knees. I tried not to cry, but it was no use. Delbert lit two cigarettes and passed me one. He put his hand on my shoulder as the gusts rushed up before the rising tide. I remembered what Grandpa Dunny had taught me. *Get up Grandpa. Stand full in the face of it. Let it touch you. Feel the life in it.*

But he never moved and the day could no longer wait

for him. I went back to the house and called Auntie Netty. Soon the aunts and uncles were all over the beach. Grandpa was taken from his beloved bay and Delbert drifted away when he had done all he could do. I watched him walk down the beach with his head down, his arms slack and his feet dragging. I knew that Grandpa had been right about Delbert Crane.

The family gathered in Grandpa's house. Auntie Netty made tea. We all sat in the kitchen and everyone looked at me the way they did when my mother died, as if I were still the prairie orphan who couldn't look after himself. Everyone murmured the standard phrases of Grandpa's life: *He had a good life. Oh, how he loved his grandchildren. A special spot for the boys, you know. He's with our dear mother now. And dear Megan has her father back. Yes, a good life. He loved his trees. He quit smoking his pipe. No, he didn't. I'm sure of it. When was it then? He liked his hair. Oh, you know Dad; he never liked to pay for a barber. No, not ever. I can see him now coming down the lane with his cane. Did he always use it? Oh, yes, he was never without it. I think that he just liked the look of it. He loved his porridge. We had it everyday growing up. I'll never forget it. He said that it'll stick to your ribs. Yes, I remember that. Quite a storyteller. They weren't all true, were they? And his pipes...* Finally they couldn't go on.

There was no formal service for Grandpa Dunny. It seemed to me that there could be no tribute worthy of him, that nothing believable could come from a stiff chaplain reading from his notes about an unacquainted life. A piper wouldn't do. I believed that the aunts weren't up to it. My mother's funeral and Grandpa's proud Scottish ceremony had left an emotional brand to last a lifetime. The thought of his death roused a thousand pipers in me, marching over every hill and dale as he might have said. He was my symbol of a reverent man. Words fell flat.

My Grandfather, Dunmore McLeod was put to rest

beside my mother in the Ross Bay Cemetery on July 11th, 1971. The epitaph on his gravestone was chosen by the aunts.

He mattered most to those who loved him

I didn't like it. I imagined him grimacing when the stonecutter set it above his head. One day I would change it.

In his will, Grandpa left the house, property and bonds and such to the aunts. They agreed that I could stay in the house until I finished school and have the use of his Volkswagen Beetle until I earned enough money to buy it. That was generous I thought, but I knew the Bratt brothers wouldn't be caught dead in it. So I needed a part-time job to help pay my way and Uncle Reggie to help me get my driver's license. The loving family duly relieved the *wee house by the sea* of the prized pieces of Grandpa's life, his collections of books, memorabilia, sketches and paintings. Yet his cane, carved from the wood of the Fortingall Yew, I claimed as my own and hid it under my bed.

I was thankful to stay in the house for a while longer, though at times I wondered if it was the family's way of keeping me on the periphery of their lives. I never fit in with them. They never seemed to know what to say to me, as if I were still newly arrived from another country and could not understand the local language. I didn't mind the estrangement. It wasn't their fault. Parry Bay had been a safe place for me, but things never last. Even the gifts and promises of the trees left me. And it seemed as if they were nothing but the expression of my deficits.

The silence in the evenings was unsettling. I kept looking for him, listening for his mutterings. I couldn't sit for long before I had to get up. A deep sense of restlessness moved me from room to room in search of something I could never find. *Columbo,* and *I Love Lucy* reruns could not ease the festering itch that was driving me mad. I could see *his* words; feel them like welds on my skin.

I began to notice Delbert out along the beach. He would sit on a log and light a cigarette. Every now and then he would look my way. I decided he was inviting me to join him. So one night I headed down the beach toward him and it wasn't long before his hand came up.

"I see you're staying in the house," he said as I came up to him. He offered me a cigarette. It was the first thing that he did now.

"Just for a few months," I said finding a spot on his log.

"Are you going back to school?"

"Why?"

"I don't know. Some kids just drop out."

"You think I should drop out?"

"Fuck no. I think you should do whatever the hell you want."

"How are your ribs?"

"Well, I'm back at work. But I don't think I can finish the canoe."

"Still going to Amchitka?"

"Damn rights we're going."

"That's pretty cool."

"Hey, man, you don't have a job, right?"

"No, not yet."

"I'll make you an offer."

"What?"

"I'll give you a couple cedar blocks," Delbert said, his rising enthusiasm, "and a plan of the art work for the prow and stern. I'll pay you if you can carve it for me. You're an artist, aren't you?"

"Yeah, I might be able to do that."

"I'll give you fifty bucks."

Just then I wasn't thinking about the money. "How about that busted up gun?"

"You want Hoot's old pistol?"

"Yeah." How easily it came, that slow pitch that I never expected.

"What the hell for?"

"I'm thinking of visiting the prairies. Look up some old friends. Shoot a few prairie dogs."

"You wouldn't shoot a fuckin' prairie dog."

"Just target practice."

"I'll never forget the sight of you holding that thing against that dumb logger's head."

"He probably won't either."

Delbert laughed. "All right, sounds like a fair deal to me." Then he turned to me gravely. "Your uncle's a pig, right?"

"Yeah."

"He's teaching you how to drive."

"Yeah, so?"

"What would he think about you having a gun?"

"Not much," I said.

"Your old man's still back there, isn't he?"

"I guess."

"You won't do anything stupid, will you?"

"What did my grandpa tell you?"

"Nothing. Seriously, he didn't say anything. Just... that it was bad."

"It's been seven years."

"That's a long time. Things change."

"Yeah, and some things don't."

"We can follow everything back to the sea, man, if we could go back far enough."

"What does that mean?"

"It doesn't mean shit. Hey, I guess it means that we can still do something."

We sat there like friends with our easy talk, smoking until the sun went down and the herons left the pools and a chill crept up our backs. There was such simplicity looking out over the water. Perhaps we ask questions that we don't know we ask, I thought. Then Delbert stood up and flicked his cigarette butt out over the stones. It arced red and tumbled and died in a spray of embers.

"Got to get up early," he said.

On the way back to the house, I couldn't help but wonder what question Grandpa Dunny had asked on that perfectly blue day by the sea. I was sure that he had. But would I ever know the answer?

CHAPTER TWENTY-SEVEN

I worked on the blocks of cedar with a mallet, a chisel and fine finishing tools. The studio was littered with chips and filled with the aromatic smell of cedar. The radio played an accompaniment of summer songs – "Rain Dance" by The Guess Who and always The Doors. It was satisfying work. The hours and days passed by in a seamless stream of focused concentration. Delbert inspected my work when he got home after a day of banging nails. He had a remarkable sense of Nootka art with its imaginative relief and subtle traces of woodwork left by the chipping away of wood. Delbert knew what he wanted – an eagle head and tail, and he guided my hands until the pieces were done. At the end of the summer we carried them to the canoe. Delbert fastened them to the prow and stern with dowels and metal stripping. We added red and black paint to the relief work in tribute to the exacting ways of the Nootka. When it was finished we stood looking at it for a while, sharing and savouring our accomplishment. One day I painted Delbert and his canoe, a moment that had to be captured and honoured.

Delbert wasn't a typical hippie after all. Ideology was lost on him. He rarely spoke of what the world needed, but like Albert Bigelow, he knew what he had to do. He never lectured me or told me how to live my life. He recognized that I needed to figure that out for myself.

At the end of the summer I was invited to dinner on Cedar Hill Road. It had been a long time since I had been there. I was nervous knowing what I was about to tell them. I had my learner's license and parked the Bug in front of the house. I saw the curtains open to frame Uncle Reggie's big head. I met him at the door.

"Every time I see you, I think that you've grown another foot," he said light heartedly. "Come on in and join the rest of the redwoods." I ducked away from the concussion of his laugh.

Soon we were all sitting around the dinner table with hands reaching and grabbing, a kind of survival of the fittest. The cousins were all the size of their father now. It seemed like I was a guest at a football banquet. The food was disappearing fast, thick cuts of ham and scalloped potatoes.

"Boys," Auntie Netty reminded them, "save some for Calan for goodness sake."

I watched them look up at their mother with mystified gapes. Oddly, Jimmy never made eye contact with his mother or anyone else. His plate wasn't heaped like his brothers. I could see that Jimmy was having problems. His oversized clothes hid a thin frame. No one said to Jimmy, *have more*. He had long hair and wore an army surplus jacket. The others had their hair cut short. Then I noticed how they watched him with worrisome glances. An unease and tension that no one seemed to be able to speak to filled the room. Auntie Netty fidgeted with her napkin until she could no longer stand it.

"Larry's going to the University of British Columbia," she said to me. It seemed to burst from her mouth.

"That's cool," I said.

"What is it you're taking, Larry?" she asked.

"Psychology," Larry said, uninterested.

"That's right," she said, "it's so exciting."

"You can start with this bunch," Uncle Reggie said.

"And Buddy's staying here," Auntie Netty said. "He won a sport scholarship at the University of Victoria."

"No big deal," Buddy said.

"At least it kept you in school," Uncle Reggie said to him.

"You should see him play soccer," Kenny said.

"And you should see this one play soccer," Auntie Netty said motioning to Kenny. He won the *Soccer Boy* award. I'm sure he will be following in Buddy's footsteps."

They never said anything about Jimmy, as if he didn't matter. I wanted to say something to him, ask him what he was up to. Auntie Netty could see the question forming on my lips.

"What about you, Calan?" she said.

"I want to go back to Saskatchewan," I said.

"Saskatchewan?" I could see she wasn't expecting that.

"That's quite a ways from here," Uncle Reggie added.

"I have to see it again," I told them.

"And when do you plan to do this?" Auntie Netty said.

"Before school starts," I said. "I don't plan to stay long. Don't worry, I'm not going to spend another winter there." I laughed but I was alone – like Jimmy.

"Where will you stay?"

"I have a friend… in Clavet," I said. Lying was easy with them. They knew nothing.

"You'll need money."

"Not much," I said.

"You're so young to be going off by yourself," Auntie Netty said.

"I don't know about that old car," Uncle Reggie said skeptically.

"It's about time I did something on my own," I said bolstering the timbre of my speech. "I think it'll do me good.

I know the little Bug's not fast, but it'll get me there and back."

My talk seemed to appease them. I sounded so mature and grounded. Auntie Netty fretted over me like a mother as Uncle Reggie voiced his concern. I was surprised that they cared that much. At the end of dinner, as plates and thumbs were licked clean, Kenny said: "Jimmy plays guitar in a band, Purple Mushroom. He quit school."

Jimmy never looked up to acknowledge it. I could feel the air leave the room, vacuumed of all hope for him. It seemed as if he had undertaken some evil pact to hurt them, assail them with their greatest fear – a family struggling to hold on to a son. I wondered how long it had been since Jimmy sat down at dinner with his family and what the cost was to them all. I followed Kenny's cue.

"Hey, Jimmy, cool name," I said. "I bet you play like Jimmy Page." He looked up.

"Not quite," he said.

On my way out the door Auntie Netty pressed a handful of bills into my hand. Standing there I caught the painting of the dying swan on the living-room wall. I wasn't afraid of it now. She hugged me and let me go.

On the way back to the house I stopped at the Ross Bay Cemetery. It was a peaceful place evoking an uncompromising order of things completed. No more arguments or lists of things to do. Death solved everything, it seemed to me. There were fresh flowers on Grandpa Dunny's and my mother's graves. I knew Auntie Kate had placed them there. I had seen her there a few times but I had left her alone. I had come to say goodbye, to say that I was going to return to where it all began – to Gray Farm filled with its shadows and misery – to Clavet where a girl had declared to the world: *Janet loves Calan Gray.*

The last morning came and I locked the house and packed the Bug. Then I sat and waited for Delbert. I had asked him if I could borrow a sleeping bag. A light rain fell. I listened to it pattering on the roof and watched raindrops tracking crookedly across the windshield. Delbert tapped on the window. I popped the hood and got out.

"It's rolled up inside the sleeping bag."

"Thanks," I said. I took the bag and crammed it in with my other stuff.

"This was a good place to live," he said.

"Yeah, maybe I'll buy it one day." I got back into the Bug and rolled the window down.

"You never know." His face was long and I saw sadness in his eyes.

"How do you get by on your own?" I asked him.

"It would be a real drag without Gloria, that's for sure."

I nodded, realizing my aloneness, experiencing my old sense of isolation. Not even the Bratts could help me now. "Got to go," I said.

"Be smart," Delbert said.

"Good luck on your trip up the coast."

"Watch the news. Who knows what you'll see."

"I'll be looking for the *Albert Bigelow* and that fine canoe." I turned the key. The engine rattled then settled down. I let the clutch out and jerked up the driveway. In the rear-view mirror I saw Delbert's arm go up. I sounded the horn. I was sad to be leaving Delbert. I had grown to enjoy his company in the evenings along the beach, sharing cigarettes and conversation, until the stars appeared like guests. At the top of the driveway I stopped and reached into the backseat for *Trees of the World*. I opened it, removed Janet's card and tucked it in the sun visor.

BIRCH

CHAPTER TWENTY-EIGHT

I felt an immediate sense of freedom as I left the Bratts to grapple with the will and submission of boys becoming men. I was on my own, but with my liberty came uncertainty. I could see now that it wouldn't be easy to retrace the journey I had made with my mother and Grandpa Dunny, to step away from the life of comfort in Parry Bay. I had a lot of time to think as I waited for the ferry and then crossed the strait to the mainland. I began to doubt the very aim of my trip. My emotive declaration seemed lost somewhere in the complexities of my life. The profundity of loss had muted my battle cry. My mind conspired against me. I shook a little with panic.

The Bug came to know the way along the fertile flood plain and through the mountain passes where it had a hard time of it. Then the radio gave out. Led Zeppelin's "Black Dog" faded at mid-riff. I had to stop. Nothing made sense anymore. I pulled over at the Spuzzum Cafe and sat in the parking lot. Shadows from a tilted world rose steeply from the river smothering the sun. It was cool in the early afternoon and I felt stupid. It all seemed a mistake. It wasn't too late, I thought. I could turn around and be home before the sun went down. I could sit on the deck until Delbert came onto the beach for a smoke. We would talk about the *Albert Bigelow* and nuclear testing, music and the ways of loggers.

I got out, opened the hood and removed the sleeping bag. Then I got back into the car and set the bag on the seat next to me. I untied the drawstring and slowly unrolled it. My hand stopped when I felt the hard outline of the Colt. I was excited, but more fearful now. I could feel my heart beating in my ears. My hand found the pistol. I pulled it out. There was a box of shells and an envelope. Inside the envelope there was a note with a folded twenty-dollar bill.

> *Thought you could use some cash.*
> *Delbert*
> *I sat there with the gun out of sight between my legs. Everything felt wrong. My life felt wrong. What did I think I was doing? Was I going all the way to Saskatchewan just to pull up in front of the house and find him in the barn and shoot him in the head like he did the cats? Was that it? Could I do such a thing? I had wanted to, for so long.*

I put the gun back in the sleeping bag, rolled it up and retied the drawstring. Then I reached above my head for the card. Its corners were rounded and its colours were a little faded, but I could still see the pond, the trees, and the swans, and I could still read Janet's words. I was alone. I had no grandfather to guide me now, but I knew that I wouldn't have listened to him even if he had been there with me. Looking at the card calmed me. I went inside and bought a pop and a bag of chips. I could go on now.

The sun was going down over the Cariboo Mountains when I pulled into a cafe in Valemount. I sat at a table by the window and had a supper of french fries and gravy smothered in ketchup. The waitress watched me curiously as I ate. Then

- 212 -

she asked me if I wanted a cup of coffee when she came for the dirty plate. "Fresh pot," she said. I remembered when Grandpa Dunny started me on a morning cup. There was always a pot of coffee on the stove. He drank it all day long. I liked it because of the added years it seemed to give me. I turned my cup over in its dish.

"So where are you going?" she asked, pouring my coffee. She was an older woman with tired eyes who seemed to know I was just passing through. There was no one else in the cafe. It seemed I was her last customer before closing.

"I'm going to Saskatchewan," I said.

"Your family there?"

I was confused by the question. It was simple enough, but I couldn't affirm it. "No, I have a girlfriend," I told her.

"What's her name?" she asked.

"Janet," I said, creating a fiction to relieve a waitress of her boredom.

"Have you been apart long?"

"Since I was ten," I said.

She looked at me, puzzled. She was doing the math. "That's a long time," she said.

"Yeah, about seven years."

"Cute," she said. She wasn't impressed by my small measure of my honesty.

Some music played in the background, George Jones – "She Thinks I Still Care," a melancholy song that must have set her mood. There was someone in the back, a man about her age. She looked back once in a while. I didn't feel like staying much longer. She put the coffee pot back behind the counter and came back to my table. The top buttons on her blouse were undone. She leaned over.

"Would like anything else?" she asked me.

I caught myself looking into the milky mounds of her breasts, at the brassiere that cupped them. I had a stupid look on my face, but I didn't want whatever she was offering.

"No offense, but you're old enough to be my mother," I said as blunt as I dared.

"Oh, sonny, you know nothing."

"I know I'm just a kid."

"You were looking at me."

"Don't think so."

"All you young ones like your mother's titties."

"Can I have my bill?"

"Sure, why not. You were looking."

"No, I wasn't." I could see the cook watching us. He knew something was going on. He most likely had seen it before. He was big and I was nervous. I got up and fished for the twenty-dollar bill that Delbert had given me and gave it to her. I kept my head down as she went to the till and brought me my change. She didn't say anything more. I went out the door and ran to the Bug like a thief, as if I had stolen something. I was glad to see the cafe in my rear-view mirror. I wondered if that scene played out over and over in every small town. Did the happiness my mother wanted even exist?

I spent a fitful night curled up in my sleeping bag in the back seat at a rest stop outside of town, dreaming of that lady trapped like my mother in a life she didn't want. Finally the new day came, a pale glow over the Rocky Mountains. When you first come off the prairies the Rockies appear blue in the distance like something impenetrable. Coming out the other side, with the mountains looming behind me, the horizon at once fell in a heap to the earth and I felt again the impossible breadth of the sky.

I drove all day on the Yellowhead Highway, through Edmonton and into the afternoon where lean prairie towns were sewn into a grand tartan of shades and patterns of harvest. I had to stop for gas in Vermillion. I bought a tin of peanut butter, some raspberry jam, a loaf of bread and something to drink in the general store. I bought a butter knife for a quarter. Then I drove a few miles out of town and pulled off the highway where a few trees grew beside a picnic table. I made myself a sandwich, laying the jam down thick and licking the crusts where the jam leaked out. It wasn't much but it filled my belly. I sat at the picnic table and washed my supper down with a root beer. A grasshopper leapt onto the can of peanut butter. Then I lit a cigarette and watched cars go by.

With an hour or so before the sun went down, I walked a short distance out into the prairie. A warm wind began to move through the birches. Clouds were stacked along the prairie margins. Several prairie dogs watched me from their hills. A pair of hawks wheeled in the far sky. I stopped and stood in a space that I had forgotten. It seemed so quiet under that old blue dome. How strange to feel such stillness now. The top of my head felt light, spacious. I turned around and around wondering what had changed. I stood and watched the sun go down. I wondered if Delbert was sitting on the beach watching the same sun.

When the stars came out like chrome sparks against the cosmic vaults, the sky was familiar in its breadth and intensity. It was a piece of the universe that had belonged only to me, and always would. I looked long into the night sky until my neck ached and I had to turn away. It was getting cold. I needed to get back. I pissed with my back to the wind. I couldn't see the Bug. I turned in every direction. I saw only the stars and their infinite blinking. I was lost.

I walked out in every direction and back. No cars came down the highway. I lit a match and it quickly blew out. I stood wondering what to do. The wind rose and gusted, a tempest in my ears. I knew enough not to march out into the darkness. There were swales and ditches and ponds to get mired in. Then something appeared in the distance – the white trunks of the birches, the dull glow of bark. I leaned into the wind and fought toward them but I wasn't making any ground. There were no landmarks, only the trees, fixed, suspended in a dark dimensionless space. They could have been anywhere, far out into the prairie. But still I went to them with my eyes tearing. All at once the trees were near. Their branches clattered and I saw the unmistakable shape of the Bug.

I spent another cramped night in the back seat. In the early morning the sun fanned out over the prairie touching and warming everything without discrimination. It found me without the feeling in my legs. I hobbled out of the Bug. There was frost on the windshield, patterns of leaf blades and stems shrinking, melting. I put on a sweater and walked up and down the parking area until my legs felt right. There down the highway was Clavet. I thought I might be there by noon. The thought of my return now made me feel sick. I never had a plan. Behind me, I could feel the birch trees watching.

CHAPTER TWENTY-NINE

I remembered Dr. Mudd as I passed through Saskatoon. He had wanted to send me away to an institution for the mentally ill. I had buried the memory of the letter and what *he* thought of me. He agreed with my father that I was something to throw away. It's strange how things come back from unexpected associations – the shape of a building, a street or the bridge where my grandparents went over. My mother had wanted me to know the tragic story of my father's family.

South of Saskatoon a sign read: *Clavet – 2 miles.* It shocked me to see it. I had begun to think that I would be driving forever and never come to it. But there it was in the distance. I slowed the Bug and pulled over onto the shoulder. I wasn't feeling well. My stomach was nervous. I was surprised to see the trailer was still there along with the stairs where Janet used to sit. I could almost see her there, her little hand waving as we passed. There was a for sale sign in the front yard nearly obscured by tall grass. The trailer hadn't changed much. It had always looked sad. It seemed vacant now. No one could possibly live there, I thought. I turned back onto the highway and drove past it slowly, looking for Janet. I kept on going, knowing there was nothing to be found in that hurting place. I despaired at not seeing her. But how could I have believed that things would stay the same, that she meant what she wrote on the side of the wall and would be waiting for my return?

The only thing I could think of now was stopping at the Clavet general store. I was sure to get the lay of the land from Mrs. Daisy, if she was still there. I parked alongside the store facing the wall. It had been painted. There were bikes on kickstands and bikes lying in the gravel. Another generation of town kids and farm kids was riding to the store for cold pop and penny candy. I got out. The same flat light at noon. Butterflies rose from the ditches. Barn swallows perched on telephone lines while dragonflies hunted and hovered as they had done for a million years.

A dry heat filled my lungs as I took a long anxious breath before I went in. Inside I was greeted by a scene that seemed frozen in time. The water cooler that had been filled with pop had been replaced with a coin operated can dispenser and a magazine rack stood where the popsicle freezer used to be. Lazy Daisy was sitting on her stool behind the counter like she always did. She was heavier now and her hair all grey, but she still wore a patterned summer dress, covered with daisies of course. She was busy taking dimes and nickels from the local children. They turned away, happy with their treats and left the store.

She looked up and saw me standing there. I waited for her. I could see she was sorting through her files of kids who had passed through her store, the ones who left Clavet, the ones who grew up. Then her face lifted in recognition.

"Now, Calan Gray, is that you?" she said, her elbows resting on the counter.

I stepped forward tentatively. "Yeah," I said, "it's me."

"It has been a long time. Look at you – so tall."

I nodded. There were things I wanted to ask her.

"Well, what are you doing back here?"

"I thought I would just pay a visit."

She paused then. There were things that she wanted to ask me. "Sorry about your mother, Calan," she said. "That was a shock, at her age."

"Yeah." As the past leaked in, an awkwardness settled between us.

"Shame," she said.

I stood there wondering if I should say anything more about it, but there was nothing that I cared to add. Except for one thing. "What ever happened to that girl that lived in the trailer up the highway?" I asked.

"Oh, Janet Smith," she said with a frown. "She's still there with her mother."

"It looks like the place is for sale."

"The town had to take it over. Unpaid taxes. The mother had her legs amputated. That poor lady. They're putting her in a hospital in Saskatoon and she won't be coming back. Won't last till Christmas, they say. It's about time that they put an end to it, living like that. A sad thing to see that girl pushing her mother in a wheelchair down the highway. And looking after her all those years."

"Do you ever see her?"

"Janet?"

"Yeah."

"Well, she's been working part time at the hardware store all summer. She delivers feed and other supplies. Smart as a whip, that girl. She finished high school a year a head of her class. Tops in the province. Go on down there and see her. I remember that she was kind of sweet on you."

"Yeah, maybe," I said. It embarrassed me to hear it from Mrs. Daisy, but still it made me feel good. Then she looked away. I thought the conversation might be over, but there was something else on her mind.

"Are you thinking of visiting your father, Calan?" she asked carefully.

"Don't know for sure," I lied.

"There're things that you should know about him."

"Like what?"

"He's not a well man, your father. The Mounties have been over to Gray Farm more than once, I can tell you. Once he ran an unfortunate brush salesman off the property with a rifle. But there's something that might trouble you more. There's been a long-standing rumour that goes back to when your father was just a boy. Not many talked about it over the years. People wouldn't say anything about your father. They were afraid of him. So it was almost all forgotten. I tell you this now because of something my husband Roy learned not too long ago. He was visiting an old friend at the hospital, a retired policeman. He was dying and spilling everything he knew like he was making some kind of confession. He told Roy that Macklin Gray was no hero trying to save his sister from the frozen pond at the back of their farm. Her name was Ida, I remember that much myself. You probably know the story, Calan. Ida broke through thin ice when she was skating with your father one winter. It seems the policeman always suspected that your father never tried to save her, that he watched her drown and never did a thing. He said that where she went through wasn't too far from shore. He could have reached her with his outstretched hand. The water wasn't that deep. There were no tracks in the snow to show he had tried to reach her. It was the cold that did it. A child won't last long soaking wet. No one could prove any of it.

"You see, Calan, Ida was retarded. She was what they call a mongoloid child. The policeman said that he might have let her drown because of the shame back then. The Grays never talked about her. They kept her inside. Sometimes when they had to go to town, people would stare. That's what the policeman said. He said it wasn't losing Ida that drove the Grays to kill themselves. No, he suspected they feared what their son had done. That's what did it. And he was the policeman who pulled her out of the pond."

I was stunned by her account. It wasn't the story my mother had told me. His cruelty had begun so young. A couple came into the store and Mrs. Daisy took up another conversation with them. She always said too much. Then I heard her say, "that's Calan Gray," as I turned away and went out the door into the glare of the sun. Could it be true? It wasn't so hard for me to believe. It was awful to hear a story so chilling about your own father. It didn't make me hate him any more, as if hate had levels, as if there could be a hierarchy of loathing. Her story only reinforced what I thought he was – a sad excuse for a human being.

I drove down Main Street. It looked the same to me, but the grain elevators that loomed over the town were gone. A lone dog padded diagonally across the street. The town seemed deserted, stuck and immobile, everything muted and exposed. The hardware store was on a corner. I pulled down a side street and parked in the shade. I had a good view of the back of the store. Janet was standing in the back of a pickup truck tossing sacks around. I knew it was her. I recognized her wild hair. She was wearing jeans and what I imagined had once been a white t-shirt, now covered in dust and grime. I checked my face in the rear-view mirror and brushed my teeth with a finger before getting out of the Bug and sauntering over in her direction. I stopped now and then to look down the street and behind me, so that I could watch her. I began to worry. What if the whole thing was just my foolish fantasy after all, a story that I had been telling myself?

I worked my way to the building and hid around the corner. I wanted to run the other way. Then I bent down to pick up a penny that was lying in the gravel. I put it in my pocket. I was a mess. When I dared to peek around the corner of the building, she was standing in the truck bed, straddle-legged and staring down at me.

"What are you doing here?" she said straight out.

"Don't know for sure," I said like a moron. Standing there with my hands in my pockets, I looked up at her against the glare of the sky, her face in shadow.

"I thought I would never see you again," she said.

"Yeah, well…"

"Do you want something?"

"No."

"Then what?"

"I just came to see you."

"Don't think so."

"What do you mean?"

"You didn't come back just to see me, did you?"

"Uh…"

"Why would you?"

"I don't know."

"You came back to see your father."

"Maybe."

"I never thought you would."

"Why?"

"Just didn't. I know why you left. Everyone did."

"Yeah, I came back to see him. I'm not going to lie about it."

"So why did you come to see me?" She jumped down from the truck and walked right up to me.

Man, was she pretty. Her eyes were clear blue and her freckles were all but lost to the summer tan on her cheeks. I wanted to kiss her right there on the spot. Dirty shirt and all. "Because I wanted to thank you for the card," I said.

"Oh, yeah, I felt bad for you."

"I still have it."

"No way."

"It's in my car." I ran across the street to get it.

"Wow, you do have it," she said as I handed it to her. "I painted this, you know."

"Yeah, I thought you might have. I look at it all the time."

"You do?"

"I thought about you a lot."

"I didn't think you cared one bit about me."

"Well, I'm here, aren't I?"

"Then take me for a drive in your fancy car after I get off work."

"Sure."

"Meet me at my house. In about an hour."

"Okay."

"Calan Gray. Right here in front of me. You always did come slow to a water-hole." She flashed me a smile, then spun around and jumped back onto the truck.

Janet was all grown up and as bold as can be.

CHAPTER THIRTY

I didn't know where else to go so I drove up and down the streets. As I passed Clavet School I wondered about Philip and how he had managed the years given his limitations, if that's what they were. Then I drove east of town, pulled part way into a field and parked. Combines sat idle nearby, waiting. All about me the shifting grain and the dance of light in the fine heads. Yet my eyes were searching for the wild places, as if they knew the value of such things. In the distance I saw the green thickening of trees. They seemed to be a remnant of a time that I could never retrieve. I thought of Jules Bear and the past rushed in. I remembered the people and their songs in the trees. That day. Could it be I was parked on that very track that led to the bones of the cats – and beyond to Gray Farm?

The gun was still wrapped in my sleeping bag in the back seat. It was a tangible thing awaiting my orders. I remembered my thoughts of the inanimate objects that evening aboard the *Albert Bigelow*. I knew it wasn't the gun that does anything. It's the finger and the brain at the end of it. I supposed that logger was worried about both. I felt uneasy about going to the trailer. I had a heap of worries now that I just couldn't sort out. Janet posed no difficulties in my mind. I was worried by the things I could never tell her. Now that it was time to go, I sensed that she might be more than I could handle.

Her trailer always felt mysterious sitting there as if nothing in the world cared about it. I was even afraid of it, but I also knew it was not evil. I parked in the driveway. There was a bike leaning against the side of the trailer. As I got out of the Bug I heard the swish of long grass at my feet, an ocean sound that took me to Parry Bay for an instant then brought me back. I continued down the worn path to the front steps. A wheelchair ramp rose alongside the trailer. I knocked on the front door but my knuckles only grazed it. I rubbed my palms on the legs of my jeans while I worked on my nerve. Then I knocked again and Janet answered right away.

"Come in," she said, "I'll just be a minute."

"Sure," I said.

"Mom, it's Calan," Janet said then disappeared.

I stepped into a dark chamber with squares of light revealing windows, remote and inadequate. I could smell something stale, organic. Where was she? I could hear a television. My eyes adjusted to the room and there, before me in a reclining chair, sat a heavy woman in a housecoat. She had stumps for legs and there was a black cat on her lap. A wheelchair sat beside her. She looked up. I was startled to have her eyes leap at me like that.

"Hello, Calan, I knew that you'd be back."

"Hi," I said. I stuffed my hands in my pockets and waved with my elbows.

"Would you like to sit?"

"No thanks," I said, keeping a polite distance.

"Be right there," Janet called out from somewhere.

I could see the room now. The television sat in a corner and everywhere there were stacks of magazines and newspapers. A plant attacked a window, struggling for the light.

"Forgive the mess," Mrs. Smith said, "we don't have many

visitors. The nurse comes by most days but she's not really interested in us. She's a kind enough person, but I sense that I'm more of a job to her. I can tell she doesn't like to get close to people. I understand that. Likely she's seen a lot of death in her life. Poor dear. I suppose she can see mine coming around the corner." She laughed.

Janet came out. She was wearing a blue checked blouse. "You'll be okay for a while?"

"Just fine, dear, don't worry about me. I won't move."

"Funny lady," Janet said.

"The only way to be, don't you think so, Calan?"

"Yeah." A chuckle lost itself in my dry mouth. My tongue dammed my throat.

"So, what would you like for dinner, Mom?"

"Pork chops and onions would be nice tonight with mashed potatoes and corn. And mushroom gravy of course."

"Her favourite," Janet said.

"Off you go now," Mrs. Smith said. "Nice to finally meet you, Calan."

"Oh, yeah."

"Come on," Janet said, grabbing me by the arm.

She took me around to the back of the trailer. She held my hand. It was an astonishing moment to be conscious of, to be with a real girl in the real world and not just in my imagination. We came to a pond buzzing with insects. A muskrat with its slick mahogany back glided in the dark water. Black birds settled on the cattails and sang.

"Look familiar?" she asked me.

"Sort of."

"The card," she said.

"Yeah, look at that, the same trees."

"Birch," Janet said. "My mother calls them Lady of the Woods."

"Where're the swans?"

"They're here," she said. She turned to me, her smile fearless.

We went back to the Bug and drove out into the late afternoon. The end of summer was near and the prairie was dressed in its copper lamination. Janet knew of a place to stop that wasn't far out of town. We followed a dirt road until we came to a slow moving stream where willows ran thick over the water like a trellis. We parked, rolled the windows down and listened to the sounds of the earth.

"Is your mom dying?" I asked after a few minutes.

"Dying, who told you that? Oh, let me guess."

"I just thought…"

"No, she's not dying."

"Sorry."

"It's not your fault. She's been unable to walk since the accident. Her circulation is bad. She lost her legs. It's hard. But she does fine. We're going to lose the house, but she thinks it'll be better. Now she can go into a place that will look after her. She said, 'now you can have a life, Janet,'" her mother's voice rising easily to her lips.

"She seems kind of happy."

"There were so many people who were mean to us. I think they wanted us to leave Clavet. But she just met that with her will. That's what she taught me. I'm always amazed by her."

I listened to her, astonished by her clarity. It seemed that no one took the time to know her. When she stopped talking I still felt the lingering effect of her words. They settled over me warm and innocent.

"Have you ever been with a girl, Calan?"

"What do you mean?"

"Have you ever made out?"

"I don't know."

"You don't know?"

I had memories of that night with the Bratts. "Why are you asking me that?" I said dumbly.

"Well, we could make out."

"Like kiss you?"

"More if you want."

I looked around. There was no one for miles. I leaned over and kissed her. It wasn't a long kiss, but I liked the taste of her, the soft warm feel of her lips and the sweet smell of her skin as I pressed close to her. I wanted more of it so put my arm around her and kissed her again. The feel of her tongue shocked me.

"Have you ever made out?" I asked her.

"Ricky Olsen tried to get in my pants once when he was drunk. I wouldn't let him. Just because he was a good hockey player he thought I should do whatever he wanted."

"I never liked him much."

"You can feel my boobs if you want."

"Sure."

"We need to get in the back seat."

I didn't know what Janet was going to do next. It all came so easily for her while I felt cramped up inside doubting everything. Grandpa Dunny had never given me any instructions, but I did have the good sense to climb in the back seat with her.

She undid the buttons on her blouse, unhooked her bra and leaned back against the window. I thought I would jump out of the Bug and run madly out into the prairie, I was so excited. She was so willing and so natural. Her breasts waited for my eager hands. I suppose she knew I was shy and there was not enough time for me to get beyond just sitting there. When I saw her nipples I thought they were perfect. I remembered the waitress in Valemount. She knew that I would like nipples all right, but there was nothing motherly about Janet's. Janet in her nakedness was as pure and beautiful a creation as had ever existed for me. She was a woman-child offering her body to please me. I moved close to her so I could put my hand on her breasts and squeeze a little. But before I could touch them, she made a face.

"What's the matter?" I said.

"I just felt something hard," she said.

"Well…" I said.

"No, something behind me in the sleeping bag."

"That's just my book of trees."

Before I could do anything about it, she reached around and pulled the sleeping bag free. The gun fell out and thudded onto the floorboards.

"What's that?"

"A gun," I said. The mood changed.

"Why do you have a gun?"

"Just like to have it."

"I'm not touching it," she said.

I picked it up. "Nothing to be afraid of."

"Calan, tell me why you have it."

"No reason."

"You're turning red."

"I'm not."

"You are too."

"It's not a big deal."

"Then why won't you tell me?" She put her bra back on, buttoned her blouse and climbed into the front seat.

"There's nothing to tell you."

She turned to me and something in her eyes cut through my armour and my bullshit. "Tell me that it's not about your father."

I sat in the pool of my invention, the story I had told myself, that I needed to redress the things that *he* did. I could never fool Grandpa Dunny and now there was not a chance that I could lie to Janet. I could feel her moving away, the wonder she had offered me unsteady now and about to topple, collapse.

"He killed my mother and my grandpa," I told her like a confessional. "He wrote me letters, short insane notes, challenging me to come back. I don't know why, maybe to finish me off. He hates me more than anything. And I hate him. And I'm not going to let him hurt me anymore. No more."

"You came back to kill him?"

"It's not that simple."

"You have a gun, Calan. He's dangerous. Everyone knows it."

"Yeah, I have a gun. I know what it can do."

"Do you? What about the rest of your life?"

"Sometimes I don't care."

"You can go back. Leave right now."

"Can't."

"You can just let it go."

"That's what my Grandpa Dunny always said."

"It's true."

"I heard that he let his little sister drown. He's no good."

"I heard the story too. My mom thinks that there's always more to a story."

I thought about what she had said, the story surrounding her mother. "What more could there be?"

"The car accident that killed my father also killed my little brother. It left my mother paralysed. I was unhurt. Why was that? Perhaps I was spared to look after her."

"Didn't know about your brother."

"There's always more."

I hesitated, then told her something I had never told anyone else. "I had this thing. I could talk to trees. I could hear them. My father thought that I was crazy. The hate in his eyes when he would look at me. He was going to send me away. Get rid of me like garbage."

"Nothing weird about talking to trees."

"You don't think so?"

"My mother talks to the Lady of the Woods. When we almost lost the trailer to a grass fire, she thought that the trees protected us somehow."

"What?" I remembered that day from long ago.

"You know, she prays a lot. Not in a religious way. She told me that after she almost died in the accident, there was nothing for her to be afraid of anymore."

"I don't know. Do you believe her?" I had my doubts. There was something to fear in the empty space of prairie.

"We have to go. Want to stay for dinner?"

"Sure, I love pork chops."

"No, no pork chops," she said. "We always talk like that. It's a game we play. I'll open a can of soup."

"All right." I climbed back into the front seat. She was looking at me.

"What are you doing, Calan Gray?"

"I don't know," I said with my head down.

We drove back to the trailer. There was little talk between us. In that brief time by the stream she had me think about what I was doing, so plain, a quality she had that seemed made for me. I remembered the day when I prayed to the trees to watch over her. I remembered the time when I lived among the shiver and tremble of leaves. Now I wondered if all was lost.

CHAPTER THIRTY-ONE

It was hot in the trailer. I lay on the worn out sofa in the front room with the cat. I couldn't sleep. Janet gave me a thin sheet after she helped her mother to bed. She knelt down beside me and told me that life could end at any time. It didn't matter how old you were, she said. I knew she was disappointed in me, but she didn't try to talk me out of going to Gray Farm. Lying in the dark I knew that there was no going back. My return was moving me where I needed to go. I had found more love and honesty in that confined trailer than in the fine urban house of the Bratts.

When I left in the morning the trailer was cool and Janet and her mother still asleep. As I went out the door the cat purred as it arched against my leg. I drove into the waking prairie, heading east past Clavet, stopping, starting, remembering until the absolute burn of my journey forced me to stop and heave my sour belly into a grassy swale. Somehow I managed to get back in the Bug. I reached over into the backseat for the sleeping bag and removed the gun. I loaded it and put it under the seat.

I crept by the Olsen farm. There was someone near the barn. They were our closest neighbours, but they might just as well have lived in another country. I felt no need to renew our acquaintance. No dust kicked up from the dirt road as I drove on. Nothing announced an approaching visitor, salesman or returning son. Gray Farm seemed remote and isolated. It was insubstantial against the horizon and not a home I ever thought I would return to.

I turned down the driveway and saw the white house and the barn behind it as well as Grandpa Dunny's shack. The poplars that had been sick were now tall and green, their high limbs slowly swaying in the prairie breeze. I crawled along the drive in low gear, alert and watchful. I turned at the house and there he was, bent over a stack of wood, an axe in his hand and a length of wood on a block. The devil himself rose up in front of the car. I had never imagined to find him so suddenly and so disadvantaged. I braked. My foot came off the clutch. The car lunged and stalled. He stood not ten feet away from me, his fierce, distrusting eyes boring into me like the hauntings he had visited upon me in my dreams.

He had his shirt off and was covered in a sheen of sweat. I was shocked by his appearance. He was unshaven. His eyes looked driven back into his skull. His body was emaciated, his once imposing muscles reduced to ropes under a taut hide of skin. He drove the axe into the block and reared back as he tried to account for the unknown entity before him. All at once his eyes widened as he recognized who it was. He started toward me. I reached under the seat for the gun but my fingers couldn't find it. I opened the door and faced him for the first time in seven years.

My skeletal father came barely up to my shoulders. He looked me up and down. He was so close I could smell his smoky breath. He seemed like a creature outlawed from the world. I wasn't so much afraid now as shaken by the muted cadaver of the man he had become. What illness was consuming him? I wondered. Yet his fists were rolled hard and the veins in his slick forearms stood out like twisting blue cords.

"What are you doing here?" he asked with that same meanness that was always thick in his voice.

The answer was not so simple as I stood there, his eyes on me like a hand rising up against my throat. "Thought I would come by," I said.

He looked. "You've grown some."

"Yeah, that's what everyone's been telling me."

"You can drive."

"Yeah." He didn't think it was possible.

"You have no reason to come back, boy. You left for good."

"There're things that I need to do."

"You'll find no answers here."

"I'm not looking for answers."

"Yeah, well you sure the hell are standing here aren't you?"

"Yeah, I'm here."

"If you came back to show me how big a man you are, then get to it."

"Get to what?"

"Maybe you want to hurt me."

"I've thought of that."

"Go ahead. It don't matter much. I'll be dead soon."

He looked nearly dead already with his pants falling off of him and the end of his belt lolling like a dog's tongue. "What's wrong with you anyway?" I said.

"Nothing at all, the doctors tell me. No sickness they could find. Still my weight has been falling off me for three years. Soon there'll be only bones while the doctors say that I'm fit as a fiddle."

He was about used up. Every bone in his body pressed against his skin as if they were caging something that was trying to escape. I didn't feel sorry for him. "You wrote me those letters."

"That's a fact."

"Why would you do that?"

"Is that what brought you here?"

"Part of it."

"I had nothing good to say. You all left me here. You weren't going to say a word."

"Why bother to write then?"

"I didn't know what else to do."

"You wanted me to come back, didn't you?"

He turned and walked over toward the barn. His shirt hung on a nail on the open door. His back to me now. "You were going to send me away, old man!" I shouted out to him.

That stopped him, my accusation jerked him back. He stood there in a half-turn, glaring at me contemptuously through the corner of his eyes. Then he turned away and continued on into the barn. There was no time now. I knew what he was about to do, what he had wanted all along. Everything he had wished for was falling into place. I turned back to the Bug, flung open the door and reached under the seat. I took the gun firmly in my hand, the loaded pistol, following his every wish, ready now and willing to shoot him dead.

I strode across the yard to the barn with the gun, my arm stiff with the lethal authority of it. I stopped at the barn door. The light from the sun projected the shadowy shape of the doors onto the straw floor. Sparrows chirped. Their wings ruffled in the rafters. I raised the gun and held it with both my hands. He walked out from the shadows into the light. I cocked the gun. He froze, staring into the barrel of Hoot Larsen's Colt .22. I was defending myself, my life. It would be a mercy killing. I would rid the world of the poison running cold inside of me. I would shoot Gray Farm in its foul heart. My finger found the cold curve of the trigger. All at once his hand came up. He wiped his chest and arms with a cloth cleaning off the sawdust and sweat.

"You weren't right in the head, boy," he said bluntly. "The doctors said it plain."

"I'm not retarded," I told him, "they were wrong. My mother and my grandpa cared. That's why we left."

"They shouldn't have done that."

"My grandpa died because of you. I swear…!"

"He was a fool."

"I loved him!"

He laughed, mocked me with the gun waving in his face. "What do you know?" he sneered.

"I know that you didn't deserve her." I was crying now, the gun uncertain in my hands. "You shouldn't have hurt her. She just wanted to be happy. You bastard, you ruined it all!"

"Put the gun down," he said in that commanding tone that I remembered. "You know nothing."

"I know that you let your sister die."

"What did you say?" His eyes flared. He cocked his head, measuring me, calculating, preparing to meet me.

"Don't you fucking move!"

"What do you know?"

"The newspaper called you a hero. But you just watched her die."

"No."

"You know it's true."

"No."

"The policeman said so before he died. He said you let her drown. A little girl."

"That's not what happened."

"He said you made it all up. Your mother and father knew what you did. They knew it. That's why they killed themselves. Admit it, you fucking, pathetic bastard. Say it or I'll shoot you right here. Just like you shot the cats. You're dying because of what's inside you!" I beat him down, pummelled him with the truth, smashed him and drove him back.

"No, no," he said shaking his head. "No, he's lying. You better watch your tongue with me, boy!"

"You'll listen to me now. It was murder to let her die like that. She was handicapped. I know it's true. You don't deserve to live…"

He dropped the cloth, fell back against a post and folded inward. He slid down, his face twisted, his teeth bared. He clutched his heart. His eyes rolled back into their vacant pits and it seemed that death was going to take him without my bullet. He writhed on the dirt floor like something alien that could not live in the world. He lay on his side, his knees drawn up to his chest. I lowered the gun and watched his last breaths, waiting for his end. An unlikely, mournful sound like a whimper came from his lips. Tears from his eyes. I came nearer and stood over him, wary of any deceit he might contrive. I felt nothing but my fury, my retribution. I turned for the door and the sun. I wanted to leave it all behind now, to walk away from his grave, the tomb of Gray Farm.

But I didn't take a step. His hand reached out and grabbed the cuff of my jeans. He wailed and the sound echoed against the walls. It was seized by the high ceiling and thrown back down, hollow and dire. He wouldn't let go. He had never held me so without rage or violence. Then I heard something in the distance – no words, but a muted remembering. *There is more.*

I knelt down. There was dirt in his mouth and bubbles of mucus. He was helpless, a human being who needed my help. I looked at him, trying to find what it was that I feared. Where did he keep it? Could it be cut out with a knife? I had to do something. In all the years that I had imagined this moment, I was always the victor. I would make him sorry for what he did to my mother and my grandpa. I would make him sorry for ever laying a hand on me. I would see him bleed. Yet I put the gun down and picked him up like a child in my arms.

He didn't weigh much. I carried him out of the barn, across the yard and into the house. The kitchen was silent and hollow without my mother's hands and her longing gaze out the window. I carried him into his bedroom and laid him down on his bed. His open eyes watched me.

"I could call the doctor," I said.

He shook his head and turned away from me. He was filthy. He smelled. His fingernails were black and untrimmed like claws.

"I'll run you a bath," I said.

He turned to wave me off with his hand. I wondered if he had had a stroke or something. He didn't seem capable of speech. I stood in the bedroom I had never been allowed to enter. There was a picture of my mother on a night table. She had slept beside him in another life. My rage left me. I was going to kill him. I hated him and he hated me. And there we met, with our grievances and our stories – our wounds and our pain.

I removed his boots and his socks. A heavy stench rose up foul and strangling. I left him there on the bed. There was nothing more for me to do at Gray Farm. I walked out into the yard and realized my error. I should have stayed away. Then I went out behind the barn experiencing a certain freedom that I couldn't explain. The trail to the aspens was overgrown. The grasses blew in slow waves as far as I could see. Across the ditch the fields were planted and ripening. The prairie farm a perfect illustration of its type. But eyes could see the family who had lived there once and even that picture was an illusion. I had to turn back because I was getting lost in the sad memories of what might have been. There was nothing that I could undo or fix. There were no remedies now, but regret came, unbidden, incomplete and irreconcilable. Why did I feel such guilt?

I returned to the barn, retrieved the gun and crossed the yard. I got back in the Bug, unloaded the pistol and slid it under the seat. It could have gone off, I thought. My hands were shaking. He would be dead and I would never see Janet again. I turned the key. The engine rattled and started and I sat there watching butterflies, swallows and grasshoppers clicking in the gravel. I looked in the rear-view mirror. I saw my likeness as if I were someone in an old photograph. I turned the engine off. A wind came hurtling down the driveway. The lombardy clapped their leaves as if pleased by such arrivals. Dust rose, spun and moved on.

CHAPTER THIRTY-TWO

I stood by the door. He was asleep. I wondered what had happened to him. Was he sick with fever or madness? Macklin Gray prone like that, perhaps for the first time in his life. In the stillness I could hear his breathing. A fly at the window hit the glass over and over, desperate for escape. I went over, opened the window and it flew out.

I left my father sleeping and went upstairs to my old room, my footsteps like a signature in the creak of the stairs. The room was untouched. My Roughriders pennant grey with dust. It seemed that a boy was away and all was in order for his return. I never had more than a few toys growing up – books with stories of animals and ancient times when knights fought evil and castles guarded a labyrinth of rooms and passages, of times when Kings rewarded the journeys of sons with gold. I lay down on the bed. How strange to think that it was still mine. I listened to my heartbeat and the sounds of the house against the wind, the whistling through the eaves and the strain of wood holding fast to the earth. I fell asleep.

I dreamt that I was aboard the *Albert Bigelow* in the middle of a vast and infinite sea. Janet was with me and we had sailed to stop a bomb. Soon the *Albert Bigelow* was no longer a boat but a canoe, yet still we sailed on. Then the canoe vanished beneath us and we swam until we reached the shores of Parry Bay. Then the bay turned into the prairie, the tall trees turned to willows and we flew without wings over places that I did not recognize. Then Janet was gone and I was alone. I searched but I couldn't find her. I awoke and broke the sadness of my dreams.

It was late. I went to his room and stood by the door, safe at the periphery, at the edge of his life. He was still sleeping. I listened for his breaths and looked for the rise of his chest to make sure. Then I covered him with a blanket. I thought I could leave now. All he needed was rest. I was hungry and went into the kitchen to find something to eat. There were eggs in the fridge and a block of cheddar cheese with green mould and a bottle of milk. I could make an omelette, I thought. But then I couldn't stop thinking of him. How could I just leave him and then sit down and eat his food? I resented him now in a new way. I considered what the man deserved in his life and debated the merits of indifference. I turned to the telephone on the counter and saw a phone book on the shelf below it. I had to call someone. Janet answered.

"It's Calan."

"Where are you?"

"At Gray Farm."

"So everything is cool?"

"Sort of."

"What happened?"

"Well, we had a fight. I think he had some kind of breakdown."

"Is he all right?"

"I put him in his bed. He's been sleeping all day."

"You sound worried."

"Kind of. He hasn't been looking after himself. He's covered in dirt. He hasn't washed in a long time."

"He might need someone to look after him."

"Yeah, probably."

"So help him."

"He needs a bath."

"Then bathe him."

"You're not much help."

"You might not want him to be your father, Calan, but he is."

"I never thought that I would have to do this."

"I know."

"Yeah, anyway…"

"You can do this, Calan. If he needs a doctor then you have to take him."

"I don't know."

"You shouldn't have come back."

"I had to."

"Well, did you find what you came for?"

"You're angry."

"Just look after him."

"Sure," I said.

She hung up.

How could I have thought that she would say anything different? I sat down at the kitchen table and felt the light falter outside. Isolation pressed in against the walls. The twilight of coming darkness sifted in through every crack and sill. The house seemed impotent. There was nothing to counter it, no music or laughter, and no family sharing their willingness to hope. Why did I come back? The simplicity of Parry Bay and the beach with its mysteries and the not so perfect Bratts seemed far away and irretrievable. What had I done?

Out of the bleak and silent space came a voice so unrecognizable and strange that I jumped to my feet to see what intruder was about. I turned on the kitchen light. Then it came again – a plea from his room.

Ida, don't tell. Don't tell.

I didn't want to go in there, to see him with his fits and delusions. I waited in the hallway, listening, fearful now, peering into the darkness where he lay. I flicked on the hall light. Then I went around the house turning on all the lights and lamps. I found the radio and turned it on – a country station playing Merle Haggard. Then I returned and stood outside his room with "Mama Tried" behind me.

I went into the dim room, without definition in a colourless haze. I stepped up to his bedside. His eyes were open. He looked up at me and I pulled back. I turned on the night table lamp. I could smell him. Then his lips parted to speak it seemed, but he said nothing.

"I'm going to run you a bath," I said. His eyes leaped upon me in that troublesome way – as if looking for answers or things to blame and rail against. Yet he made no gesture to deter me.

I went to the bathroom down the hall and filled the bathtub. There was grime in the sink and splatters on the mirror. The bar of soap in a dish seemed like a rock petrified from disuse. A threadbare towel with streaks of dirt like bear markings on a tree hung on a rack. I used it to clean the mirror, and the sink and faucets. In the hall closet I found a facecloth and a clean towel and set them near the bathtub. Then I returned to his room and removed his blanket.

"You have to get undressed," I said. He just looked at me. I was getting used to him not answering. I took his silence for agreement. Then his hand came up. He wanted me to leave the room. I waited in the hallway and could hear him getting out of his clothes. "Just throw them out here," I said. "They need to be washed…or burnt."

I could tell by his breathing that it was a struggle for him. I heard his belt hit the floor and then nothing. I waited. "Can you do this on your own?" I asked. He said something and I moved to the door. He was sitting slouched and naked on the edge of the bed. A fine dark hair covered his back and torso. Then he turned to me slowly and painfully, a man fraught with his humiliation.

"Boy, I can't get up," he said weakly.

"Then I'll help you," I said. He could talk at least now, but still there was a part of me that preferred him mute.

"Don't touch me," he said.

I knew that he meant it, so I remained at the door. Then I asked him again. "I can help you if you let me. There's a hot bath waiting for you. I think it'll make you feel better."

"You did this," he said.

"I'm not so sure about that," I answered boldly.

He looked at me. He could still scowl like a mean son of a bitch.

"I'll do it," he said.

But he just sat there. "Tub's getting cold," I said.

Then his hand came up like he was stopping traffic.

"I'll call the doctor," I said. "I'm sorry." I turned away, went down the hall a few paces and then I heard him calling me back as I knew he would. His stubborn declarations were failing him now.

"All right," he said.

He was grim as I led him to the bathroom, tasting a vulnerability that he had never experienced before. He wobbled and held my arm. His fingertips dug into me as he hung on.

"Don't you look at me like that," he said as I helped him into the tub.

His back and buttocks had festered with sores. His body was breaking down. I noticed the inflamed skin of his groin, raw and red. He settled into his bath. In the bright light of the bathroom, I could see the hollows and shadows eating away at him and the premature threads of silver in his hair. He shuddered there in the water and ripples ran out against the porcelain.

"You can leave," he said.

He covered his private parts with his hands, cupping his embarrassment. I put the facecloth and soap on the edge of the bathtub. "I could make you some supper," I said. "You're probably hungry. I could eat something myself." I noticed that the water had turned grey already.

"What would you make?"

"Eggs."

"Scrambled."

"You don't have much in the fridge."

"Scrambled," he said angrily, "I like them scrambled!"

"You're not an easy patient," I said. "I can see that you would be hell on doctors."

"Never asked you to come here."

"I'm not so sure now."

"You've got quite a mouth. And you need a haircut."

"It's the way I like it."

"Go on, leave me to my bath."

"You're not going to drown if I go into the kitchen?"

"I just might."

"And then I would have to save you and I'd burn the eggs."

"You're a smart ass."

"I don't mean to be."

"I'll take my eggs in the morning," he said.

"I'm hungry now."

"I have no appetite for food at this hour."

"I think you could use something to eat."

"Damn it, boy, why are you doing this to me?"

"Doing what?"

He looked straight ahead, his head shaking slightly. He grew tired with the conversation. He wasn't amused with the way I spoke to him. No one had ever said a disrespectful word to his face. Yet now he seemed to recognize that I wasn't the same kid who had wilted under him those years before. Nothing was the same. It seemed to me that no amount of scrubbing would make him clean. I was not so sure why I stayed. I never took pity on him for the malady that had a hold on him. His legacy was violence and abuse, and he was so fouled by it that I wondered if he would dissolve, the hot water rendering him down until he drained away.

CHAPTER THIRTY-THREE

In the morning, I carved the mould from the cheddar cheese with a kitchen knife. There were eight eggs in the carton and I used them all, cracking them open and spilling their yolks into a buttered frying pan. The bottle of milk was thick and sour and I poured it down the sink. I had to work the sludge down the drain with the handle of a wooden spoon. The coffee was perking on the stove.

I had heard him again in the night. After his bath I towelled him dry, walked him to his bedroom and helped him into his pajamas and into bed. He fell asleep right away. Soon there were voices coming from his room. I tried to sleep but I kept listening for him. He was calling out his sister's name as if he were trying to reach her from that dreaming place. Did she answer him? What would she say to a brother who had let her die like that? All night he petitioned her. And as I lay in my bed, I couldn't help but think of what guilt he had lived with.

I left the eggs to simmer after I stirred them well, then I added slices of cheese. I went out into the garden. Robins were running out on the lawn, tilting their fine heads as if to hear the sounds of the unwary worms. There was nothing planted where my mother had kept perfect rows of peas and beans, but there was an onion among the weeds, a survivor of an ordered world. I cut its green tops and went back into the kitchen. I chopped them up and sprinkled them over the cheese, added salt and pepper and covered the pan with a lid. Then I set the table. I didn't know why I fussed like that. It was not the anticipation of hot food that made me take such care. It was something else and it confused me. I felt mortified when I called him to breakfast. I had betrayed my mother and grandpa.

He came into the kitchen on his own and sat down at his plate heaped with scrambled eggs. He was wearing his house-coat — a faded tartan that I remembered. I could tell right away that he was more sullen than usual, his mouth pulling at his rough face. I had a sense of where things would go now. I was going to leave. I saw no point in staying any longer. I had lost any feeling for him long before that day.

We ate in intractable silence, aware of each other's presence. There seemed to be nothing between us that was salvageable. He began to lift his head to look at me, a fleeting suggestion that talk might begin. But then he would go back to his eggs. He did that until his plate was clean. When he stirred his coffee and raised his cup to his lips there was a tremor in his hand. He put the cup down and looked away. There was something on his mind but he just couldn't say it. His silence was becoming unbearable.

"I'm leaving today," I told him. "I have to get back to school."

He looked at me like it didn't matter. Why would it?

"Jules Bear is coming to get the wood," he said at last. "I wonder if you could finish splitting it. Birch splits well. Burns fast and gives off a fair heat."

"Yeah, I could do that," I said. I was surprised to hear that Jules Bear still came around. The idea that I might see him lifted me now. And there was something else. He had asked me to cut the wood. He didn't tell me to do it.

"Who taught you to cook like that?" he said.

"My grandpa."

He nodded, his unlikely recognition. "Regular school?"

"Yeah, regular school," I said, nothing more, told him none of the details of the useless trades that I had no interest in.

He seemed to think about that for a minute. Then he finished his coffee, got up from the table and left the kitchen. I watched him leave, the sound of his footsteps unremarkable now.

I cleaned up the dishes, went out into the yard and began on the wood. He was right about the birch. It split easily and clean and I tossed the split pieces onto a pile. I worked into the late morning. The heavy work felt good. Sweat teared at the end of my nose. I wiped it with the back of my hand. The sun was hot and I lost myself in the rhythm of the axe. There was no yesterday or tomorrow, only the rise and fall of steel and the thud and crack of wood – muscle and leverage and gravity – the singular movement of the woodcutter's dance.

When I was done I was pleased with my work. I looked at the pile of split birch and the blisters ripped and weeping on the palms of my hand. Then I turned. I knew he was watching me but I didn't know how long he had been standing on the porch. He had that tormented look again. I walked over to the porch and sat on the steps.

"Not used to hard work," he said, noticing my hands.

"I worked on a Nootka war canoe this summer," I told him.

"War canoe?"

"Yeah, I carved an eagle for it."

"You like the coast." He sat down on a chair and lit a cigarette.

"I've never seen such life. I would like to buy my grandpa's house one day."

"How would you do that?"

"Don't know. I'm a pretty good artist."

"I was calling out in my sleep last night."

"Yeah." I felt foolish now at my eagerness to tell him something about myself.

"That old policeman telling a story like that. Why do people suddenly want to tell the truth when they know they're dying? It's something all right."

"Just what I heard."

"No one ever said that to me before."

"You don't have to say one way or the other."

"But I'm the only one who can say."

"I suppose."

"I've been holding onto that day like a rolled fist in my belly. I've been holding on tight and praying it wouldn't leak out."

"You don't have to tell me about it."

"I don't want to. But it's leaking out."

"You can tell it."

"How does a man tell it?"

"Just say it."

He leaned forward, rested his elbows on his knees and took a long drag on his cigarette. "Damn," he said, "damn it all. Oh, I was mad that day. I always had to look after her. Since my brothers died in the war, it was left to me. Ida was a handicapped girl. I had to be with her all the time. Even when we went to town. I was ashamed to have a sister like that. The kids made fun of me. I could never have anyone over to the house. So when I had to take her skating on the pond, well, I made quite a fuss about it. I was angry and confused by the war, by Leonard and George never coming back. Gray Farm wasn't the same. I told her about the ice. Told her again and again. She understood. But she would always tell me that my face was hot knowing that it would make me madder.

"When she went through I heard the crack and her gasp when she hit the cold water. I skated over to her. She was under the ice. I just stared down at her thinking, no more Ida if I didn't do a thing. And I didn't. It's shameful that I did that. She never hurt a flea. And after it I felt like I had a dead girl living inside me my whole life. A father shouldn't have to tell his son a story like that. What kind of man am I? Don't you carry on with such a thing, boy. I've seen your anger. I suppose that's what I taught you. And I'm sorry for it. Damn you all for leaving me. But I don't blame you. No. I've done it, son. I've done it all and can't get nothing back. Not a thing." He got up and went back in the house.

I saw tears running down his cheeks, perhaps unloosened now for the first time, a man confessing his shocking crime, the world spinning compassionless in his eyes. I was like him. I began to understand. Me with a gun in my hand, a boy staring down through the ice. I sat on the steps long after he went in. I felt such sorrow. Could everything be forgiven?

I went to the barn and took his shirt down from the door. His clothes needed washing and I thought that I could do that before I left. I wasn't sure how his washing machine worked, but I would figure it out. In the barn I noticed a tarp covering something. It had wheels. Curious, I pulled the tarp back and exposed the Ford Country Squire sitting in the darkness. Perhaps it was his last new car, something that he wanted to preserve. How it used to glide down the highway while my mother and I talked until she would look off into the distance. I put the tarp back. There was something else I had to see.

Grandpa Dunny's shack was locked and I looked in through a window. Cobwebs and dust covered everything. I found it sad to see it now. How could I look into that space without remembering my grandpa's exclusion from the house? But I could remember what was good – the nights around the campfire drinking wine with Delbert and always Grandpa's wisdom. Even my mother, laughing with her sisters on Cedar Hill Road was a memory that I would keep forever, a vision of her joy.

I walked out to the edge of the field and stood under the

noon sun. I thought about the aspens in the distance. I stood there listening for them. They were coming. Yes, they were coming now. Had I returned to hear them – the language of trees that I had forgotten? Had I come back to remember, to listen to their unspoken truths, to rediscover that there is always more?

I ran my father's clothes through the washing machine and through the ringer without getting my fingers jammed. Then I took them out onto the porch and pinned them to the clothesline the way my mother had. His clothes hung wet and solitary. Even they seemed sad.

A truck pulled up alongside the stack of birch. It was Jules Bear. He got out and saw me coming across the yard with my big grin. He met me, placed his great hands on my shoulders and looked up into my eyes.

"How you have grown," he said. "I knew you'd be back."

"I never thought I would," I said.

"There are things at work that we can never know."

"Yeah, it seems that way."

"It is good to see you, Calan." He smiled with depth and sincerity.

Then I noticed the pipe in shirt pocket – and I remembered the day our train pulled away from him. "I'll help you load the wood," I said.

"That would be good."

We pitched the wood into the back of his pickup truck. His movements were slow, steady, unhurried, measured. He was heavier now with lines cut deeper into his skin. He seemed to come out of the earth, as if his feet had roots.

"I didn't think that you would ever be back at Gray Farm," I said.

He stopped and turned to me. "Sometimes men become friends forever," he said. "Nothing can change it. It is that way between us. We share our pain. We do that with another so that we might suffer less."

"He didn't blame you?"

"For a while, he was angry. Now he is tired. I can see that he has given up. When a man gives up on life, life will give up on him. He will die. It is good that you came back. I prayed that you would."

"I didn't come back out of kindness."

"But you came back. Sometimes kindness hides. But it is there."

"He told me about his sister Ida – the day she drowned."

"He never told me. I always thought that he might. But I just left it alone with him."

"He might now."

Jules returned to the pile.

"I'm leaving in a while," I said.

"You have a life somewhere."

"Yeah."

"With your grandpa."

"He died."

"I'm sorry. He knew me. And when I smoke his pipe, I know him."

"I miss him."

"He lived long but your mother had a short life. And I am sorry for that too."

We pitched wood in silence, honouring our memories. Then I looked off into the distance, a prairie habit. There was something that I hadn't noticed before. There seemed to be no preparation for the harvest. The combine was idle behind the barn.

"The wheat will be coming off soon," I said.

"The Olsens farm it now," Jules said. "Your father has not farmed for a few years. He rents the field. Ole wants it for his sons. He will not let me on it now. I come by and bring your father groceries. We smoke and watch the prairie dying red in the evenings."

Soon the wood was piled high in the back of Jules' truck.

"I give thanks to the birch for this wood," he said. "I will go see him now."

"All right."

"Do you still hear the trees?" he asked me.

I turned toward the north and the wind came down into the yard. I could feel something moving me now, pushing me away from Gray Farm. "Yeah," I said, "it's time to go."

"The earth is always speaking. But you have always known this."

"It's hard to hear it sometimes."

"We do not end at our bodies and trees do not end at their trunks. Yes, when we are not listening, we hear little."

He brought his hand up. I took it firmly and looked into his dark eyes.

"Do not forget that girl," he said to me.

"I won't," I told him.

He walked away and stepped up onto the porch. Then he stopped and turned back to me. He stood there for a moment as if to make it a gift, a perfect memory of him. I would never forget his final words to me. It was the last time I would see Jules Bear.

CHAPTER THIRTY-FOUR

I left Gray Farm without saying anything to him, leaving the way Grandpa Dunny, my mother and I had left all those years ago. He had given us little choice then. Now I was leaving on my own terms. More words were pointless. The world, it seemed, reared up and settled all accounts. I felt relieved, satisfied that I had met him evenly and that I no longer had a need to punish him with my thoughts or dark imaginings. And as I passed the house I turned to look one last time. In the window something moved. Perhaps it was just a reflection of the lombardy with the afternoon wind full in their high crowns. I could not be certain that he watched me, that he felt moved at last to see me leave. If he had regrets, then they would die with him.

I turned onto the dirt road with my windows down, my left elbow perched as if I were a veteran of the open road. Driving along the Olsen farm, I couldn't help but feel resentment for their claims on Gray Farm. Still I knew that my father couldn't farm the fields without Ole Olsen and his sons who thought the world was for their taking. I could see Bobby and Ricky with their father standing near the house. I became so upset at the thought of Ricky Olsen touching Janet that a certain chivalry began to rise within me and tempted me to pull into their driveway. I managed to let go of the impulse and moved on.

As I passed the Clavet General Store I hoped that Janet would be home. I would not give Lazy Daisy the satisfaction of the smallest measure of news for her gossip. I stopped by the trailer. Janet's bike was gone. I knocked on the door. There was no answer. I waited. Perhaps her mother couldn't come to the door on her own. So I called out.

"It's Calan."

"She's at the hardware store, Calan," she answered through the door.

"Thanks," I said. I felt bad for her until I remembered her spirit, how she met her life.

"Thank you for coming by," she said.

"You're welcome," I said, but the phrase sounded odd in my ears. It felt as though I had been thanked for nothing at all.

I headed back to the hardware store and parked on the side street. The truck wasn't there. I went inside and the clerk behind the counter told me that Janet was out on her deliveries and that she would be back in two hours depending on how the day went. I stood there dumbly wondering what to do. I wanted to go, get away. Then I noticed cans of spray paint on a stand beside me. I picked up a can of green paint and turned it over in my hand as if it had a message for me. I bought it and a can of white paint.

Now I had to stop at the Clavet General Store, not to buy anything, but to do the only thing that I could think of. I got out of the Bug, took the cans of spray paint and shook them. I had one opportunity to get it right. I turned the image of what I wanted over in my mind. Then I opened the lids and walked up to the blank wall on the side of the store.

I took the green paint and sprayed on birches and the outline of the pond, then I took the white paint and added the swans and the trunks of the trees. I used the paint to add depth and shading. I stood back to admire it. I liked the green of the trees, the glow of the swans on the water. I tried to picture Janet coming by on her bike and seeing it there. I wondered what it would mean to her. I hoped that she would understand.

Back on the Yellowhead highway I felt only the wind in my hair, the rushing landscape and the Beetle full out at fifty miles per hour. The sorry battering of bugs against the windshield made me think of the nature of things, of how nothing lasts forever. It seemed that life was a mystery, a puzzle with pieces fitted and lost, misplaced and recovered.

I felt that I had lost Janet. I could not handle the reality of her. I began to fantasize like I had before in the safety of my empty imagining. I dreamt how it would be one day when I was out along the beach in Parry Bay. I would turn slowly to see someone in the distance, a girl in a long dress with the breezes touching her. All at once she would dance and twirl and I would watch her as one might regard a deer at play in a meadow. So free, so innocent, so alive. Then she would run to me and I would catch her and carry her to the *wee house by the sea* and … Then, I thought of Delbert because I could not imagine the beach without thinking of him.

I had no recollection of driving as I thought about him and the *Albert Bigelow* – the emptiness of the prairie giving way to the rising mountains of British Columbia. I do not remember sleeping in a parking lot or a rest stop. Nor do I remember driving down through the sweeping curves, crossing bridges, westbound in the deep valleys. On and on without knowing how I navigated treacherous roads, unaware. Some part of me drove without my direct instructions. That fact occupied me a great deal and I thought on the matter all morning on my last day on the road. It felt like I had two people inside me and I became frustrated because I couldn't quite sort them out. Where were Delbert and Gloria? Did they make it to Amchitka? I needed a cup of coffee and a piece of apple pie for my troubles.

I filled up with gas in Hope, parked the Bug and went inside the restaurant. I sat down at a booth that looked out at the highway. I ordered pie and coffee. There was a newspaper on the seat and I was astonished to see my answer in the headlines.

Bad Weather Hampers Greenpeace Protest

The chartered ship, Phyllis Cormack renamed Greenpeace, was forced to turn back from Amchitka due to bad weather. It was reported that the crew of the US navy ship Confidence, patrolling the area, was sympathetic to the activists' cause. It is not known at this time if this will delay nuclear testing. Highschool students in the Vancouver region walked out of class in protest and assembled at the Peace Arch on the Canadian/American border... It was also reported that a boat towing a Nootka war canoe overturned in rough seas. There is no word of the fate of the occupants...

I was stunned by the news, shocked to read it there. There was a photograph of *Greenpeace* setting sail with her enthusiastic crew but there was no photo of the *Albert Bigelow*. "No, not Delbert!" I said out loud. Everyone turned to look at the crazy kid sitting alone. I had to get back to Parry Bay. I picked up the piece of pie, stuffed it in my mouth and slid from the booth to leave. I slopped my coffee down my shirt as I tried to take a drink with my cheeks bulging with apples and pastry, making a spectacle of myself for the patrons hunched over their hamburgers. I paid the bill and left Hope. I pointed the Bug toward the western horizon and sped on until I ran out of road two hours later.

The smell of the sea felt like home as I leaned on the rail of the upper deck on the *Queen of Saanich*. Ships in the distance plodded unhurriedly to their ports. The ocean was not so still. Small craft seemed inconsequential and daring as they rose and fell in the waves. What could happen to a canoe out in the open sea with its narrow beam and big aspirations?

I arrived at Parry Bay in the early evening and called Auntie Netty to tell her that I was home and that everything was fine. I asked her if she knew anything about the protest at Amchitka, Alaska, if she had heard any news about a boat and a Nootka war canoe that had capsized in rough weather. She had heard nothing, she said, and went on to tell me that Jimmy was no longer at home, that Uncle Reggie had thrown him out. I could tell that she wasn't in the frame of mind to listen to me talk about Delbert Crane. I promised I would see her soon.

It felt good to be near the forests once again, to see their great gathering above the high tide mark and to feel the cool wet air settling over the bay, salty and acrid. I left the house and walked down the beach. It was hard not to expect Delbert to be there. I went to his house. All was dark and still. Then I returned to the beach and sat where we always sat and watched herons coming in for the night. I could hear thrushes calling from the dusky woods. In the distance the first lights of Victoria blinked on one by one, comforting beacons for the weary, as the sun fell Mars-red into the sea. I sat alone and thought about the absence, the silence and the sudden heaviness in my chest. Where are you, Delbert? I listened for him as I listened to the trees. I listened for some clue that he was alive, for his voice rising on the night air. I listened as Jules Bear would listen. But Delbert was silent.

On November 6th, 1971, President Richard Nixon authorized the detonation of a nuclear bomb on Amchitka Island, Alaska. Finally I could hear Delbert saying, *Insanity arises from the minds of the insane.* It seemed that the world was forever changed, altered by fear and scandalous mistrust. But the sun did come up the next day as I watched from the kitchen. The order of things along the water was seemingly unsullied. I saw two people down the beach, stationary in their heavy coats, looking out over the bay. There was a good chop on the water and I wondered why they stood at that spot. And then I knew.

I threw on a coat and hurried down the beach before they could leave. They turned to watch me coming. They looked tired and lost.

"Hi," I said, "I'm Calan."

"You knew Delbert," the woman said.

"Yeah, he was my neighbour."

"We're his parents," she said.

"I'm sorry."

She looked at me as if searching for a memory of him. "So, this is where he lived."

"He loved the ocean."

"Like his father." She glanced up at her husband but he did not meet her eyes. It seemed that he was struggling just to be there. Then I saw that she held *his* hand. She was stronger.

"They found his boat smashed on the rocks off the Alexander Archipelago," he said. "The canoe was still attached to the stern by a long rope. They told us the boat rolled over. The Gulf of Alaska was no place for that boat. They haven't found them. We never met Gloria."

I remembered her waving from the wharf in Port Renfrew. "I liked her. She was gentle."

Mrs. Crane smiled, but her husband still looked bewildered.

"I gave him a book once," he said, "*Voyage of the Golden Rule*. I never thought…"

Her hand slid up his arm. It seemed that he blamed himself. There was nothing that I could say to a father in his grief, but there was one thing I could do.

"I have something," I said, "if you could wait a minute."

Mrs. Crane nodded.

I hurried back to the house, to the studio, and found the painting of Delbert and his canoe. I wrapped the canvas in a spare cotton sheet, tucked it under my arm and returned to the beach, where they stood. I held it out to them. Mrs. Crane took it.

She pulled back the sheet. I wondered if they would recognize him with his long hair and beard, with his red bandana, working his adze along the hull, cedar chips about his sandaled feet and the eagle noble on the prow. They might wonder about the ghosted figures working alongside him, the spirit craftsmen and shaman dressed in skins and cedar bark. But they would know his long face and posture, the muscled arms and legs that had grown from the boy they had raised.

Mrs. Crane now slumped at the sight of her son rapt in the things that he loved, his hands creating form and beauty. Mr. Crane took the painting and held her arm tenderly.

"He made a difference," I told them.

Mr. Crane looked at me for a moment. "Thank you," he said. Then they turned away and left the beach.

Later I went back to the house and got Hoot Larsen's pistol. I took it down to the water's edge at low tide, gripped the muzzle in my hand, reared back and flung it end over end out into the bay. I watched the ripples until I knew that it was on the bottom with the sculpins and crabs. And then I offered a moment of silence to honour my every missed direction.

FIR

CHAPTER THIRTY-FIVE

The school allowed me to paint a mural on the gymnasium wall. I was dangerous with a saw and hammer. I neglected to measure things, relying on my eye. Nothing fit or lined up. I was a *rough* carpenter to be sure. The instructor did not mince his words when he banned me from his shop. *Wood butcher,* he called me. It seemed that all my talent and ability had been saved for just one thing. I told the principal I would paint the largest Douglas fir in the world and it would be unlike anything the school had ever seen. It would have a great trunk, knobbed and riven, with converging lines to branches up in the broken crown. It would appear to the viewers that they were standing at the base and looking straight up the trunk to the very top of the tree. Some might be tempted to climb the fir, its three dimensions would trick the eye.

It was the tree that Grandpa Dunny talked about, a tree that grew along the San Juan River at Port Renfrew that we never got to see. It was a thousand years old and growing still. It took me a month to get it right. I had to climb a scaffold to finish the painting. I imagined it, its girth and form, pulled it out of my memory. I had walked along the bay until I found a good tree. I stood under it for hours until I knew every inch of it, recorded it like a photograph. I listened to it with my hand against its trunk searching for its pulse. I found no heartbeat there but I could feel the tree's energy tingling in my fingertips. I learned its language. The tree was pleased with my attention and by some grace, told me about the tree along the San Juan River. If you stood against the opposite gymnasium wall, studying the great high limbs, you might see the faces that I carefully added. You might see the spirits of people. There was always a crowd of students around the tree. Visiting basketball teams always lingered there before the game. The painting made people happy.

In March of another year, when the first cherry blossoms appeared one Sunday, I went out along Victoria harbour with my paintings. Tourists strolled along the waterfront and succumbed to the allure of my paintings. They were attracted to the standard seascapes depicting waves swelling bottle-green, foaming with white froth and spraying against the black rocks. I even had to make prints of one painting because it sold so well. It was a painting of the *Albert Bigelow* with the war canoe in tow, rising against a savage sea. I sold the prints along with a story of a young man and his dream. I didn't like to speak at length to people but I earned my keep with my art. It was all I knew, all I ever wanted now.

Early one afternoon I heard Auntie Netty standing above me on Wharf Street calling, "Calan, Calan." There were a lot of people walking by and I didn't see the face of the girl standing beside her holding a suitcase. I assumed she was just another traveller eager to see the ships and Parliament Buildings, and always the Empress Hotel. When Janet came down the stairs all I could do was shake my head, disbelieving, delighted. I looked up to Wharf Street to see Auntie Netty standing there with her arms folded, silently broadcasting her disapproval. A young man who could hear the language of trees could hear his aunt plain enough – *good god, they'll be shacking up in my father's house.* She couldn't stand to watch our reunion and left. And I knew that it would trouble her deeply to know how often I took Jimmy in.

I watched Janet with her hair falling down about her shoulders then lifting in the harbour breezes. She wore jeans and a navy blue sweater, not the long dress she wore in my dreams when we danced along the beach in Parry Bay. And she did not run to me the way she did in my imagination. She walked past me to look at my paintings.

"They're good," she said.

"Thanks," I said.

"Sold many?"

"I think I made a couple hundred bucks today."

"That's a lot."

"It's better than delivering pizza."

She was slightly amused. "Your aunt is pretty uptight," she said.

"She can be."

"I have something for you, Calan."

"Yeah."

"From your father."

"My father?"

She knelt down, opened her suitcase and pulled out an envelope. "He came to see me at the hardware store," she said. "He asked me, 'are you that girl?'"

"'That girl?' I asked him.

"'The one they're talking about,' he said, 'the painting on the side of the general store.'

"'Yeah, I'm that girl,' I said. 'The newspaper made a big deal about it.'

"'I saw that,' he said. 'The article went on to say that you're going to the university in Victoria now that your mother's in Saskatoon.'

"'I'll be leaving soon,' I told him.

"'Can you give Calan this letter?' he asked me.

"'Okay,' I said. He nodded. It seemed that talking was

difficult for him. 'I see you there looking at the wall,' I said. 'You must like it.'

"He looked at me. He didn't smile. I saw so much pain in his face but I knew that he liked it. He stood there for hours. People talk about it. The wall has become the pride of Clavet. But I think that your father is the proudest."

"So, you're going to the university," I said. It was hard for me to hear what she said about him. I couldn't comprehend his sudden interest.

"Yeah, I'll be staying in the university residence."

"How's your mom?" My blood rushed up to my head.

"She's so amazing. She went without, her whole life, so that I could go to university."

"Did you tell my aunt that you were going to stay with me?"

"Hell no. Why would I tell her that?"

"No reason. She just seemed upset, that's all."

"Probably because I told her that I was going to marry you."

She handed me my father's letter. I didn't want to open it. I wanted to keep looking into Janet's clear blue eyes.

> *Dear Calan;*
> *I'm no letter writer. I hope you destroyed the ones I sent before. They came from a stranger. I don't like him. I'm trying to sort out many things. I'm glad that Jules still has room in his heart for me. I don't deserve his kindness. Your Janet is so full of life. It made me feel happy knowing you painted that picture for her. I know nothing about your life. I'm ashamed of that fact. Don't let her go.*
> *Ole Peterson bought most of Gray Farm. Perhaps later he will buy it all for his boys. He's a good farmer. Better than me. I would like you to buy your grandpa's house. I'll arrange it all. It's something I can do now. I'll stay in the house and work when I can. My bones are sore. I'm tired most of the time.*

But some days I wake up and think things can change. It seems Life has given me another chance. I hope you don't hate me too much for what I did to you. I never earned your respect.

One day I could come out west. Just a thought. The Country Squire would like the change. Maybe I shouldn't. Maybe it's a bad idea. You'll do fine with your painting. You don't need my advice. You're a lot like your mother.

Dad

I stared at the letter. I remembered the ones he had sent me. They were cruel. But now the letter in my hand was from a different man. It seemed a letter a father might write to his son.

"Are you all right, Calan?" Janet asked. She held my arm and looked up into my eyes.

"Yeah," I said, confused. I never thought it was possible. I just didn't.

We walked a short distance along the walkway. Janet looked at more of my paintings. She still held my arm. We belonged to each other now. She stopped at a painting. It was a gravestone rising from the moss and ferns before a massive tree. Shafts of light. She turned to me, then she turned back to the painting and read the epitaph on the gravestone.

Dunmore McLeod
1905 - 1971
I am the green light in the forest
I am the wind on every shore
I am Life
I am

I felt her squeeze my arm as a wind suddenly rushed in from the harbour, spun about our feet and rose up to the street above.

Acknowledgements

I would like to thank Silvia and David at Medici's Gelateria and Coffee House in Oliver, B.C. for the privilege of being their "writer in residence." A special thanks to David Badger for his thoughtful listening and friendship.

I would like to thank my editor, Ron Smith, who brought me back to myself, to the essential of writing. I am grateful for his vast experience that helped shape this book into the vision I had imagined.

Acknowledgements

I would like to thank Silvia and David at Medici's Gelateria and Coffee House in Oliver, B.C. for the privilege of being their "writer in residence." A special thanks to David Badger for his thoughtful listening and friendship.

I would like to thank my editor, Ron Smith, who brought me back to myself, to the essential of writing. I am grateful for his vast experience that helped shape this book into the vision I had imagined.

Danial Neil was born in New Westminster, British Columbia in 1954 and grew up in North Delta. He began writing in his teens, journaling and writing poetry. He made a decision to become a writer in 1986 and took his first creative writing course with Rhody Lake. His first short story was published in the 2003 Federation of BC Writers anthology edited by Susan Musgrave. He went on to participate in the *Write Stretch Program* with the Federation of BC Writers teaching free verse poetry to children. He won the poetry prize at the Surrey International Writers' Conference four times and studied Creative Writing at UBC. He self-published his novel *The Killing Jars* in 2006, and then *Flight of the Dragonfly* (Borealis)in 2009. His poetry and fiction articulate a close relationship with the land, its felt presence in his narrative and vision. Danial lives in the South Okanagan of B.C.